# DOUBLE-DOG DARE

PICK-UP LINES BOOK 3

KAYT MILLER

Cranky Pants: Pick-up Lines Book 1

Lucky Charmer: Pick-up Lines Book 2

Double Dog Dare: Pick-up Lines Book 3

Sexy Savior: A Cocky Hero Novel

1001 Dark Nights Short Story Anthology

Holiday Mishaps Anthology

Bedhead

Redhead

Deadhead

Wedhead

FarmBoy

Game Changer

One of a Kind

The Virginia Chronicles

Our of the Blue: The Flynns Book One

Mick'sology: The Flynns Book Two

Vested Interest: The Flynns Book Three

The Importance of Being Ernie: The Flynns Book Four

The Importance of Being Kennedy's: The Flynns Book Five

Quirky Girl: The Flynns Book Six

The Art of the Game

Lainie: The Palmer Sisters Book 1

Agatha: The Palmer Sisters Book 2

Sadie: The Palmer Sisters Book 3

Cortland: The Palmer Sisters Book 4

Keely: The Palmer Sisters Book 5

Violet: The Palmer Sisters Book 6

Molly: The Palmer Sisters Book 7

The Portrait Painter

Hopeful Romantic

Thanks to Margie Dill

# DEDICATION

*To my eighty+ year-old mom who, after beta reading my first book,
said,
"You know… I think you need one more sex scene."
I love that woman!*

*And to Becky Johnson. You are amazing.*

# COPYRIGHT

This book is a work of fiction. Names, characters, places, and incidents are the product of the author's imagination or are used facetiously. Any resemblance to actual events, locales, or persons, living or dead, is coincidental.



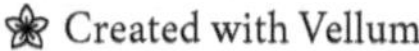 Created with Vellum

# CONTENTS

# 1

EMMA

*"Do you generate electricity with water through the process of hydropower? Because dammmmm."*

"Oh, God."

The memory of it's… it's cringeworthy. No. It's more than that. It's… it's… humiliating.

Luckily, that guy doesn't know me from Adam. I'm 100 percent positive he's never seen me before and I really hope he never will again. There's no way a guy who looks like *that* and dresses in clothes that aren't standard-issue college guy clothes is going to be seen on campus.

No way.

No. I'm safe. Safe from having to face him again. Now, all I need to do is stop the scene from running on repeat through my brain. Oh, and I'll need to get my roommate and *former* best friend to stop laughing every time I walk into the kitchen.

She can be *so* annoying.

Flopping back onto my bed, I squeeze my eyes shut in an attempt to force myself to go to sleep. It's been almost two hours since I said those words--you know the ones above that pain me to repeat--and in that time, I've done everything in my power to make the memory of it go away.

Maybe if I start at the beginning, it'll exhaust me, and I'll fall asleep...

Here goes.

Carley Dearborn, my closest and dearest friend, has been trying to pull me out of my shell for, well, all my life. We grew up in the same town and met when we went to the same elementary school. We also went to middle and high school together. We were practically connected at the hip. Even after graduation, when I told her where I wanted to go to college thanks to their excellent engineering department, she shrugged and said, "That sounds good to me." We lived in the dorms together our first year and then decided to move off campus the next.

To say we're tight is an understatement. She's the sister I never had. Okay, I've got a sister, but she and I don't get along, but that's a story for another day.

So, as I said, Carley has been trying to yank me from my hard turtle shell ever since we were kids, and for the most part, she's been successful. I've tried things I never thought I would or could.

Like swimming.

I was terrified of the water, but one day at the local pool, she took me by the hand and walked me into the water. She stayed with me in the baby pool until I was ready for more. That's the kind of friend she is. I should say *was*. This thing tonight wasn't so gentle.

No, tonight was the "last straw," apparently. At least those were the words she used when she told me we were going out tonight. She didn't even warn me like she usually does. Ordinarily, she'd give me a few days to process the idea of doing something out of my comfort zone. But she didn't tonight. Instead, she stomped into my room after she got home from class, put her hands on her hips, and said, "Tonight, we're going out and you're going to do it. You're going to approach a guy at the bar and you're going to talk to him."

The expression on her face sort of alarmed me. She looked scary. Angry. I had no idea where it was coming from since I hadn't recalled doing anything to make her that way. So, instead of arguing, I merely nodded. I mean, it was Friday night. Midterm exams were over. Sure, I had homework, but I always had homework and I could do that on Saturday and Sunday.

"Good," she said without a smile. "I'm going to choose your outfit and I'm doing your hair and makeup." She glared at me adding, "No arguments. Go take a shower."

Wow. Bossy. In her defense, I would've argued. It's my MO. You know, modus operandi. It's cop-show speak that means a particular way or method of doing something, especially one that is characteristic or well-established.

Man, I love cop shows.

Anyway, I digress… I did as she instructed, er… demanded, because I knew Carley wasn't in the mood for argument and I learned a long time ago when she got that way, it was just easier to go along. So I shut my textbook on hydroelectric power, slid off my bed, and showered.

By the time we got to the bar, my stomach was doing flip-flops. I mean, she had me in a *dress*. A dress! I never wear dresses, especially not short ones. Sure, I've worn this one before *but with leggings*, for crying out loud. It's so short, if I bent over, you'd see my undies. In addition, she gave me big hair. I'm talking B-I-G hair. It's curly and wavy and it's got so much product in it, my fingers only get in about an inch before they get stuck.

And don't get me started on my makeup. The word trollop came to mind when I looked in the mirror, but that's an insult to trollops. Sorry, trollops. She gave me what she termed "smoky eyes" but what I'd refer to as vampire eyes—all dark and suspicious-looking. I looked ridiculous. On top of that, my lips were red, *really* red. Luckily, most of the red ended up on the side of my first drink.

On top of all that—the clothes, the hair, and the makeup—she chose the swankiest joint in town for my humiliation. People don't even call it a bar. It's a "club." Believe me when I tell you, there's a difference. A bar is a place you go and have a beer. A "club" is fancy. There's a line out front to get in, and according to my former bestie, you have to look a certain way to even get inside. Cue my hideous ensemble.

The minute we stepped into the place I did a complete one-eighty to leave The Dirty Rabbit. I don't know why they call it that because there's not a speck of dirt in the place unlike most of the campus bars we've been to. No, this place was nice. Which means it's not our scene. It's not meant for college-aged people. A place like this is intended for professional people. People who don't have jobs; they have careers.

Like I said, I was about to turn and march my big butt out of the place, but Carley grabbed my arm. "Where do you think you're going?"

Looking back and up at her, I gave her my best glare. "We can't afford this place. I bet drinks here are five bucks a piece."

"*I* invited *you* here, so I pay. You know the rule. Besides, we're not going to be here that long." She released my arm and gave me a familiar look. I knew what was coming. "You're going to have a drink for courage and then you're doing it." She shrugged. "Besides, Dad sent me some money."

The eye roll couldn't be held back this time. "Of course, he did." Mr. Dearborn, better known as Daddy Moneybags, had an affair with his secretary when Carley was five, and divorced Carley's mom soon after. Since then, she's seen him only a handful times, even though he lives in Chicago--a mere two hours from our hometown. When I say she's only seen him a handful of times, I'm not joking. Example. She saw him at her grandmother's funeral, at her high school graduation (he didn't stick around for the party after), and several times by accident, like the time at the Costco one town over from where we grew up. He was with a woman. And not the one he had the affair with. A different one. One with several children in tow. To say that was awkward is an understatement.

No. Brad Dearborn is not present in her life, at all. Instead of spending quality time with his beautiful daughter, he sends her money as a parental substitute. *Lots* of money. I know it hurts her. How could it not? The money comes in handy, though, and she figures why not use it for good. Or in the case tonight, for evil.

Ordinarily, I would refuse to help her spend her dad's cash. It's not mine, after all. But tonight, I had no trouble helping her because I was going to need some liquid courage and I couldn't afford fine establishments like this one.

As a matter of fact, until this week, I had no money coming in, but I finally landed a work-study job at the library—thank goodness—because the word "broke" wasn't strong enough to describe my bank account. No, I'd say nearly destitute instead. And since my parents make just over minimum wage at a discount store in our hometown of Pontiac, Illinois, they sure aren't going to fund my night out.

Don't get me wrong, my parents are awesome. They're kind and generous to a fault. They just don't have a pot to piss in, as they say. It's one of the reasons me and my sister don't get along, but I won't bore you with all that drama.

With no fight left in me, I followed Carley up to the bar where there were two open seats. Surprising because this place was packed with people, most of whom were wearing suits and work attire. I guess it makes sense for these people to go out on a Friday night after their work week. As Carley ordered us our first drink, I took a moment to scan the bar. Most of the people here were young. I'd guess midtwenties so that was good. At least we weren't sticking out like a sore thumb here since we're both twenty-one. I felt something cool touch my fingers and looked down at the drink Carley placed next to my hand. I peeked over at her. She raised her glass and looked at me expectantly. "To new challenges."

I lifted my drink, which looked to be a vodka cranberry, my favorite, and tapped my glass to hers. "To kicking your ass tomorrow for making me do this."

"Ha!" She laughed before she sipped her drink. "Like you could kick my ass."

She's right. I'd never been able to do it. She's way bigger than me. Okay, not in the weight department. I'm pretty sure we weigh about the same. The difference is she's eight inches taller than me, so the pounds we both carry are stretched out on her. Yeah, on her they look good. On me, not so much.

Actually, Carley is mostly my opposite in everything. Like I said, she's tall, I'm not. Her hair is blonde, while mine is more of a mousy-brown hue. She's athletic, having played most sports in high school while I was more of a mathlete. Still am. She's open, spontaneous, and funny. I'm closed off, nervous, and awkward. I guess that's why we've been friends for so long. Opposites attract. At least, it works for us.

Heck, even tonight I knew she meant well. I should be angry with her, but how can I be when all she wants to do is help me. She's the one who's had to listen to me whine and even cry sometimes about the fact I've never had a boyfriend. Hell, I've only been kissed once and that, again, was all thanks to her and a party in middle school. She got a game of spin the bottle going and well, that's it. I spun the bottle and it landed on Shawn McNamara. I could tell by his expression that I was the last person he wanted to kiss, but he did it because the bottle told him he had to.

"So, let's get a couple of drinks in you and then we'll choose the guy."

I quickly downed the rest of my drink because, oh, God, she was *really* going to make me do it this time.

She's tried in the past but to no avail. Those times she even helped me prep. We talked about what I'd say once I stepped up to the guy. We rehearsed it for goodness' sake. But every time I approached a guy, I'd freeze up, turn, and walk straight back to our table or out the door, whichever was closer. Honestly, I have no idea why she thinks tonight would be any different.

"And before you chicken out like you usually do, let me tell you why it's going to work tonight. Why I chose this place."

Holding up my glass, I made eye contact with the bartender. When he saw me, he quickly stepped in front of us. "Need another one, beautiful?" Then he winks.

The urge to roll my eyes was almost too much to bear, but I didn't do it. I kept my eyes in place. "Yes."

"Be right back."

Turning to Carley, I waited for her to tell me why she chose the fanciest club in town.

"I chose this place because we don't know anyone here."

I looked around just as the bartender returned with my drink. "That'll be ten fifty."

I nearly choked at his words. "For a tiny drink?" I squeaked. Carley's right about one thing—you won't find college students at a bar like this one because no college student could afford this place.

Carley handed over her credit card, which got her a wink from the bartender.

Once he's gone, she continued. "And because we won't know anyone here, you can approach a guy——a guy that you'll never see again."

"Okay." I nodded as I took a long pull from my drink. "I can see the benefits of that." I really could.

"So, because of that, I say you should choose the hottest guy in the place." She shrugged. "I mean, why not?"

*Why not?* I could tell her about a million reasons why not, but I didn't. "I guess."

"I'm thinking *that* guy." I followed her line of sight until it landed on a guy who belongs on the cover of a magazine.

"Him?" I practically choked on the last little bit of my drink. Because *that* guy was way out of my league. From here, I could tell he was tall. Plus, he looked built like he had some muscle beneath that suit jacket. That's not the best part of him, though. It's his face… it's perfect. Like a young Paul Newman.

Now, before you think that's an odd comparison, my mom loves Paul Newman. She has every single one of his movies on VHS, and if you were to look him up—young Paul Newman—you'd agree that the man was gorgeous. This guy had the same sort of wavy, golden-brown hair. I couldn't see his eye color from my spot at the bar, but part of me hoped they were the same blue as Newman's.

*Ugh. Why was I going off on a tangent about Paul Newman?*

Because thinking about something else was calming.

Not to mention his salad dressing is pretty good. And he, well, he's no longer with us, but his company still gives away much of their profits to important organizations. And I do my best to support companies who are trying to do good in this world. Especially companies who are working to help our environment. It's one of the reasons I chose my major in alternative energy. The earth needs our help.

"Hello?" Carley waved her hand in front of my face. "Yoo-hoo. Earth to Emma."

She made me laugh. "Sorry."

"Off on one of your brain tangents again?"

That's what she calls it when I space off. "Yeah. This one was about Paul Newman."

Carley looked over toward the guy. "Ooh, he does look like a young Paul Newman. In that movie…" She snapped her fingers together like she's trying to remember the name.

I said, "*The Long, Hot Summer.*"

"Yessss." Carley slapped my arm. "That one." She glanced at the guy again. "Definitely. Newman was sexy as fuck in that one."

"He was." I nodded, all while trying to think of something else to distract my friend because my thought was, if I got her drunk and talking, she'd forget all about me doing this... this stupid, embarrassing, and self-destructive act.

She drank the last of her cocktail, clapped her hands together, and said, "Right. Let's do this."

*Crap.*

"Paul Newman is the one." She nodded in his direction.

"Yeah." She smiled brightly. "He's gorgeous." And he wasn't alone. He was with a group of about six or seven other guys. All of whom were very good-looking. They're more Carley's kind of guys. At least, they're the kind of guys who like her. She's like a bee to honey to that kind of man. If that makes any sense.

Funny, though. She doesn't seem all that interested in guys right now. It doesn't stop them, though.

"You know what?" I turned to face her again. "*You* should talk to him. He seems more your type."

"Nope..." She shook her head slowly, and I couldn't help but notice that her hair moves when she does. Unlike mine, which is more like a helmet. It's armor, I guess, which is a good thing. I need battle-ready gear. "...my sweet Emma, this is about you."

*I hate when it's about me.*

"I don't think I can do it." I mean, he wasn't alone. Those other guys... "If he were alone."

"Well, let's have another drink and we'll wait until he approaches the bar or something."

"I'm gonna need a shot," I mumbled under my breath, but she heard.

Raising her hand to the bartender, he stepped over. "Another?" he asked with a smile and another wink. My God, the guy was shameless. Plus, you'd think his eye would stick like that the number of times he winks a night.

"Two shots of tequila, please."

"Not tequila." I moaned. She knows what tequila does to me. It makes me brave.

Winky is back before I could argue.

"You need it. Now shut up and drink."

"Fine." I threw back the golden liquid and winced as it burned down my throat. "I hate you," I hissed.

"I heard that." She took her shot. "And no you don't." Looking over in his direction, Carley raised her hands so they're right below her chin and clapped. "Ooh, he's on the move," she said excitedly.

I turned my head in time to see the target of tonight's humiliation approach the bar. Except, he wasn't alone. Two of the guys from his group were with him. "He's not alone," I whined.

"Go." She practically pushed me off my stool. "Get 'er done."

"I can't."

"You *can* and you will."

I shook my head. I wish I could tell you my hair went with me, but I can't.

"Go."

I took a moment to look at the guy I was supposed to talk to. He's so... everything. "He's not the right one," I said as a droplet of sweat started to run down my forehead. "He's too pretty."

"No. He's just a guy. He probably lives with his mommy."

Suddenly, I laughed, because that was funny. Turning to Carley, I looked her in the eye. "You know dang well that he"—I pointed in his general direction—"doesn't live with Mommy." No, a guy like that... he's got his own house. Maybe a condo. A nice one.

I waited for her to tell me we could leave, but that's not what I got. "You're really going to make me do it, aren't you?"

Glancing at the man then back to Carley, I asked, "Do what?" I didn't know what she was talking about.

"Fine. But just remember you made me do this." She sighs. "I double-dog dare you."

I was suddenly frozen. I couldn't breathe. Or blink. *"What?"* The word came out as a screech.

"You heard me." She was starting to sound like the angry Carley from earlier. The one who stood in my bedroom doorway and commanded I go out tonight.

"Really?" That time I sounded squeaky.

"Really. I've coddled you for far too long. I'm proclaiming this a double-dog dare situation."

*A double-dog dare situation?*

"You're invoking the triple D? *For this?*" I had to concentrate on my air intake because I was seriously shocked. "It's not *that* bad?" I mean, seriously? We hold the triple D with high esteem. It's so revered, we've never actually used it.

"Yes, it's *that* bad. I've been trying to get you to talk to a guy for two and a half years. You're a junior now. You're going to graduate in a year and eight months. What kind of best friend would I be if you left here without talking to a stupid guy?"

"I talk to guys."

"Those nerds in your engineering classes don't count."

"Hey." I was about to defend those nerds in my engineering classes when she held up her hand.

Excuse me? *She's giving me her hand?*

"They're nerds. Just like you."

"Hey!" This time I had to defend myself, at least.

"There's nothing wrong with being a nerd. You're going to make three times more than me when we go out into the work-force. So I don't feel sorry for you. But we can hash that stuff out tomorrow. Right now." She placed her hand on my shoulder. "Right now, you're going to march your little tushy over to that hottie and you're going to talk to him." She gave me a warm smile, then she did it again. She pulled out the big guns. "I double-dog—"

"I *know*," I said, so loudly, the people around us could hear so, I repeated quietly, "I know. You double-dog dared me." Which meant, I had to do it this time. *I had to.* It's the promise we made to each other in ninth grade. If we double-dog dared the other, we *had* to do it. It is rare, sacred, and once uttered, unbreakable.

The only good thing about getting this over with… the sooner I did, the sooner we could leave and the sooner I could go home, change into my comfy clothes, and eat my weight in some kind of cookie, which *she* was going to buy now that she was forcing my hand. It's the least she could do.

Sliding off the stool, I pushed my dress down as far as it would go, which wasn't very dang far. I reached up and attempted to do something with my hair, but it wasn't going anywhere. Taking in a lung full of air, I released it slowly.

"Quit dicking around and go." Carley's voice turned all growly on me. I didn't like it.

"Fine," I gritted my teeth and growled. She was starting to irk me.

Taking a step, then another, and another, I made my way around the corner of the bar and spotted him waiting in line to order. He was easily the tallest one by several inches. Not even his buddies were as tall. I took another step but this one felt like my feet were in quicksand. The closer I got, the harder it was to walk. And to breathe. My heart pounded in my chest so hard it felt like it was gonna jump right out.

I flinched when someone spoke into my ear. Carley. "I know you're freaking out right now, but *you can do this*. Remember, you'll never see him again."

I nodded because I couldn't speak.

"Ask him what his sign is."

His sign? She's talking about his Zodiac sign. I'm into that. Well, we're into that. Both Carley and I read our horoscopes every day, and wait one gosh-dang minute. Turning to face her, I asked, "Did you read my horoscope today?"

Carley smirks. "Of course."

Now it all made perfect sense. The reason she was dragging me out here today. The urgency was because my stupid horoscope said something about romance and taking risks. "Carley...." I practically growled her name.

"What?" She looked a little surprised by my reaction. "This is meant to be. The stars say so. Now go." She touched my shoulder and gave me a gentle shove. "*Go.* And if you don't want to ask him his sign, use one of those pickup lines you read about."

Oh, right. One of the other times she's tried this, I prepared by looking up cute things to say when you first meet someone. I paused for a moment to think. Sure, some of them were pretty raunchy, but there were a few I really liked. I even wrote one of my own. One that fits me perfectly.

"Right." I nodded and took a more self-assured step toward the man. The closer I got to him, the more I realized he was a *man*. He's definitely not a boy like so many of the guys, the nerds, I take classes with.

When I was less than a foot away from him, I looked down at his feet. He was wearing dress shoes. Nice ones. I could also see from here that his pants were black, the same color as his dress shirt. Taking a small step closer, I leaned in, closed my eyes, and took a whiff.

Yes, I realize that was probably weird to smell him, but I had to know.

Answer? He smelled good. *Very* good. Like musk and spice.

Before I could lose my nerve, I reached up and, with my pointer finger and tapped him on the shoulder. I watched in slow motion as he turned his head, but he looked above me. So I did what I could to draw his eyes down. I raised my hand and waved in front of his face. It worked. His head tilted down until our eyes met.

Holy shite. His eyes were blue. Probably not as blue as Paul's but pretty dang blue. I'd categorize them as steel blue. It goes along with his expression, which I'd categorize as a steely gaze. I'd also like you to know that he's better-looking up close than he was far away, which is saying something, because he was flipping gorgeous from across the room.

*Oh, crud. I can't do this.*

It was too much.

I glanced back at Carley. She was leaning against the bar, her left elbow resting on the wooden surface, her right hand on her hip and her expression? If I told you her brow was arched so high it's nearly at her hairline, would you believe me? Plus, she's not smiling.

This is it. I have to do it. "No excuses this time, Emma."

"Huh?" He speaks. It's too bad I didn't have time to explain because I did it. With bravery I didn't know I had, I said what I needed to say. "Do you generate electricity with water through the process of hydropower? Because *dammmmm.*"

*I did it.*

I said it.

*I can't believe it.*

Except... time froze. It stood still as he stared at me. He blinked. I had no idea what to do next. I mean, I had no plan after I said what I said. I guess I assumed he'd chuckle, look at me adoringly, then he'd hug me or something.

That's not what happened.

Instead of the hug I so desperately needed, he blinked some more then said, "Uh... what?"

Ordinarily, when someone asks me a question, I answer it. Correctly. In this case, his 'What?' was asking me to repeat my previous statement, which I was hesitant to do.

"Huh?" I gave him a few blinks of my own. When his eyes met mine, I was struck rather dumb. And believe me when I tell you, I'm *not* stupid.

"What did you say to me?" he asked again.

*Wow, he's got a nice voice too.* The man was the entire package.

Instead of doing what I should--you know... run--I repeated myself. My personalized pickup line. "I *said,* 'Do you generate electricity with water through the process of hydropower? Because dam.'" This time I didn't emphasize the last word because now that I repeated it, it sounded really stupid. The two guys standing with him must agree because they started laughing.

Great.

Not only that, but the guy I just said those words to smiled, rather smugly, if I were being honest. I watched as the smug smirk on his face morphed into a toothy smile. It's like he was about to laugh at me too.

I was right. It did change into a laugh. A chuckle, I guess is how I'd describe it. It was mortifying. Suddenly, he wasn't so good-looking anymore.

Not in the least.

2

ELI

"Well, *she* was fucking interesting."

That statement came from my best friend and teammate, Cody. I've known him for a few years, so I know what he really means. "Interesting" to Cody isn't a compliment. He thinks she was weird.

Ordinarily, I'd agree, except for the fact there was something about her that intrigued me. Maybe it's the fact that she's not like anyone else in this place. That and she made me smile. Something very few people have been able to do lately.

"She was definitely interesting." Except *I* mean it like it's a good thing.

It's too bad she ran off.

Literally.

She turned and ran into the sea of people.

"Come on, man." Cody slaps my back. "Plenty more where that came from."

He means girls. There are plenty more of them. He's right. The minute we got a table, they started circling us.

I reach for the beer he's holding in front of me. "Right." I follow him back to the table where it's surrounded by the usual puck bunnies. There are *always* bunnies and I'm not going to lie, I'm over them. It's old. Played. Not that I've been with all of them, I haven't but a fair share, though none of them had that thing that makes me want more than a night.

Now, don't get all pissed off about me saying something as insensitive as that. I'm sure they're all nice girls, but I haven't met a single one that gave me pause.

Now… that girl tonight. She gave me pause. I was ready to dig in there, get to know her, but before I could even say another word, poof, she was gone. One minute there was this intriguing little gem in front of me saying the most ridiculous line and the next she was in the wind.

*Damn.* I'll probably never see her again. And that sucks.

## 3

EMMA

"'LET'S GO TO A BAR WHERE NOBODY WILL KNOW US,' SHE SAID." I pause. "'It'll be fun,' she said. 'I *double-dog dare* you,' she said." Believe me when I tell you that I say all of that with my snarkiest voice.

"I never said *anything* about fun," Carley says with a grimace. "I know you too well to think any of *that* last night was going to be fun."

I'm sitting on our one and only stool at our tiny breakfast bar, glaring at my best friend while eating a bowl of generic extra-sugary cereal because I deserve it. With a sigh, I shove another spoonful of processed goodness into my mouth. "Myeah," I say with my mouth full. After chewing fast so I can get the rest out, I add, "But you had to know I was going to crash and burn. And if that's the case, why'd you *make* me do it?" I mean, she asserted the sacrosanct triple D.

"I already went over that. Twice." She's eating a yogurt and a piece of dry toast. Who does that? Who eats dry toast? "It had to be done. Your stars were aligned."

I shake my head and shove another spoonful into my mouth, still glaring at her. *Stupid horoscope.*

"Say it again."

Now she's just being rude.

I shake my head again.

"Please?" she says way too sweetly. "One more time?"

"God." I slam the spoon onto the counter. "This is it. The last time."

Holding up three fingers like she was a scout—she wasn't—she says, "I swear."

"I hate you."

"You love me."

"Fine." I close my eyes and repeat the words that will haunt me for the rest of my life. This time I do it so fast, I don't bother taking a breath between words. "Doyougenerateelectricitywithwaterthroughtheprocessofhydropower?Becausedam."

She lowers her head. I can tell she's doing her level best to hold in her laughter. "No, you said, '*dammmmm.*' You really emphasized the last word."

"Dammmmm." I give her the evilest eye in my arsenal. "Better?"

Now she laughs… so hard some of her yogurt ends up on her workout top. Good. She deserves that.

"Witch," I mutter. Sliding down from the stool, I set the bowl in the sink and run some water over it. "I'll let you wash my bowl as payback."

"No problem." She's still laughing and it's annoying as heck.

"I'm glad I can provide you with so much joy."

"Hey." Carley reaches out and touches my arm. "Em. No."

"I get it." I do. I get that she can find amusement in my struggles.

"No." She's no longer laughing. No. Now she's blocking my exit. "Emma. No," Carley says, shaking her head. "I'm not laughing *at* you."

"You're laughing *with* me?" God, I hate that expression. "Because, if you haven't noticed, *I'm* not laughing."

She squeezes my shoulder. "You didn't do anything wrong. You just said that pickup line, turned, and ran."

"I said it twice."

"It doesn't matter."

It matters to me. "Sure." I nod, then give her a fake smile. "I need to get in the shower. I start my job at the library today and I can't be late." I *need* this job.

"Okay." Her voice is soft. I can tell she's worried I'm going to stay mad at her. She knows me--I tend to hang on to my anger for longer than is healthy. Just ask my sister. "But we'll talk later, right?"

"Right." Because Carley knows I'll get over it. Especially when my best friend is involved. I know she's got my best interest at heart.

"I'll bake cookies while you're at work. They'll be ready when you get home."

"Which kind?" I mean… I'm not an idiot. Carley makes the best cookies and since she refused to stop and get any last night….

"Your favorite."

"Oatmeal chocolate chip with coconut?" I didn't need to tell her—she knows my favorite—but it feels good to say those five little words anyway.

"Exactly."

"Fine." I sigh, then give her a weak smile. "I'll look forward to those."

"I know you will, Em."

She's right. She knows me better than anyone. Heck, she may know me better than I know myself.

"Em?"

I turn my head on my way to my bedroom. "Yeah?"

"You'll never see that guy again."

Famous last words.

"CAN I HELP YOU?" I ASK, NOT EVEN BOTHERING TO LOOK UP FROM my *Hydrology & Hydraulics* textbook.

"Yeah. I need to reserve a study room."

I sigh and shut the book, making sure to place my bookmark in the crease first. Pushing myself up from my slumped position at the study-room reserve desk at the college library, I grab the sign-up notebook. I've only been working for an hour or so, but there's not much to the job except signing people in who want a study room, getting their student ID, making sure they only stay the time allotted, and handing them back their ID when they leave. Easy peasy. "Name?"

"Eli Baxter."

"What time?"

"Now."

*Ugh.* This guy…. lucky for him, it's Saturday afternoon and there's nobody here right now. According to my boss, Albert, "Saturday's are d-e-a-d, dead."

"Your lucky day." I hold my hand out. "ID?" See? I'm like an old pro already.

I feel the card slide into my palm as I pick up a pencil. When I start to write down his information, I glance at the photo on the card. And choke.

"Hey…," the guy says, sounding concerned, "You okay?"

"Yep." I lower my head and do my best to swallow down the lump that's just formed in my throat.

"'You'll never see him again,' she said," I mutter softly to myself.

*I'm going to kill Carley.*

After writing quickly, I turn away from the guy, the one from the bar the night before, and grab a study room key. I can't let him see my face. Not that he'd recognize me. I mean, I've got my glasses on, for one. For another, my hair is a rat's nest on top of my head, not all big and curly like last night. Plus there's no makeup on my face whatsoever, so it's doubtful he'd recognize me. No matter, I do my best to keep from actually looking at him. Without facing him, I'm able to hand him the key. "Room 3B. You've got two hours."

"Thanks."

I can tell he hasn't left yet. I mean, I sense him. And smell him. He smells the same as last night--maybe better. I glance back and see he's just standing there. "Yeah? Is there anything else you need?" I do my best to provide good customer service without revealing my face. I bend down like I'm getting something from below the desk. Since I'm new, it's probably not a bad idea to check out what's hidden below the counter. Just doing my due diligence. Getting to know my new workplace. Etcetera.

"My ID?"

"You'll get it when you check out."

"Oh. Right." He pauses. I can feel his eyes on me. At least on the top of my head. "Excuse me." He pauses. "Do I know you?"

"Nope."

Now, I'm pulling out a bunch of junk from beneath the counter like I've got a job to do. It's gross. I wonder when the last time someone cleaned this out. I'm pretty sure I see papers from the turn of the century.

"Yeah. I'm pretty sure I know you."

"Nope."

"You haven't even looked at me so how do you know we haven't met before?"

"I just do. Saw your ID card."

Wow, I spy something ancient in the back of the cupboard. Reaching in, I can't believe my eyes. "Is that an original MacIntosh?" I'm talking to myself but loud enough for the guy to hear.

"Let me see."

Ignoring the voice above me, I wrap my fingers around the

small, tan box and slide it forward. "It is." I'm sort of in awe. Once I've got it to the front of the shelf, I wrap my arms around it and lift. Setting it on the counter, I stare. "Wow."

"That's from 1984," says the guy I wish would just run along to his study room. His head leans forward as he reads something on the back of the tan computer. "A 128K."

"Yeah?"

"Apple's first personal computer." He reaches out and turns the thing to face him. "Is the keyboard and mouse down there?"

Dropping back down, I end up halfway in the cupboard. "Yep." I drag those out with me. Setting them on the counter, I smile up at him and regret it. Because it's then I realize I've given myself away.

"You've got…" He points to his nose.

"What?" I wipe at my nose quickly.

"And…" He points to his forehead.

"What?"

"You're all dusty."

Crap on a cracker.

"You've also got something crawling in your hair."

"What?" I shriek. "Is it a spider?" Holy crud. A *spider?* That's all I need to hear to make me freak the heck out. So what do I do? I scream. I scream and then grab at the top of my head. I'm running from side to side in front of the counter, yelling, "Get it out. Get it out."

Full disclosure. I have an intense fear of eight-legged critters.

"Hold still," Eli says, chuckling.

"It's not funny." A tear slides down my cheek. "Get it, get it, get it."

"If you hold still, I will."

I stop moving, but my arms are stiff, and my hands are in fists at my side. The single tear that escaped has multiplied.

"Got it."

I don't believe him, so I look up. "You did?" I say with a sniffle.

"See?" His voice has softened to a near whisper. "Got him."

"Oh." My voice sounds pathetic and a little soggy. I look at his open palm and see a dead bug. Not a spider, thankfully, but more like a little beetle. "Thank you."

"So, I saved you," he says with a smirk. A cocky one.

"Yeah." I snort. "You're a real superhero." My sarcasm is on full display.

Before I can think, he reaches into his backpack and retrieves something. I watch as he slides on a pair of dark-rimmed glasses.

"Holy Clark Kent," I whisper. This guy in glasses is better than anything I've ever seen. In. My. Life.

He must hear me. "See. I *am* a superhero."

I snort again at his words. "Shut up."

I guess whatever I said is funny because he laughs, loudly. When he stops, I distract myself by fiddling around with the old-timey computer. I've plugged it in and attached the keyboard and mouse to the main box. Pressing the Start button, it chimes to life. "Wow. It works."

"That thing was cool. It changed the world, but you can't do much on it—maybe type a few things on it. There's not much on them—some games, a drawing program, that sort of thing."

"Really?" I look up at him. "How do you know all that?"

He shrugs. "Com sci major."

"Computer science? You're a *nerd*?"

He points to his eyewear, then nods down at my textbook. "Guilty. What's yours? Hydraulics?"

No way is this guy a nerd. At least not any nerd that I've ever seen. The illusive "hot nerd" is just that. Mythical. "Oh." I look down at my textbook. "Environmental engineering with a focus on hydropower."

He blinks at me. No, he's staring. And I know why. Because I just gave myself away. *He knows.* "I see. What do you want to do with that degree?"

"Save the planet." Ugh. Why did I say that?

"Now who's the superhero?"

I giggle. I can't help it. "Not me."

"So, what is it about hydropower that will save the planet?"

It sounds like he really wants to know. "Hydropower is a climate-friendly energy source."

"I see. How does it work?"

"Oh." I titter. "It generates power without producing air pollution or toxic by-products. Using hydropower avoids approximately two hundred million metric tons of carbon pollution in the US each year, equal to the output of over thirty-eight million passenger cars."

"That's a lot."

"It is." I smile brightly. I love my major. I could've chosen other areas to study but I've always been fascinated with water. I'm an Aquarius *and* a Pisces, having a birthday on the cusp, both of which are water signs. Therefore, water is my jam. *Just don't make me swim in it.* The few times I've been to Chicago, I've always wanted to spend the majority of time at the beach. Just sitting by Lake Michigan soothes me.

Someday, I hope to visit the ocean. Now, that's a dream....

"That major sounds liked it'd be *dammmmmmm* hard."

Oh, balls.

*He knows.*

4

———

ELI

It's *her*.

The one from the bar last night. I clocked her as soon as she walked in the front door of the library, then watched her head over to the library information desk. A few minutes later, a Justin Bieber wanna-be approached her and led her away through some office doors in the back. A few minutes later, she came back with that same Bieber jackass. Discreetly, I watched them head up the stairs to the second level. I was tempted to get up from our table and follow her then, but I waited. When the Biebs returned without her, that's when I decided to I search for her. I mean, at the very least, I wanted to know who she was.

It took me over an hour to discover her at the study room reserve desk. I've never used a study room before. I don't know why I've never tried it. I'm constantly looking for places to study without being bothered by people.

Looking down at her, I can't help noticing she's not wearing all the makeup. And her hair isn't all big and puffy either. Well, it is at the top. The hair she wore down last night is now piled on top of her head in the messy way girls wear it now. I have to say, she's even more adorable than she was last night. Sure, she's...

27

unique. The word *peculiar* comes to mind. But she's so fucking cute with her big glasses and her hair extra messed up after the insect incident.

"Umm…."

I give her a smile and it feels so foreign to me. Probably because there hasn't been any reason to do it. Not until now. "So it *was* you last night?"

Her face flushes to hot pink. It looks like it may be warm to the touch. "I don't know what you're talking about."

"No?" I lean forward and rest my elbows on the desk. "You sure about that?"

"Positive."

God, this girl. I'm pretty sure there's a bead of sweat on her forehead. "Well, that's a shame." I'm going to get her to fess up if it's the last thing I do.

"A shame? Why?"

"Because…" I lean in closer to her. Just as I'm about to say something provocative, I feel my body lurch to the left.

"There you are," says the person who, literally, just ran into me.

Oh, shit. I left our table on the first floor of the library and didn't tell anyone where I was going. "Hey, Lacy."

"Did you get us a room or something?" She giggles. I watch as she looks at the library girl. "I guess we're going to '*study*.'" She says raising both hands and using two fingers in each hand to create air quotes. Then she makes a big deal out of winking, giving the tiny girl behind the desk the impression we're going to use the room for other things.

"Where's Cody?" I look back over my shoulder.

"He's still at the table. He's into my roommate Kendra."

I feel like I need to clarify with this girl. The one behind the desk. "We're really studying." Looking over at Lacy from my psychology class, I say, "Come on." I turn toward the study rooms. Before getting too far, though, I turn back to the library girl. "Hey. What's your name?"

Her face is no longer pink, and her expression has morphed into a frown. Luckily, she answers, "Emma."

"Emma," I repeat. It fits her. Emma is a name that belongs to a sweet girl with a pretty face and beautiful smile. Yeah, it's perfect. "Nice to meet you, Emma."

"Uh-huh," she says, dragging the old MacIntosh back off the counter. "You too."

She sounds a tad sarcastic. Why does that bother me? Hell, I'm not going to let it. "Talk to you later."

"Yep." She's now gone, no doubt putting the ancient computer back where she found it.

"Bax," Lacy whines. "Come on."

Reaching for my phone, I send a message to my best friend:

**Me:** I'm up on the fourth floor. Study rooms. Room 3B.

I only have to wait a second before he sends me his smartass response.

**Cody:** Have fun "studying," dude.

5

EMMA

"I'm going to kill you, Carley." I'm hiding in the small office behind the desk with my phone to my ear, whispering my empty threat into my cell phone.

"Why? What'd I do *now*?" Carley sounds a little miffed.

"You said I'd never see him again."

"Uh-huh." She sounds a little distracted. That is until she practically screams in my hear. *"You saw him?* The guy from last night?"

"Yes," I hiss. "He came to the library. He's a student here." And I'm pretty sure an athlete of some sort because he was wearing a long-sleeved T-shirt that did nothing to hide his big arm muscles. Not only that, it had our school logo on the front and "Hockey" printed below that.

"No. Way." Her voice is sort of breathless. "Did you talk to him?"

"I had to. He wanted a study room."

"On a Saturday?"

*That's what I thought too.* "He's a nerd. So, yeah."

Carley begins to cackle, which makes me regret calling her on

31

the phone. Now that she's started laughing, she's not going to stop. "A nerd," she says wistfully. "Oh, shit, Em. You're hilarious."

"He's a com sci major. He knows all about computers. He's a nerd."

"Well"—she's decided to calm down—"a nerd, huh?"

"I also think he may play hockey."

There's silence on the other end of the line.

"Carley? You there?"

"Yes." She breathes into the phone. "I'm processing."

So I wait. I peek out into the room to make sure nobody needs me. When she finally speaks, I want to roll my eyes. "He's *the one*." Her words are weirdly enthusiastic. "And it makes perfect sense."

I'm gonna go ahead and ignore the second sentence. I know what's coming. "What one?" I know what she meant, but I can't just agree with her now, can I?

"The one you need to bag and tag." She rushes through that sentence then adds, "Your horoscope said—"

"First of all... *gross*. Bag and tag? I don't want to hunt him down like some poor, defenseless animal." And she has my curiosity piqued. I didn't have time to read my scope today. "What did it say and which one was it? Pisces or Aquarius?"

"First of all, *he's* not defenseless and it was Pisces. Aquarius was way too stuffy today. It said..." I wait for her to do whatever it is she's doing. "It says, 'Try new things today and you may find sexy fun where it never existed before.'"

I don't know what to say to that. "So my new job is trying new things and because I had the misfortune to run into the guy I humiliated myself in front of last night... you're calling that potential sexy fun?" I mean...

"Of course."

"Did I happen to mention that he's here with a woman?"

"Uh, no."

"Well, he is--so that blows your whole theory to bits."

"Oh, ye of little faith…."

I'm about to argue when I hear the bell on the desk chime. I already hate the thing. When I hear it, my body stiffens and I feel a little like shoving the silver bell thing down the throat of whoever rang it. "Thank you, Pavlov."

"Pavlov? What are you talking about?"

"I gotta go." Speaking of Pavlov… "Someone's ringing that bell at the desk."

"Ah, Pavlov. Gotcha. See ya. We'll finish this convo up tonight. I'm baking your cookies right now."

"Ooh. Sweet. Thanks."

When the bell rings again, this time much more annoyingly repetitive, I hang up the phone and step out and see the blonde girl from earlier. "Here." She hands me the key. "We're done."

I look up at the clock. Only thirty minutes has elapsed. "Okay."

Holding out her palm, I slide Eli's ID into it.

"We're going back to my place." She winks at me again like she did earlier.

"Good for you." I mean. What do I say to that? Besides, for some reason, the whole idea of her and him makes me feel sad inside, which is crazy because he belongs with someone that looks like her--blonde and beautiful.

"Right? I've been trying to bag and tag that guy for two months."

And there you have it. The reason I never want to hear that expression ever again.

"He's been a tough nut to crack." She snickers. "Get it?" She blinks at me. "Nuts?"

"Oh." I pretend to laugh, then I give her that trigger pointy thing with my right hand and make a clicky noise with my mouth. "Got it."

"It's been awfully hard work though," she says in a whisper. She looks behind her, then leans closer like the two of us have some sort of secret. "I've actually had to study for this stupid psychology class." Her eyes roll so far back in her head I sort of fear for their return. "That's the class we have together."

"Okay." I'm really not enjoying this conversation. I don't know why she feels the need to tell me all of this.

"You know. You'd be sort of cute if you'd—"

"That's enough, Lacy." I practically jerk from my spot at his voice. I didn't even see Eli approach.

"What?" She turns to face him. "I'm just trying to help a girl out."

"She doesn't need your help."

Lacy snorts. "Uh, yeah. She kind of does." He looks back at me and gives me a forced smile. "No offense."

I shrug, because what am I supposed to say to that? It was offensive but whatever. I'm used to that kind of thing.

I guess Eli's not in the mood to disagree with her because all he does next is hold his hand out flat and ask, "Did you get my ID?"

"Got it, babe," she coos as she slides it slowly into his palm. The way she does it was kind of seductive if you can be sexy with an ID card.

"Later, Emma," he says, walking away.

"Mm-hmm" is all I seem to be able to say. Because... bummer.

---

"So..." Carley sets a plate of cookies down in front me along with a glass of milk. "Start at the beginning. Tell me everything."

Grabbing the cookie on top, I shove it into my mouth and point at the chair across from me. "Omkay," I say with my full mouth. You know, I really need to quit doing that. It's very bad manners to talk while food is rolling around inside my mouth. Swallowing, I begin, "He came in a little after one."

Carley takes one of my cookies, leans back in her chair, crosses her legs, and listens all while eating one of *my* cookies. Grasping the plate, I pull it off the table and onto my lap. Arching my brow, I dare her to say a word all while I think to myself, *Mine.*

Once that's settled, I tell her the story of his arrival and the MacIntosh. I even fess up to the story about the bug because she's had to save me from bugs a time or two. She laughs at that part, probably because she's seen me freak out.

After I tell her everything that happened, even the part about Lacy offering to give me a makeover, she asks, "So, do you think they went home and… you know… fucked?"

I shrug. "Probably." Why wouldn't they?

"How does that make you feel?"

"Lucky her?" I blink a few times.

"That's it? You're not angry? Jealous?"

"Why would I be? He's way too good-looking for me. He'd never think of me like that." Even if I did have a fantasy last night about him falling madly in love with me despite my faults, those were dashed the minute the blonde bombshell sidled up to him. "I'm not his type."

"Aw, Emma."

"No pity. You know I hate pity."

"I just feel bad. You're adorable and he was hot. I'd love for you to land a guy like that."

"My God, Carl." I snicker. "He's not a plane."

She laughs. "A plane."

"No." I shake my head. "It wasn't meant to be."

Sadly.

6

———

ELI

"Tell me why we're here, *again*," my best friend, Cody, says with a sigh.

"To study."

"We can study at home. Why do you keep dragging me here? These study rooms give me the creeps."

"The creeps?" I frown at him. "That's a bit extreme, don't you think?" He doesn't respond, he merely stares at me. "Look. If we go downstairs, you know people are going to bug us. We won't get a damn thing done and I've got a paper to write."

"If we go downstairs, yes, we'll get attention, but the right kind of attention—from the laaaaadies."

"You"—I jab my finger into his chest—"need to study. You're failing your biology class, remember?"

"How can I forget? Coach has been up my ass about it."

"Which is why we're here. I'm looking out for you."

"*Suuuuure* you are."

"Believe what you want, but this is the best place to focus on our homework. When we're done, I'll buy you a beer."

"Fine." He sighs. "Deal. But none of that cheap domestic shit. I want the good stuff. An import."

37

Slapping him on the back, I approach the desk doing my best to act nonchalant. I've been here the last three days hoping to see Emma again, but no such luck. Maybe today will be the day. Or, hell, maybe she only works weekends. I scan the area looking for her or for anyone who can get us a study room. When *she* comes around the corner, I smile. "Emma."

I must have surprised her because she jumps about a foot off the ground. In the process, she spills whatever she had in the cup she was holding.

"Balls," she mutters as she wipes off something brown from her light-colored top.

I chuckle at the expression. *Balls.* "Sorry. I didn't mean to startle you."

She looks up at me. "It's okay. I'm super clumsy."

"What was in your cup?" I say "was" because most of it is either on her university sweatshirt or on the floor.

"Hot chocolate," she says, swiping a hand down the front of her oversized top. She mumbles something else, but I can't quite make it out.

"I'm sorry." And I mean that because I swear, she looks like she may cry over the loss of her beverage. Hell, I'm tempted to drop everything and run down to one of the campus coffee shops and get her a new one.

"Who's this?" Cody asks, stepping up to the counter.

"Nobody," I mumble.

Ignoring me, Cody smiles at Emma. "Hey there, munchkin. Can we get a study room?"

*Munchkin?* What the ever-loving hell?

Her sad face suddenly morphs into something else. Irritation. "Please don't call me that."

"What?" He looks surprised. "Don't call you munchkin?"

"That's derogatory." You'd think Emma is the one who said that but nope, it was me.

Cody slowly turns his head until we make eye contact. With only his mouth, he silently forms the word "Derogatory?"

"It is." I shrug.

"Fine." He sighs. "I'm sorry, shortcake."

My head rotates quickly to Emma. I'm not sure what I expect, but it's not her responding with a shrug then, "I guess that one's better, douchenozzle."

Okay. That's it. That's the fucking funniest thing I've ever heard. So I laugh. And laugh. Loudly. "Douchenozzle." I slap Cody on the back, but I can't stop laughing.

"Funny," Cody says giving Emma a dirty look. "Consider yourself the winner of that round."

"Oh, I won the battle, but you're supposedly going to win the war?" She arches her pretty brow.

"Something like that."

"Uh-huh. Sure." She holds out her palm. "ID?"

I hand her mine and watch her write down my information. When I get the key, she says, "You've got 3B again."

"Thanks."

"Um…," she says, sounding hesitant.

"Yeah?" I look down at her and smile, because there's just something about her that makes me happy.

Pointing at Cody's shirt, she asks, "Do you guys play hockey?"

I look over at my friend. He's wearing one of our standard issue hockey team tees. "We do," Cody says proudly. "I'm the best forward the school's ever seen."

I chuckle because the guy is damn good but, the best? Nah. When she looks at me, I shrug. "I'm a defenseman."

"Are you a good player too?"

Cody snickers, but I ignore that. "I'm okay."

"Where've you been hiding, sweetheart?" Cody leans on the desk and runs his hands through his long hair. "*Everybody* knows about the hockey team." He points at me. "And that guy right there? He's destined to play in the NHL."

"NHL?" she asks, furrowing her brow. "What's that?"

Cody's expression is priceless, like someone just told him there wasn't a Santa Claus. "Uh, seriously?" Cody's voice gets loud and a little squeaky like he can't believe what he's hearing. "You don't know what the NHL is?"

Emma doesn't respond. She just waits for the answer to her question. So I say, "It stands for the National Hockey League."

"Oh, um. Right." Emma's face has turned a deep shade of pink.

She's embarrassed. I didn't mean to make her that way. I need to say something. "Don't listen to that jackass." I slug Cody in the arm. "Hockey is all he ever thinks about."

"But not you?" Emma asks me.

That's a good question. "I think about it, but it's not my entire world."

"What the hell are you talking about?" Cody has turned to me and the glare he's giving me says it all.

"It's not. I've got to think about a future that doesn't include hockey." I mean all that. "I can't count on making the pros." Better question––do I really want to?

"I call bullshit," my only true friend at this university spits. "If you put your mind to it, you'd make it. Your dad—"

I'm not talking about my father right now. "Was a great player, yes." Believe me, he never lets anyone forget that. That and how disappointed he'll be if I don't make the pros. But, in order to get this conversation to end, I add, "I'm doing my best, but I'll never be as good as he was."

Before Cody can say anything more about me and hockey, I wave at Emma, then take big strides away from the desk toward the study room. Once there, I insert the key into the lock.

"*Her*?" he says from behind me.

"What?"

"*That* chick?" I look back just as he gestures toward the check-out desk.

"What about her?"

"She's the reason we've been coming here practically every night." It's not a question.

"I wouldn't say that."

"You don't need to, man. It's written all over your fucking face. You're smitten."

Smitten? That's probably a good word for it. "I don't really know her." But, after her comeback just now—*douchenozzle*—I'm going to do my damn best to change that.

"She's not the type—"

I don't like where this is going. "To what?"

"She's no puck bunny."

What he means is, she's not one of the women who hang out after hockey games in order to hook up with one of us. "Definitely not a puck bunny."

"That chick will take a lot of work. She's got high-maintenance written all over her."

The look of irritation on my face can't be helped. It's directed at the man who's supposed to be my best friend. "What the hell do you mean by that?"

For the first time since I've known Cody, I see something I never thought I would. Sympathy. Or maybe understanding. "She reminds me of my little sister. Kids, guys especially, have been really mean to her for as long as I can remember because she has always carried a little extra weight."

"Hang on…."

He shakes me off while holding up his hand. "Let me finish. I think it's bullshit. My sister is cool as fuck. Believe me. I've kicked as much ass as I could without getting myself into too much trouble––so if you like that girl, you need to go into it knowing she's probably gonna be skittish. You'll have to treat her with kid gloves."

"Maybe I'll start by *not* calling her shit like shortstop."

"It was shortcake, and that term wasn't meant negatively." He smirks. "Who doesn't love shortcake? It's sweet and delicious."

I growl at his words, because I don't like what he's insinuating.

"Yeah. I get it. She's definitely the reason we've been here every night. You should've told me. I would have come along just to witness the downfall of the *playah* formerly known as Eli 'Bax' Baxter." He gets a huge smile on his face. "Yeah." He nods. "This is great for me."

"What is?"

"Now that you're out of commission, I'll get all your leftovers. More of the lovely ladies for me."

"God, you're an ass." But he makes me laugh anyway.

"Nah. I'm just shrewd."

Okay, that makes me chuckle again. There's nothing shrewd about Cody.

"She's cute, man."

"Emma?" Yeah. She is. Even more so than on Saturday. Today, her hair was in a ponytail at the back of her head. It gave me a better look at her face and her neck. I love a woman's neck. Plus, her shirt isn't as huge on her today. It gives me another look at her body and reminds me of the night at The Dirty Rabbit. She had on that tiny dress. Yeah, Emma should absolutely stop hiding that cute little bod. At least from me. Deciding we need to be done with this conversation, I slap Cody on the back. "Come on. Let's study."

He doesn't answer; he merely makes a growly, groaning kind of noise. The guy hates school, but he's got to keep his grades up if he wants to play hockey. And believe me when I say, the team needs him. He really is an exceptional forward.

## 7

## EMMA

"Well, that was interesting," I mumble to myself after the guys step into the study room.

"What was interesting?" Glancing behind me, I see my coworker Ava.

"Those guys." I point toward room 3B.

"The hockey players?"

How did she know?

"That tall, blond one has been here every day this week."

She's talking about Eli because the other one has brownish red hair. "He has?"

"Yeah." She steps up next to me. "Next time he comes, let me sign him in." She wiggles her eyebrows. "He's just my type."

I look over and up at her. She's a good six inches taller than me. And pretty. Really pretty. "Oh. Okay. Sure." Looking over toward the study room that now houses Eli and the other guy, a sense of sadness washes over me, because Ava's right. The two of them would look amazing together. Any fantasies I've had about me and Eli Baxter are ridiculous. I need to let them go. "He wants to play in the NFL."

"You mean the NHL?"

I have to think about what I said versus what she said. "What's the difference?"

"One is hockey. The other is football."

"Oh." I release a short laugh. "Right. It's the hockey one."

"I know. I looked him up. Jack Baxter was a goalie for Wisconsin. He was drafted to play for Chicago, but in his very first professional game, he tore something in his knee. He never played again."

"Oh. That's too bad." I guess. I mean, it sounds sad. I look back over at Ava. "You looked all that up after you helped Eli this week?"

"I sure did. I did my research. If he and I are gonna get together, I need to know more about him."

"Sure." I nod. I get it, even though it bothers me to think about the two of them together. Stepping around the desk like I'm going to do something work-related, I whisper to myself, "Shake it off. Quit living in a fantasy world, Em." Because there's no way a guy like that would ever give me a second look.

"You're talking to yourself again," Ava deadpans.

"Oops." I do it all the time. Too much, apparently, if she's figured that out after only working with me for a couple of days. "Sorry."

Ava winces. "God, Emma. You're so weird."

"I know." She doesn't need to say it. I already know.

---

"Hi, honey, I'm home," Carley says after slamming the door shut to our tiny apartment. After stepping into our living room, she flops down next to me on the sofa. "How was your day, dear?"

The girl is funny. She says that kind of stuff all the time. "Fine. And you?"

"Hellish. I had a trig test that I totally flunked."

"Why didn't you say something? I would have helped you study."

"You were busy."

"You know I would've helped you."

She shrugs. "I'll figure it out." I watch as she switches from sitting to lying back on the couch so that, now, my head is on one end and hers on the other. Our legs are overlapping in the middle. "Tell me something good." She sighs.

"Well, Eli came to the library again today."

"Eli?" She quickly sits up and grabs my ankle. "The hot guy?"

"Eli and another guy." I scoff when I mention the second one.

"What's wrong with the other guy?"

"He's a tool. He called me munchkin."

"Oh, hells no." Carley shakes her head. "Did you give him hell?"

She knows me and how much I hate being called one of those horrible names for short people. "Eli told him not to call me that so instead, he called me 'Shortcake.'"

"What an asshole."

"Douchenozzle." I say with a snicker. "That's what I called *him*."

"You called him douchenozzle?" Carley has scooted closer to me; my legs are now on her lap. "To his face?" she squeaks.

"I did." Remembering it makes me snicker. "Eli cracked up." He has a great laugh--deep and rich.

"Then what happened?"

So, I told her the rest, about the hockey stuff and also about Ava.

"No." Carley shakes her head. "Don't you dare go get her if Eli shows up while you're working. She's a worthless bitch. She was in my ed psych class. We had a group project..." Carley sighs. "She's one of those who doesn't do her part on group projects so people like me have to do her shit too." I hear a growl.

"I hate people like that." I really do.

"Right?" I want to laugh at the fact that Carley just went way off track when she adds, "Besides, she'll chew him up and spit him out. Then you'll never see him again."

"But she's—"

Holding up one of her fingers in front of my face, she waggles it back and forth and says, "Don't you dare say you're not good enough for him." She squeezes my ankle. "Because I know how that brain of yours works, Em. You think because Ava looks like a *Sports Illustrated* swimsuit model that she should be with Eli––but that's not true."

"They match."

"That's not a thing, sweetie. People don't end up together because they 'match.'"

"Think about their babies. How pretty—"

Holding up her right hand this time, she shakes her head. "That's also not a thing."

"Maybe not, but one thing is certain, guys like Eli don't date women like me."

"Oh, really?" Carley says with a scowl. "Guys like Eli don't date beautiful, smart, funny, classy women?"

"Classy?" I giggle after that one. "I'm *so* not classy."

"You are. You never cuss. You drink tea from a fancy cup, you-you—"

"It was my grandmother's teacup. I drink out of it because I loved her, and I miss her. It reminds me of her."

"Let me finish."

I sigh, exasperated.

"You hold doors for strangers, you help old ladies cross the street, you'd give a person the shirt off your back if you thought they needed it more than you and—"

"That's not about being classy. That's about being a good person." I'm proud of that part of myself. I try to be a good person.

"You're generous."

I guess she's giving up on the classy thing—probably a good idea.

"Just stop." I've rolled my eyes about twenty times in the last few minutes and now my eyeballs hurt. "I get what you're saying, and I thank you, but I stand by my claim. Guys like Eli Baxter don't go for girls like me."

Moving my feet off her lap, she stands. "Not true."

It is true. And the sooner she realizes it, the sooner we can move past all of this stuff with Eli, and I can get back to my life of books, school, and the knowledge that I'll probably live alone with a hamster or two. I refuse to accept the "crazy cat lady" label so hamsters it is. Ooh, wait… make that a guinea pig.

8

ELI

"WE GOING TO THE LIBRARY AGAIN?" CODY ASKS AFTER A HELLISH practice. One where our coach thought it'd be fun for us to do a hundred laps and that was after a full-on scrimmage.

It's been a week since the last time I went to the library to use one of their study rooms. I'm not sure why. Maybe because whatever thoughts I had about that girl, Emma, are probably not good ideas. Shaking my head, I say, "Nah. I'm beat." That's no lie. I don't know what got into Coach Montross today, but he had it in for us. "What was up Coach's ass today?"

"I think he heard about the party."

"What party?"

"The one you blew off Saturday."

"So, he kicked *my* ass for something I had nothing to do with?" Actually, he kicked everybody's ass.

Cody shrugs. "There was some nudity."

"What?" God, these assholes need to grow up.

"And social media."

"What the fuck, dude? You guys filmed naked women?" That's appalling. I mean that.

"Nah, man. We--" He points at himself. "A few of us, the players were naked."

"Jesus," I mumble. "You put your naked asses on social media?"

He shrugs. "Seemed like a good idea at the time."

"What about now? Does it seem like it was a good idea *now*?"

"For me? Sure. But I'm hung like a horse." Then he laughs. "Not so much for Buck and Sam."

Sadly, I get what he's saying. "You're a dumb fuck. You want to get drafted, man, the last thing you need is that kind of scrutiny."

"Boys will be boys." He shrugs again.

"You watch." I point at his face. "That'll come back and bite you in the bare ass."

"Maybe." Cody keeps shrugging this shit off when, for a guy like him, a good player—maybe even a great player, who needs every bit of help he can to catch the eye of a pro team—this kind of bullshit will have them passing him right up.

"Pull your head out of your ass, man." I wave him off as I walk toward Coach's office. "I'll catch you later." Cody merely shrugs again, grabs his bag, and leaves.

Raising my fist, I'm about to knock when his deep voice yells from within. "What?"

Turning the knob, I open the door and poke my head inside.

"What, Baxter?"

"For the record, I wasn't at that party last weekend."

"I know."

What the fuck? "So you knew and you still—"

"You're part of a team," he says, interrupting me. "When one of you fucks up, all of you fuck up."

I've been playing hockey since I could walk so none of that's a shock. "I get it." I nod. "I just wanted you to know I wasn't there. If I had been, I'd have stopped it."

"I know. So next time go."

I get what he's saying, but the last place I want to be is

surrounded by a bunch of drunk assholes. I've had my fill of that. But I guess I've got to think about "the team."

"Yeah. Sure."

---

"MAY I HELP YOU?" I'M DOING MY BEST TO LOOK PAST THIS TALL girl to catch the eye of the petite brunette who I *know* just saw me, then ducked into an office back behind the desk. Yes. I changed my mind about the library. After I left Coach Montross's office, I decided I needed to study. Well, okay, I wanted to see if she was here.

"Yeah. Get Emma."

"Oh, she's about to leave. Would you like me to get a room with you?" She snickers. "I mean, *for* you."

"She's off?" I take a step to my right to see if Emma's come out of the office yet, but this chick keeps moving with me blocking my view.

"Who? Emma?" The woman's voice sounds too high-pitched.

"Yeah."

"*You* want to talk to *Emma*?"

What the hell is this girl's problem? I finally look at the woman who's doing her damn best to get my attention. She's pretty, and a little too desperate. "Can you get her?"

Throwing her hands up like she's frustrated, she stomps back to the office that Emma disappeared into. Moments later, Emma steps out, her cheeks are flushed a deep pink I'm starting to get used to. "Eli?"

"There she is," I say with a smile. "You off now?"

"Uh, yeah." Stepping toward the desk, she looks back at the other girl who's following her so closely, I'm surprised Emma doesn't feel her hot breath on the back of her neck. When she reaches the desk, she places her hands on the top and waits.

"Wanna get a cup of coffee?"

"Oh." She looks over her shoulder again. That girl is still there, hovering.

"Do you mind?" I ask Emma's rude coworker.

"No." She shrugs and stays put. "Emma can go whenever she wants. Her shift is over."

She didn't get my meaning, but I don't bother explaining. "Coffee?" I ask Emma again.

"If you don't want to go, *I* will."

I repeat. What is wrong with that girl? "I asked Emma."

"Sure. Yeah." Emma shrugs. "I could use some coffee, but I don't have a lot of time. I've got a ton of homework tonight."

"Emma." The tall girl practically screeches. "You are the biggest idiot."

"Hey!" I'm not going to stand here and let someone talk to Emma like that.

"What? The hottest guy on campus asks her out and she says she doesn't have time?"

"It's just coffee," both Emma and I say simultaneously.

"There's no such thing as 'just coffee,'" the tall girl snaps.

Ignoring her comment, I look down at Emma. "Ready?"

"Let me grab my stuff. I'll meet you on the main level."

*Finally.* We need to get away from here as soon as humanly possible.

"See you there." I smile and turn and practically skip out of the room to the main set of stairs. The smile remains all the way down to the lobby and when I see her heading my way, the smile turns into a grin. My God, what is it about this girl that makes me want to do a goddamn jig?

Doing my best to keep myself in check, I take a moment to really observe her. She's walking toward me, but she's not looking at me. Hell, she's not even looking up. Her head is down and she's practically dragging her backpack on the ground. The damn thing is so stuffed it's got to weigh a hundred pounds.

Taking quick steps, I reach for her bag as soon as I'm close enough. "Here. Allow me." *Allow me?* What kind of shit is that? No matter, my act of chivalry has gotten her attention. She's finally looking at me––she appears to be surprised.

"Oh, no, I can carry it."

"I've got it." I lift it and grunt as I sling it over my shoulder. "What the hell you got in here, an anvil?"

I guess what I said was funny because a sweet giggle escapes her lips. "Pretty much everything I own is in there."

"So, there's a bed and sofa?" I wiggle my shoulder. "Feels about right."

Her giggle turns into a full-fledged laugh and I've got to say, I don't hate it. Not in the least.

"Coffee?" I say as I point to the library exit. "Let's go to Brewster's."

"Oh, um, that place is sort of expensive. Why don't we—"

"It's on me."

"No." She shakes her head.

"I invited you for coffee. I pay."

She blinks at me. I can practically see the wheels turning in her head. "I guess that's how my roommate and I handle things like that too." She snorts. "She had to pay that night at The Dirty Rabbit."

And there we have it. She's opened the door for us to talk about that night and her one-of-a-kind pickup line. "Speaking of––"

She holds up her hand. "No. I knew I shouldn't have mentioned that night. We're not talking about my utter humiliation at making up the worst pickup line in history. Not in this lifetime."

I chuckle at her assertiveness. This girl is fucking adorable. "No?" I shrug or I try to with her thousand-pound bookbag over my shoulder. "That's too bad. I was going to tell you about one of *my* best pickup lines."

"Oh?" She looks up at me and blinks. "*You've* got a pickup

line?"

"Sure." Although, I've never had to use it. Girls do just what Emma did that night. *They* approach *me*.

9

---

EMMA

"You've got a pickup line?" I don't believe it. Heck, I don't believe I'm walking across campus with the best-looking guy I've ever seen. Not only that, *he* asked *me* to grab a coffee. It's surreal. I'm tempted to send Carley a text just to hear what she's got to say on the matter, but that'd be rude.

"I've got one or two, yeah."

I stop walking because I need to focus on this for a second. "Oh, yeah? Let's hear one." *Where the heck did this courage come from?*

Eli stops walking too. When he turns to face me, I've got to look up to see his pretty face. "All right. How 'bout this one." He clears his throat like he's gearing up for something big. "Are you a computer keyboard? Because you're just my type."

Okay. That one is hilarious. To prove it, I throw my head back and crack up. I guess my laughter is contagious because Eli does the same. It goes on for several minutes, long enough to draw attention to ourselves as other students pass by. I don't care though. Because this feels good. Cathartic. Sure, Carley and I laugh at stuff, especially at each other, but I haven't laughed this hard in a long time. Heck, laughing tears are coming out of my eyes so I wipe them away. "That was awful," I finally say.

"Really?" He turns to continue our stroll to the coffee shop that's just across the street from campus. "That's the best one in my arsenal."

"Well, that's a shame." I start to giggle again. "I heard a computer nerd one before. What was it?" I tap my chin, then reach out and place my hand on his forearm. A zinging sensation spreads from my fingertips up my arm. Ignoring that feeling, I quickly pull my hand back and say, "Oh, I remember." I look over at him and smirk. "Is your name wi-fi? Because I'm really feeling a connection."

He groans. "That's terrible."

Snickering, I say, "I think it has the makings of being a pickup line classic."

"No way."

I shrug because I don't have a rebuttal. I will in an hour when I'm alone and on my way back home. That's always when I think of witty comebacks. Not on the spot. No. Not me.

"Here we are." Eli grabs the door handle of Brewster's and holds it open for me. "After you."

I step inside and breathe in the aroma of freshly ground coffee, plus the scent of baked goods. This place is known for its fancy coffees but more so for their pastries.

From behind me, Eli places his hand on my shoulder, which causes me to jump a little. "Smells damn good in here."

"It does." I wish I was one of those people, those women, who can just flirt and talk to guys, but I'm not.

We walk side by side until we're in line. The place is kind of busy for this time of day. Apparently, everyone else on campus decided it was coffee time. "Get anything you want." This time his voice is soft and close, like he's bent down to say something private, just to me.

"Oh." I read the board. "I'll just have a small, black coffee."

"No." He's still close. "I had a feeling you'd do that." Drawing himself up to his full height, he says, "If I had to guess, I'd say you were more of a frappe kind of girl."

That couldn't be further from the truth, but I'm curious why he thinks that. "What kind of girl likes frappes?"

"Oh." He turns fully to face me. "It depends on the flavor, I guess, but a frappe girl is someone who's pretty, creative, spontaneous—"

I snort at that last word. Well, all of it is pretty far off from the truth.

"What? You're not spontaneous?"

"I'm none of those things."

Eli's mouth morphs from a smile to a frown instantly. "You're *very* pretty." We look at each other then. "I don't know about the other things, but I know that for sure."

I'm blushing like a fool. My face is suddenly hot as can be. So it's time to change the topic. "Well, I don't care for iced coffees as a rule."

"Well, then… tell me, Emma…" He blinks. "What's your last name?"

"Perkins."

He nods. "Well, tell me, Emma Perkins, what's your absolute favorite coffee drink?"

"It varies." It really does. "Today the Foggy London Town Tea sounds really good."

"Wow." He shakes his head. He mumbles something I can't quite make out, which troubles me. So I ask, "What's wrong with my choice?"

"Nothing." His smile returns. "You just surprised me and it's a good thing."

"Oh." I blink a few times. "What're you getting?"

"Espresso."

"Wow. You'll be up all night."

"Good. I've got a lot of homework."

Oh, if that wasn't a hint, I don't know what was. "Well, then, let's get our coffee to-go so you can get home."

"No way." He shakes his head. "Homework can wait. Let's relax and talk a bit."

I don't respond. Instead, I look ahead and see the line has moved quickly. It's already our turn to order. I stand next to him as he orders our coffees and several of the sweet pastries from the case. "We're going to share those," he looks down at me and states matter-of-factly. "And don't give me any guff, Emma Perkins."

I'm not sure why he keeps saying my entire name, but I like it.

I like it a lot.

Somehow, we find seats––two big comfy chairs in the back corner of the shop. They're placed so close to each other the arms are touching. Curling up into one, my body is leaning to my left so I'm close to Eli. Holding up the plate with the sweets, I reach out and take an apple tart. "Are you sure? That one is the most fattening."

I quickly drop it on the plate and retract my hand until it's in my lap. I know I'm blushing again. "Oh. Right."

His face changes again. His smile is now in a straight line. "No. I'm sorry. I was only joking." Pushing the plate closer to me, he says, "Please, take the one you want."

"No." I shake my head. "I'm not hungry." I've learned the hard way that humiliation is very filling.

"Damn it, Emma." He's now scowling. "Please. It was my attempt at humor, and it failed miserably." He stares at me. "Please? If you don't eat it, I'm throwing it away."

With a sigh, I reach out and take the apple tart and set it on a napkin. "Happy?"

"No," he says softly. "I shouldn't have teased you like that. You're…"

"What? I'm what?" Already fat? Stupid? Ugly? Naïve?

"You're sensitive."

*Sensitive?* That's *not* a compliment. It's right up there with overly emotional and high maintenance. "Okay." I unfurl my legs and scoot to the edge of my seat. "On that note." And the other one. "It's been swell. But I need to go."

"What?" he says loudly. "Why?"

"This—" I point to him, then back at me. "—is weird. Maybe I'm just being 'too sensitive.'"

"Weird?" He blinks a bunch of times. "What's weird about two friends having coffee together?"

And there it is. Two words that are very familiar territory for me––the friend zone. "Friends." Because of course we're only friends. Why else would *he* ask *me* for coffee? Heck, maybe he was going to ask me to set him up with Ava. Or he needs help with some homework… "Well, *friend,* I need to go."

"What about your tea?"

Just then, Eli's name is called up to the front. "At least take your tea with you."

I nod because I don't know what to say. I could use the tea.

"Good." He reaches out and touches my shoulder. The zing happens again, but I force it out of my mind. "Wait here. Don't move."

I do as he asks. Well sort of. I step over and grab my backpack, slinging it over my shoulder. *Then* I wait on the spot until he returns with my cup saying, "I didn't mean 'sensitive' in a bad way."

I raise and lower the shoulder that isn't weighed down by the backpack. "No worries." I can't look at him right now. I feel my eyes burn and know that means there are tears threatening to leak out.

"I *am* worried. I––"

*What? He what?*

"I guess this was a bad idea."

I need to go. *Now.* Before the tears start to fall. I will not let this guy see me cry. No way does he need to know his words hurt me. "Okay. Well, I'll see you around." Hopefully he takes the hint and doesn't come to the library anymore. Otherwise, I'm going to have to quit my job ————and I need it. I need it a lot.

"Bye, Emma Perkins."

"Goodbye, Eli."

1 0

---

ELI

What just happened? We were having a nice time at the coffee shop one minute, the next I call her sensitive and it's over? Wait, before that I teased her about the pastry. The "sensitive" comment only sealed my fate.

*What is wrong with me?*

Why did I make a comment about her choosing the pastry with the highest caloric value? Hell, it wasn't even true. I'm pretty sure the coffee cake with extra frosting on top would have been the most fattening. "God. I'm such a fucking idiot," I say and in full voice so everyone sitting at tables around me hear me.

"Yeah, but you're hot so I'll let it slide." I look to my right and search for the owner of the voice. When I spot her, she's smirking. She's my age. Dark hair. Beautiful. I should smile and flirt with her, but I can't. I don't want to. Because she's not Emma Perkins.

Emma Perkins. The girl who makes me smile and laugh and feel like I can conquer the world just by talking to her. And that happened after only speaking to her for an hour. But I blew it.

Shaking my head, I set my coffee down, grab my bookbag, and leave the coffee shop. I wasn't lying when I said I had a shit ton of homework, but that's the last thing I want to do right now. Instead of doing what I should, I pull the phone out of my back pocket.

**Me:** Wanna get a beer?
**Cody:** Hell yes. Meet you at Paradise in 20?
**Me**: Sure.

Paradise Lounge is one of the bars close to campus the team likes to frequent, which means there's going to be puck bunnies. But I don't care about them. I just need a beer with my friend. Let's see what he thinks about my fuck up with Emma.

---

"YOU FUCKED UP," CODY SAYS RIGHT BEFORE BITING INTO THE biggest cheeseburger I've ever seen.

"Is that a quadruple burger?"

Chewing, he nods.

"You're going to die of a heart attack at age thirty if you keep eating like that."

With his mouth still partially full, he smiles and nods at his food. "What a way to go, though." He points at my grilled chicken sandwich. "Life's too short to eat healthy all the time, man."

"I like grilled chicken." I do.

"You didn't even get fries."

"I--" He's right. Instead of arguing, I reach across the table and grab a handful of his fries and shove them in my mouth. "Happy?" I say, chewing on the fried potatoes.

"Asshole." He wraps his arm around his plate and pulls it in until it's pressing on his chest. "Hands on your own goddamn food."

I smile and continue to chew until I wash it down with the rest of my beer. "So, what can I do?"

"Pay me back. Buy me another side of fries," he says with a pout.

"No, dick. About Emma."

He shrugs. "Apologize."

"I did."

"Grovel."

"Grovel," I say to myself. I've never had to do that, but I've seen my dad do it plenty. The guy fucks up constantly. It's not a good look and one I'd prefer not to emulate, but maybe Cody's right. "I could grovel."

"Are you gonna buy me some more fries then?"

"No." I laugh. The guy doesn't need any more grease. "I'll buy you a beer, though." Not that he needs more beer either.

Cody frowns. "Fine."

EMMA

"I'm sorry."

I look up and have to blink because I can't believe my eyes. It's Eli and he's holding a bunch of flowers out in front of me. A huge bouquet. Something I've never gotten in my entire life. And this one, well, it's beautiful, with flowers in every color of the rainbow, and there are so many different kinds. It's amazing.

"Are those for me?"

"Of course."

"Why?" I'm still staring at the flowers.

"Because I was a jackass yesterday. I thought I was being funny and clever; instead, I was insensitive and boorish."

"Boorish?" I snort. "Who says that word anymore?"

"I guess I do." Eli shrugs. "If the shoe fits."

"I don't think 'boorish' is the right word."

"No?" His head tilts to his right slightly. "What word would you use then?"

I tap my finger on my chin. "What about churlish?"

"Churlish?" He gently places the flowers on the counter, then reaches behind him and pulls out his phone. I watch as he taps away for a few seconds, then stops. Reading something, he nods. "I'll accept churlish. But ill-bred has a nice ring to it."

I snicker.

"Oh, how 'bout common?" He reads more. "There's also coarse, ill-mannered, rough, low-class, unrefined, and vulgar."

Shaking my head, I respond, "You weren't vulgar."

I guess my comment catches him off guard because his head jerks up at my words. Then he laughs. "But the rest of them are okay?"

His laughter makes me laugh. "Yeah. They all fit."

"Fair enough, lovely Emma Perkins."

Holding out his hand, he says the word I hate most in this world. "Friends?"

Placing mine in his, we shake. "Friends."

"Good. Can I get a do-over on the coffee?"

"Oh." I'm not sure that's a great idea. "Do you think that's wise?"

He's quiet for a minute. "Maybe you're right."

I don't know why, but I was hoping he'd argue that point with me.

"Dinner, then."

I nearly choke. "D-Dinner?"

"Saturday night."

"Uh--" It feels like there's dust in my eyes, I'm blinking so much. "Dinner?"

"Yeah. Wear something nice."

I look down at my oversized U of Wisconsin-Madison sweat-shirt, then back at him. This sounds like a date. I'm this close to asking him if it is, when that guy he was with the other time steps up to the desk, slaps Eli on the back, then says, "Hey, tiny dynamo."

*Tiny dynamo?* What the heck?

I don't know why, but that one makes me laugh, though I'm still able to say through the giggles, "I've never heard that one before, ya wanker." I add the last bit in a terrible English accent, so it sounds more like "wankah."

Both guys break out into full-on laughs, which draws the attention of everyone else in the place. Trying to keep myself from losing it, too, I place my finger over my lips and make the universal librarian sound. "Shhh."

Bad move because that only makes them laugh harder.

"Emma?" I stiffen up at the voice of Mr. Lane, my boss's boss. He's not a nice person.

Turning to face him, I plaster on a fake smile. "Yes, Mr. Lane?"

"I could hear you all the way on the other side of the building."

"I'm sorry, Mr. Lane."

"Keep it down."

"Yes, Mr. Lane."

I turn to face the guys and can't help noticing they're no longer laughing. Hell, they aren't even smiling. "Sorry, babe."

That came from the wanker. Too bad, because hearing Eli call me "babe" would be a dream come true.

Leaning on the desk, Wanker moves closer. "I'm Cody." Then, he winks. Like a wanker.

"Cody."

"I figure you should know my name since you and my boy here"—he slaps Eli on the back again. Hard enough to push him off-balance a little—"are going to be spending some time together."

I look over at Eli as he asks, "So, Saturday night? I'll pick you up at seven."

"Seven." What the heck is wrong with me? *Shake it off, Em. We're friends. This is his way to make up for the whole fiasco in the coffee shop. Nothing more.* "Sure."

Holding his phone up, he looks at me. "What's your number?"

I give it to him. I hear mine chime from somewhere behind me. "Now you have mine. Text me your address."

"Okay." I smile, but it's only half of one.

"Great." Eli's smile looks real. "It's a date."

*What?* It's a date? No. No. That's just an expression. We all say it. Heck, I've said it to Carley before. *He's just teasing. Of course, he is.*

"Okay. See you Saturday." In two days.

"Great," he says again.

"Great." This time it's Cody. "The two of you are riveting, but I've gotta go. There's a hottie studying alone down on two. I'm about to keep her company." With another wink, he's gone.

"I hate when guys wink," I mumble to myself, but I guess Eli hears me.

"Yeah?" He's looking at me like he's really curious. "Why?"

"It's smarmy."

Eli reaches for his phone again and types something. He reads, "Ingratiating and wheedling in a way that is perceived as insincere or excessive." He nods. "Yep. Cody is definitely smarmy."

I cover my mouth and snicker.

---

"You can't wear that," Carley says, sitting from her perch on the couch. This is the sixth outfit she's vetoed so far. "I've only got one more." I look at the clock. "He's going to be here in fifteen minutes."

"Let's see the final option and we can choose the best of the worst." She rolls her eyes. "We're going thrifting this week. You need to have clothes to wear out with this guy."

"Do not." This is a one-time thing. "He's only taking me out to apologize."

"Sure." She shoos me away. "Go. Let's see this final option."

I was really hoping some of the others would have worked out, because this last one is way too, well, girly. In other words, it's *not* me. It's the reason I told Carley she had to stay out of my closet and remain on the couch for this. She would have picked this up first while I'd prefer to wear one of my legging-slash-tunic combinations, but she said I looked like a mom instead of a hot, single chick.

Ha! That's a joke.

No matter, I race into my room and grab the dress my mom bought for me to wear to my cousin's wedding last year. It's black, which is its only redeeming quality. Honestly, I don't know why my mom chose this dress for me. It's short and sort of low-cut. Not even close to my mother's usual style. Unzipping the back, I step into it and pull it up past my hips and over my boobs. Sliding my arms into the short sleeves, I hope and pray I haven't gained too much weight since the last time I wore it. Reaching back, I contort myself enough to get the zipper up halfway. After stepping into the short heels that go with the dress, I rush out the living room and give Carley my back. "Can you zip me?"

"What is that?" She sounds disgusted as I hear the zipper go up.

"What is what?" I turn and face her.

"Why the hell didn't you put that on first? We would have been done hours ago."

"It's short." I point to the fact that the hem ends midthigh."

"Yeah. It's the perfect length."

Ignoring her, I point to my cleavage. "It's too low-cut."

"Bullshit." She stands up and touches the sleeves. "You'll want a sweater. Wear my little black cardigan with it." She twirls her finger in the air. "Spin." I do. I turn 360 degrees. "That silhouette is absolutely perfect for you."

"Mom said they called it fit and flare."

"It's perfect." She then runs into her bedroom, returning with the cropped cardigan sweater.

Sliding my arms in, I frown. "I'm going to stretch it out."

"Shut up." Carley pulls my hair out from beneath the sweater and smooths it down. She flat-ironed my hair and did my makeup again. I told her I wanted it light and natural and that's what I got except for the red lipstick. "Your coloring is perfect for bright red," she'd said as she applied it.

The knock on the door makes me jump about three feet in the air. "He's here," I whisper, but it comes out husky.

"He is." Carley smiles brightly. Touching my face, she adds, "Your first official date."

"It's not a date."

She takes hold of both shoulders and leans in close. "If he's wearing a suit and tie, it's a date."

"He said dress up." I roll my eyes. "I--" Before I can finish, he knocks again. "You get it," I say to Carley. I'm so nervous, I may pee my pants. Well, in this case, panties.

"Coming," she says. loud enough for him to hear, but to me she adds softly, "I hope it's you that comes tonight."

"Shut up." I laugh as I slap her on her arm. "So gross."

"You'll see just how *not* gross it is." She gives me a sly look. "Hopefully soon." Before I know it, she's at the door with her hand on the knob. "Ready?"

I nod even though inside I'm shaking like a leaf. And after I see the man at the door, I know my nerves are well-placed. I'm about to say "wow," but he beats me to it.

"You look beautiful, Emma Perkins."

"So do you." My voice sounds breathless. Probably because I am. I can barely breathe at the sight of him.

Carley laughs from somewhere in the room. I'm not sure where she went because I can't stop looking at Eli in his dark gray suit, white dress shirt, and gray patterned tie. He looks gorgeous. Like he did the night I humiliated myself--only this time, the jacket and tie only make him look more handsome.

"Shall we?" Eli holds out his elbow like some prince in one of my fairy tales.

"Sure." I reach out and touch his elbow and feel that spark again.

"Don't forget your clutch." Carley steps over to me and hands it off.

"Oh." I nearly choke saying that little word. "This is my room-mate and best friend, Carley."

"Nice to meet you, Carley."

"You too." She pats my ass. "Now run along and have a nice *date*."

The bitch emphasized that word on purpose.

Without missing a beat, Eli says, "We intend to."

1 2

ELI

"Your roommate is pretty." It's the first thing I say the minute we step out of her apartment and by her reaction, I know it was the exact wrong thing to say.

Because she stops walking not three feet from her door. "Oh." She's blinking furiously and her face has turned a shade of pink I've only ever seen on a cupcake. "Do you want me to set you guys up?" She clears her throat. "You two would look perfect together."

"Emma—"

I don't get to finish because she's already back at her apartment door with a key in her hand. "I should have thought of that." She's mumbling but I can hear her.

"No. Emma..."

In seconds, she's got the door reopened and she's stepped through. I follow her because I've got to do my utter best to fix this.

"You forget something?" Her roommate is sitting on the sofa with a remote in her hands.

"Uh." Emma's voice cracks. "He likes you." Then, before I can say a goddamn word, she's gone. She disappears into a door at the back of the apartment.

"What'd you do?" The roommate is now standing a foot from me. She looks angry. Really angry.

"Nothing. All I did was mention that you were pretty."

"You idiot." Her voice is a growl. I'm not going to lie, she's intimidating. "You fucking, fucking idiot."

"I didn't mean it like it sounded."

"How did you mean it, dumbass?"

"Wow. Knock off the insults. I was just making conversation."

She rolls her eyes so hard it looks like it hurts. "Try talking about the goddamn weather or her hair or her dress. She tried hard to look pretty for you." She growls again. "Have you ever gone on a date before?"

"Yes."

"You must suck at it because the last thing you do is talk about another girl." She stomps over the couch, picks up the remote, and turns off the television. "That's dating one-oh-one."

"She didn't let me finish. I was thinking you'd be a good match for my teammate Cody." But now that she's ripping me a new asshole–– Wait, yeah, she'd be perfect for Cody.

"Cody Williams?" she asks with an arched brow.

"Yeah."

Waving me off, she continues, "This isn't about me. You need to go in there…" She points in the direction of the door Emma disappeared into. "…and try to salvage whatever this is you've got with Emma." She points at me. "Wait. Do you want something with Emma?"

Do I want something with Emma? "Yes."

"What do you want?" She's still pointing. "If you're just trying to get in her pants…."

"No." I shake my head. "I can get laid anytime."

With another hard eye roll, Carley sighs. "Please don't say something like that to her."

"I wouldn't." Well, I probably would since I keep putting my foot in my mouth.

"Go." She gestures toward Emma's door. "Tell her what your intentions are so she knows what's going on with you two. No more misunderstandings."

"Right." I stare at her for a second, then I ask, "You want me to go into her room?"

"Knock first." Carley mumbles something like "Fucking idiot" under her breath but I can hear her. Yep, she and Cody would hit it off.

"Right." Sliding my hand over my tie, I step around the couch and down a short hallway. I know she's watching me, so I point to the door and look back at Carley.

"That's the one."

Raising my hand, I knock softly.

"Go away, Carley."

Her voice sounds soggy. She's crying.

Shit.

I knock again.

"Carley. I'm not in the mood."

I'm startled by a whisper in my ear. "Just go in."

"You sure?"

"Positive."

Reaching out, I turn the knob and expect it to be locked. It's not. When it clicks open, I push it open slightly--enough to see that Emma's lying face down on her bed. The dress she had on has been replaced by black stretchy pants and what looks like a T-shirt.

"Emma?"

She must not have expected me because she practically jumps off the bed, wiping her face with the bottom of her T-shirt, revealing porcelain white skin on her stomach. "Eli?" she croaks. "I thought you left."

"No. I--we need to talk."

"It's okay." She gives me a fake-ass smile. "I get it. You don't have to explain anything."

"No?" I move into the room and press the door shut behind me. "I think I do."

"Eli…."

Stepping close to her, I look down at her blotchy face. The little bit of eye makeup she had on is now sort of running down her face making her look like a pretty raccoon. Reaching down, I swipe my thump beneath her eye. "You've got a little makeup."

"I do?" Turning away from me, she bends to look into a small mirror. "Great," she grumbles. "Can this night get anymore terrible?"

"Terrible?" Wow. That breaks my fucking heart. "I wanted tonight to be special."

Emma stands and slowly turns to face me. "Well, it was *especially* terrible." She doesn't smile. I wish she would.

"I'm sorry. I wasn't… I didn't mean to say that about your roommate. I didn't mean it the way you think."

"She's really pretty and super nice—"

"Will you please let me speak?" I didn't say that in anger, but I'm getting tired of her assuming the worst from me.

Her head moves up and down slowly.

"Out in the hallway, I was going to say that she and Cody would be a good fit, but you jumped to the conclusion that I wanted to date her. Hell, you had your door unlocked and you were in your bedroom in two minutes flat.

"I just figured—"

"You figured I was there to hook up with your roommate when I was there to take you on our first date. A first of many." I pause. "At least I was hoping it was the first of many."

"As friends." She's not asking.

"Is that what you want? For us to be friends?"

Her head moves up and down. "I want us to be friends."

"Is that all?" I hope to God she says no to that question.

"It's what you said you wanted."

"When?"

"At the coffee shop, at the library, everywhere."

Placing my hand on her cheek, I run my thumb across the softest skin I've ever touched. "Emma Perkins?"

"Yes?"

Leaning down, I touch my lips against hers. When I pull back, I see Emma's eyes are closed and her mouth is waiting for more. So I do it again. Only this time, when our lips touch, I move my body closer and wrap my free arm around her and rest it on her lower back. Our bodies are touching. She fits against me like a perfect puzzle piece. Her breasts rest below my pecs and when her arms wrap around my waist, I sigh into her mouth. Using my tongue, I enter her mouth and hope she responds in kind.

When she does, the hand that was on her cheek slides into her hair. It's soft as silk too. Everything about this girl is luxurious. Pulling back, I rest my forehead on hers. "Emma Perkins?"

"Yes?"

"I want to be more than friends."

"Okay."

"Yeah?" I smile down at her. "You sure?"

"I'm sure."

"Oh, and Emma?"

"Yeah?"

"You autocomplete me."

I feel a slap on my ass, and laugh when she says, "That one was dumb."

"Sorry." I chuckle before leaning in for another kiss. This one was even better than the first two.

13

—————

EMMA

THIS IS SURREAL. I'M SITTING ON MY SOFA IN MY LIVING ROOM pretending to eat the pizza that Eli ordered for us. Netflix is playing some movie on the laptop in front of us, but all I can think about is Eli's hand resting on my upper thigh. That and the fact the lights are off, and my roommate decided to go to the library. *On a Saturday night.*

But I digress.

I'm doing what the kids refer to as Netflix and chilling. With a guy. And not just any guy. With *the* Eli Baxter. With the Eli Baxter who says he wants to be more than friends. With *me*.

See what I mean? Surreal.

"Do you like the movie?"

I'm jerked from my thoughts about how big his hand is and the fact that he's started gently stroking it up and down my leg. "Huh?"

"I said, do you like the movie?"

"Oh, yeah. *Love* it." *I like his hand on my leg more.* I nod like my life depended on it.

"How 'bout the pizza? You like that too?"

I just keep on nodding. "Mm-hm. Delish."

"You haven't taken one bite. Not one." The smirk on Eli's face says it all. "And you haven't been paying attention to the movie. I've asked you several questions and you've ignored me."

"Oh." I smile to buy myself some time. "It's because I'm *so* into it."

His palm leaves my thigh and moves to my face and rests on my cheek. "You're a terrible liar." I watch him move closer until his lips touch mine. It makes me forget about the paper plate holding my pizza slice in my lap. Turning, I feel it slide off onto the floor, but I couldn't care less.

Wrapping my arms around his neck, I pull myself closer to him. His warm hand moves from my face to wrap around me to my lower back until we're pressed together. His heart is beating almost as hard as mine is.

"Em," he whispers in my ear. I feel his hands move up and down my back. When one of them slides forward and over my breast, I squeak. One of his fingers sweeps across my nipple, which makes a moan escape. A sound I've never made in my entire life.

"This okay?" he asks as he does it again until my nipple is hard as stone.

"Yes," I hiss as he does it several more times. It makes me want to bite him. So I do. Not hard, right below his ear.

"Shit." Eli moans this time. "Yeah. Bite me."

I do it again in the same spot, then take his earlobe in my mouth and nibble.

"Fuck."

I'm on my back on the sofa before I even know we're moving. His hand moves beneath my T-shirt until it rests on my bra-covered breast. With a tug, I feel the cup of lace being pulled down and his hand sliding gently over my exposed nipple.

"Eli," I pant.

"This okay?"

I like that he asks me if what he's doing is all right with me. "Yes."

His mouth covers mine in a kiss so heated, I want to melt. I think I might. I touch him too. Down his back, over his firm butt, then back around to his chest and stomach. Every part of him is hard and muscled. I'm tempted to move my hands lower, but I'm not ready. Cool air hits my stomach and I realize he's pulled my top up. I should stop him.

"God, you're so fucking pretty."

Well, shoot. I should stop this, but when his mouth latches onto that same nipple he was touching a few moments ago, I'm in no state to tell him to stop because I never want it to end.

The second I hear a key in the lock in the front door, I'm both sad and a little relieved. "Shoot." I quickly move to a seated position while pulling down my shirt. I look over as Eli does his best to get situated too. He's doing it gingerly. When I see his pants and the tent in the front, you know, crotch region, I realize his issue. Reaching to my left, I grab a pillow and toss it into his lap which generates a yelp from him.

"Sorry."

"No." He shakes his head, making a gasping sound. "It's okay." Resting the pillow that matches our '80s floral couch over his lap, we both look up as Carley steps into the apartment. The minute she sees us, she smirks.

"Sorry if I interrupted you, but the library closed so I had to come home."

"N-No problem." I'm still really turned on and a little dazed, to be honest. "Glad to see you."

She snickers. "Sure." Pointing to the hallway, she adds, "I'm heading to bed. Night."

The second her door shuts, Eli tosses the pillow on the floor and leans back into me.

"Uh, Eli?"

*God, I'm an idiot.*

Squeezing his eyes shut, he sighs. "Right."

"Sorry."

His eyes open and a sincere smile spreads over his face. "Don't be sorry, Em."

"You sure?" I look down at his lap and see it hasn't gone down at all.

"I'm sure." Leaning closer, he kisses me softly. "I need to get home anyway. Early practice tomorrow."

"On Sunday?"

"Every day."

"Oh. Wow." I had no idea.

Standing, Eli holds his hand out for me to take. Once I'm in front of him, he asks, "Can I call you tomorrow?"

"Sure." I nod. "Yeah."

Handing him his suit jacket, I walk Eli to the door. He kisses me again and waves as he steps out into the hallway. Shutting the door, I lean against it and sigh.

"You look satisfied." Carley must have heard him leave because she's standing at her open bedroom door.

"I'm not sure satisfied is the right word."

"What is the right word?"

"Happy," I say with a broad smile. "I'm happy."

After I brush my teeth and get a glass of water, I slide into my bed. As I'm reaching for my bedside lamp, my phone chimes.

**Eli:** Sweet dreams, beautiful.

**Me:** You too.

**Eli:** I'm beautiful? LOL

**Me:** You are. But I'll use handsome instead.

**Eli:** That's better.

I decide to leave it at that. But add:

**Me:** Night.

**Eli:** Night.

# 14

ELI

WHAT THE HELL JUST HAPPENED? I MEAN, I'M NOT UNHAPPY WITH everything that went down with Emma tonight. I just never expected to ask a girl on a first date and end up being her--well-being something more significant in the same night. Was it too fast? Do I need to back off or is this exactly what I need? What I want? I've got to process this—maybe talk it out with someone who knows me. Reaching into my jacket pocket, I pull out my phone and text Cody. Since he's out partying, I agree to meet him at Paradise for a beer. That place is gonna be packed but hopefully, we'll find a spot so we can talk for a while. Then I need to get to bed. I wasn't lying when I told Emma I had practice in the morning. I need my sleep.

As I wait for Cody at the bar, I send a quick text to Emma.

**Me:** Sweet dreams, beautiful.

I stare at my phone as she sends me a reply. I chuckle at our short text exchange and smile from ear to ear as Cody takes the seat next to me.

"So, why are you calling me at eleven o'clock on the night you had a date?" Cody's left eye is arched like he knows something's up.

"We ended up staying in."

"Oh? I thought you had reservations at the fancy Chez Robert place." He mispronounces "Chez" as always. No matter how many times I've told him the 'z' is silent, he insists on emphasizing it.

"Chez Paul. I did." And I forgot to call and cancel them. They're not going to be happy with me but since my dad almost always eats there when he's in town, I think they'll forgive me. Nobody gives the great and powerful Jack Baxter any grief.

"So? What happened?"

"She…" I'm interrupted by someone bumping into my right side, then sliding their arms around my neck. I feel lips below my ear a second later.

Fucking puck bunnies.

I reach up and take her hands in mine and unwrap her from me. "Do you mind?"

"Not at all." She smirks.

God, I'm sick of this shit. Why did I suggest Paradise? "My buddy and I are talking right now."

"Oh." She titters. "I'll catch you later, then, Bax."

No, she won't. Ignoring her, I turn to my best friend.

"Whoa. You're really into that girl, aren't you?"

"Can I just tell you what went down tonight?" I want to talk this out. See if he thinks it's as crazy as I do. So I start at the beginning. At the part where the date became a non-date.

As soon as I tell the entire story, Cody's first response is "Is her roommate hot?"

Of course, he picks up on that. "Yes. She's just your type." I scoff, exasperated. "Can you stay on topic, please?"

"Sure." He sips his beer. "You made your girl cry? On your first date?"

Okay. Not surprising he jumps to that. "It was a misunderstanding."

"That you got squared away by telling her you want to be more than friends. Then you proceeded to Netflix and chill on her couch." He's not asking.

I nod anyway.

"So you were about to go on a hot first date and ended up sitting on the couch like a couple of old fogies." Cody chuckles.

Well, I wouldn't call us old fogies. Not when I remember having my mouth on hers while my hand was up her shirt and my palm was cupping her tit. A tit that was the perfect size. It was pretty and pink too. Oh, shit. My dick's reacting again at the mere thought of it. Time to change the subject.

"It wasn't bad."

Cody stares at me for a several long seconds. "You've got a girlfriend now." Again, that wasn't a question.

"I think I do."

"What's your dad gonna say?"

The fuck do I care? "I'm sure he'll be pissed, but it can't be helped."

"You'd better not let him get wind of it."

My father thinks women are a distraction. According to him, my one and only focus should be on hockey and making it onto an NHL team. "*I'm* not gonna tell him." Because I don't need him driving up here so he can get his nose into my personal business. I'm sick of it.

Cody places his hand over his heart. "He won't hear it from me."

"Good." I'm weighing the options of going home or staying for another beer when another woman approaches me. This time, she slides between my open legs and throws an arm around my shoulder. "You want to get out of here?" she asks seductively.

"No." Yes. But I want to do it alone.

"Ah, now, come on, Bax." She juts out her bottom lip. "Don't be a party-pooper."

Party-pooper? Who says that shit anymore?

"He's taken, beautiful," Cody says in his smooth, creepy way. "But *I'm* available."

"You're Cody, right?" She slides her arm off me and turns to my friend.

"I sure am. Cody Williams at your service, milady." He even bows a little. God, the guy has no shame.

"Well, Cody." She giggles. "Since your friend is such a downer, I'd be happy to take you up on your offer. Your place or mine?" Between the two of them, they've brought back lines from '50s cinema. And not in a good way.

"Yours." He picks up her hand and kisses it. "Shall we?"

"We shall." She giggles again.

I watch the two of them walk away. The minute they're out the door, I slide off the stool, throw a twenty on the bar, and leave.

15

EMMA

It's been three and a half days since my date with Eli.

Well, I guess it wasn't technically a date. Not after I made a spectacle of myself in the hallway and in my bedroom. No, date isn't the right word. It doesn't matter. It's been three and a half days since I last saw him. Or spoke to him. He told me he'd call me on Sunday, but he didn't. That was okay because I knew he was busy with hockey practice and being a computer programming major.

I get it.

But when Monday came and went and Tuesday was the same, well, I've resigned myself to the fact that that whole thing with Eli in my apartment Saturday night was entirely imagined. He got a little action and that was all he wanted.

*Oh, crap.*

Wait one second... What if he--what if I'm a terrible kisser? What if he was turned off by my, well, my body? Goodness knows he saw some of it. His hands felt quite a bit of it.

Slapping a hand over my face, I groan. No. I'm going with the first one, because I felt how much he enjoyed touching me, so it had to be my kissing skills, or lack-thereof. Of course, he wasn't impressed "I'm so embarrassed."

"Why?" Ava asks, stepping up next to me at the library counter.

"Oh." I didn't realize she was here. It means my shift is almost over. "Nothing."

"It wasn't nothing. You groaned like you were in pain. Why are you embarrassed?"

Should I tell her?

No. She's not my friend.

"Just going back over a test I just took. I did terrible."

Ava's expression is unreadable. When she shrugs, I know she's going to let this whole thing drop. Looking behind her, she looks back at me as she pulls her phone out of her pocket. "Hey, check this out. I saw our boy at Paradise on Saturday."

*Our* boy?

"I took a couple of pictures." Ava makes a scoffing sound. "The guy is such a player." Turning her phone to face me, I see a photo of Eli. It's easy to tell it's him. He appears to be wearing the same suit from Saturday night. There's a blonde girl wrapped up in his arms, kissing his neck. I glance at his face and he seems to be okay with it. I mean, he's not fighting her off. His hand is resting on her arm and everything.

My face heats immediately. Embarrassment like I've never felt before sweeps through me. "Wh-What time was that?"

She peeks at the photo. "Time stamp says 11:23."

He left my house a little before eleven. He sent me a text fifteen minutes or so after that. Wow. He didn't waste any time. I guess when I told him I wanted to stop, he needed more.

"Moral of the story?" She smirks. "Stay away from *that* guy unless you're just hoping for a hookup."

"Right." I do my best to smile. It's difficult though. "Of course. We're just friends." I swallow the lump in my throat, and it hurts it's so dry.

"Oh, speak of the devil," Ava whispers. "The man himself."

I look up in time to watch Eli saunter closer. My initial reaction is to smile at him but then I remember the picture and the smile drops. I don't bother scowling. I'm not his girlfriend. It was just the two of us watching TV. A couple of kisses––a hand up my shirt. Nothing more. Why would there be more?

"Hey, beautiful."

Okay. Now that hurts.

"Eli." It's all I can muster; my voice sounds strained.

"What's wrong?"

"Nothing?" I force a smile across my lips.

"You sure?" His handsome face actually looks concerned.

"Positive. Need a room?" I grab the black binder notebook that holds the sign-up sheets.

"I, uh… was hoping you were getting off soon."

"Nope." I fake smile again. "I'm working late today."

"No, you're not." Ava decides right then to butt into my business. "You're off in like five minutes."

"Oh, great." Eli's smile is too pretty.

"Well, I was supposed to be off, but they asked me to work on a special project." God, I'm a terrible liar.

"What special project?" Ava needs to get a life and stay out of mine.

I turn my head so only she can see the scowl that's crossing my face. "I'll tell you about it *later*."

"Oh." She snickers. "Right." She turns to Eli and says, "You looked like you were having a good time at Paradise on Saturday night."

"Paradise?" Eli blinks a few times. His head slowly moves down until he's looking me in the eye. "I met up with Cody."

Like I care.

"Sure, you did," Ava singsongs. "Who was she?" She holds up her phone and shows Eli the same photo as she showed me.

"See?" She snickers. "You looked like you were having a really good night."

"I…" Eli looks at me again. Now he knows. "She was just a puck bunny. She hugged me, then I pushed her away."

"Puck…" I start, my voice husky. So much so I have to clear my throat. "…bunny?"

"Girls who are into hockey players. *Any* hockey player."

"She's pretty." I mean, I can only see her back and a little of her face, but from that she looks like they'd match.

"*You're* prettier."

Oh, now I know he's full of it. And it makes me mad. "Yeah. Right." I turn and make my way into the little office behind the desk.

Inside the office, I step past a chair just as I feel a hand on my arm. "Em."

I squeeze my eyes shut and do my best to gather myself. "No." I shake my head. "It's okay, Eli." Turning around, I'm now facing him. When I look up, there's concern written all over his handsome face. "I'm sorry. I didn't mean to cause any drama. You can go out with whoever you want. I… this means nothing."

"It's not nothing, Emma."

"Well, I had no right to assume you and I were--"

"What? We're what?"

"A thing." I don't know what to call it. "An item." I guess I'm funny because he laughs. It makes me embarrassed--again. I'm sure tired of feeling that way. "Never mind." I turn and bend so I can grab my bookbag, but Eli beats me to it. Picking it up, he throws it over his shoulder. I feel a little sorry for him because my bag is heavy. But only a little.

"So you *are* off work?"

I've got no reason to lie to him. "I am."

"Can we go somewhere and talk?"

Why would he want to talk? I sure as heck don't have anything more to say. Even if I did, he'd probably just laugh.

"Please?" His voice sounds almost vulnerable. "Em?"

Well, crud. "I have a few minutes."

"Great." His hand that was on my upper arm reaches down and takes my hand. He pulls on it until I'm following him out of the little office and around the desk.

"Night, Ava," I say as he pulls me along.

"Emma?" she asks, but I shake her off.

Now I'm practically jogging to keep up with him. "Slow down," I grumble.

"Oh, sorry." He chuckles nervously. "I forgot your legs are a lot shorter than mine."

Whatever. "Where are we going?"

"Let's go down to the archives."

The archives are the darkest, dustiest, and dingiest part of the library. It's the place they hold everyone's dissertations and theses. You know, the things no one ever reads again. "Well––" I can't think of an argument, so I follow his lead down the weird set of stairs that lead to the bowels of the library. Once there, Eli pushes open the door, reaches to his right and flips a switch. A few lights flicker on and I have to wonder how he knows about this place. I mean, he knew right where the switch was. I'm about to ask him when I feel his hands slide beneath my armpits and I'm lifted into the air. There's enough light to let me see I'm being moved to my left. When he sets me down, something cold hits my bottom. I look down and see a short filing cabinet.

"Eli––?"

I don't get to finish that either because his mouth is on mine so fast, there's no time for me to question him. His arms wrap around me and his body finds its way between my legs. My crotch is lined up perfectly with his. I hate to say this, but I don't mind it.

When he pulls away from my mouth, his lips move across my cheek down to my neck. "That picture was nothing. I pushed her away. Ask Cody." He nibbles on my ear, which makes me tilt my head away to give him more room to work. My goodness, it feels good. "I met Cody there to talk about *you*." Eli's mouth moves back to mine. "All I can think about is you." His tongue swipes at my mouth. "Open those pretty lips for me."

I can't refuse. I guess I'm weak. Or stupid. When I open my mouth, I feel his tongue seeking mine. I don't hesitate. I kiss him right back. And it's good. *Really* good. I feel it through my entire body. We're lined up together and his hardness is pressing against me, making me squirm. I press myself into him and hit that spot. The one I discovered on my own. Moaning at the feeling, I do it again.

"You like that." Eli sounds breathless.

"Yeah." I really like it.

"Good. Now rub that sweet little pussy against me, Em."

His words make me stop, suddenly. "Uh..." I mean, do I want to be doing that? In the archives?

"Please." Eli kisses my neck, then he suckles. When his palms make their way down to my butt, I feel him add pressure there until I'm pressed against him closer than before. I moan at the sensation.

"Eli."

When he presses into me, I moan again.

"Is this okay?" he asks as he does it again.

"Yessss." I wrap my arms around him and hold him so close and so tightly, it feels like we're one. "Eli. More."

He's begun to press against me rhythmically. Each time with a bit more pressure than the last. He's hitting that spot that's taking me higher and higher until--until. "Eli," I squeak. A feeling of euphoria rushes through my lower half. "Eli," I say rather breathlessly.

His grasp on my bottom is firmer now and he thrusts faster, then suddenly stops, releasing a moan that vibrates through my body. "Emma," he whispers in my ear. "Wow."

When he starts to laugh, I stiffen up. *Why is he laughing?* Doing my best to push him away, I scoot my bottom to the edge of the filing cabinet. "Let me down."

"No. Em—"

"Let me down." I look up into his eyes. "Please. Let me down."

"Not until we talk."

"That's what you said when you brought me down here." But I need to know. "Have you brought other girls down here?"

He's quiet. Too quiet.

"Yes."

"Great." I feel so frigging stupid.

"Look." He's still got his hands on my hips. "I really wanted to talk, but once we got in here, all I wanted to do was kiss you."

"Oh." Should I be falling for all of this? His lines?

"Yeah. Oh" He chuckles. "I'm sorry I dry-humped you in the archives." He looks remorseful.

*That's* what dry-humping is?

"Can we talk about Saturday night?" he asks softly. "I'm telling you the truth. Cody will vouch for me."

Of course he would; he's his friend.

"Cody won't lie for me, if that's what that look on your pretty face is telling me."

"I believe you."

"You do?"

I nod. I'm still not so thrilled about any of this. "You said you'd call on Sunday…."

His face is unreadable. All he's doing is blinking. Then— "Shit." Lowering his head, he rests his forehead on mine. "I forgot. I had practice, then homework…."

"I understand." I do. I really do. I get busy.

"I thought about you all day. Hell, for the last three and a half days."

Okaaay. What am I supposed to do with that information?

"*You* could have called *me*."

I quickly shake that suggestion off. "No. You said you were

going to call *me*." The ball was in his court as far as I was concerned.

"You won't call guys?" He's looking at me like he's sincerely asking.

"I––that's not what I said."

"Even after we dry-humped in the archives?" He chuckles again. "Will you call me after we did that?"

There's a rush of heat on my cheeks. Hopefully it's too dim in here for him to see. Doing my best not to sound nervous, I say, "It's not that."

"So, you're a traditionalist?"

I don't know what he means by that. "You said you'd call…" I sigh. "It's just manners. It's nothing to do with traditional or non-traditional or gender or equality. It's just manners." And even though my parents are poor as church mice, they've always thought manners and politeness were important. And kindness. That's a big one.

"I get it." Eli takes a half step back. "Manners."

"Yep. Manners."

"So, when I tell you I'm going to call, I need to call."

"That's the gist of it, yes."

"Manners," he says, then smiles. "Got it."

"Good."

"I'll call you later." He's got his hands beneath my armpits, helping me down from the filing cabinet.

When I've got both feet on the ground, I'm a little unsteady. Righting myself, I place each of my hands on his arms. Looking up at him, I arch my brow at him. "You'd better."

"I will." He bends down to kiss my mouth softly. "I promise."

16

ELI

"Manners," I repeat as I drive home. After our little talk in the library, Emma took off saying she had stuff to do. I'm not sure how to take it all. I mean, I'm used to women who want to spend every waking (and sleeping) moment with me. But Emma's not like other girls. She seems to be the opposite, and it's confusing.

Example. I offered to take her to dinner tonight, but she refused saying she was doing something with her roommate. When I asked if she wanted a ride home, she shook me off on that too. I can't figure her out.

As I pull into the driveway of the house I share with Cody and one of the other guys on the team, a house my dad purchased for me, my phone chimes. Thinking it might be Emma, I reach for it and am about to hit that little green circle when I see who's actually calling. "Dad," I mutter. Do I want to talk to him? No. But, if I don't, he'll keep calling. And calling. I hit the green icon. "Hello?"

"Son," my father, Jack Baxter, says loudly. I must be on speaker phone.

"Dad."

"How's practice going?"

95

See there? That's all he cares about, hockey. I mean, the guy didn't ask how I was, how school was going, nothing. He never does.

"It's going fine. How are you and Mom doing?"

"We're good, honey." I hear my mom's voice coming from somewhere in the background. See? Speaker phone. "How are classes going?"

There you go. My mom cares about other things besides hockey. She's had to, otherwise I think we'd all go insane because all my father ever thinks about is hockey.

"They're good. I've got As in all of my classes so far."

"Wonderful." At least she's proud of my academics.

"Never mind that. You need to focus on your workouts. Next year's your year, Eli."

He means next year is my year to enter the NHL draft. Something I'm honestly not sure I want to do. Sure, I like hockey. I enjoy the sport, the competition, and the guys on the team but is that what I want to do for a living? "I'm able to focus on more than one thing at a time, Dad."

"Bullshit," Jack Baxter grumbles.

"Jack," I hear my mom say in her soothing voice. The one she uses when she knows my dad is going to go off on some hockey tangent. "We talked about this."

"Helene." His voice sounds far away, which tells me he's now turned to talk to her. "Eli needs to put everything he has into hockey right now. He doesn't have time to pussyfoot around. He needs to focus. He's going to have one chance at this. I won't let him fuck it up."

*Focus.* That's a word I'm pretty goddamn sick of. I've heard it repeated so many times by my dad I could puke.

"We promised him, Jack. He wanted to go to college. We agreed as long as he continued with hockey. He kept up his end of the bargain. Now, let's let him decide for himself."

"He wants to program goddamn computers, Helene." My

dad's voice gets louder, and it's filled with contempt. "Do they even *need* programmers anymore? Isn't everything done by robots now anyway? How's he going to make a living? I'm sure as shit not going to support him forever."

I'm rolling my eyes hard all while thinking it's like I'm not even on the phone anymore. "Dad—" But he's still going.

"The only reason I agreed to his college bullshit is because he'll get exposure playing for the Badgers. Even if he ends up on an AHL team somewhere, he's still going to make more money than he ever did programming old computers."

"Dad." He's so clueless about what I want.

"Jack."

Mom and I are both trying to get him to let it go. I've heard the same song and dance from him for years.

"Just do what I asked you to do, Eli," my dad growls. "Get your fucking stats up and don't get distracted. Distraction is the worst thing for a player of your caliber. I've seen better guys than you get caught up in other mundane shit and miss their chance. You've got to *focus*."

There's that word again. "I'm doing it. I'm working hard. I'm focused. I swear." *Jesus.*

I'm ready for this call to end when he adds, "Your mother and I are coming up for a visit soon."

Great. "Okay. When?"

"We'll have to let you know. I've got some stuff going on here."

My parents live in Chicago. I guess I do too. We've lived in that city since my dad was drafted by Chicago. The year I was born. I'm glad because I love the Windy City. My friends are all there and if I'm being honest, I kind of like my solitude. The idea of moving all over the place with a bunch of stinky guys doesn't appeal to me in the least. Even this university was a stretch for me. The only reason I'm here is because my father played for the Badgers, and he figured if he caught the eye of the pro scouts here, so would I.

"We love you, honey." My mom's voice sounds so sweet compared to the loud bark of my father.

"Love you too." And I do love her. And him. He makes it difficult, though. All he can think about is hockey and me making it to the NHL like he did. But I'm not him. I'm good but he was *great*. Some of his impressive stats here at Wisconsin have never been matched. I'm nowhere near as good as Jack Baxter.

I get the reason he's like this because his career was cut short. His first season, he got the starting spot when the actual starting goalie broke his foot. In Dad's first game, he went for a puck and ended up tearing the hell out of his knee. Dad didn't let it stop him. After several surgeries, physical therapy, the doctors determined playing was no longer an option. So, he took some of his NHL money and found a niche in Chicago's real estate market. His name alone brought him clients, but his tenacity and smarts made his company what it is today—the largest commercial and residential real estate company in the city. Hell, in the state. To say he's successful is an understatement.

After the call is over, I realize I'm still sitting in my car in the driveway. Pushing open the door, I grab my shit and head inside to an empty house. Cody must be out and about. Mark, our other roommate, spends most of his time at his girlfriend's place so that's nice. Not that he's an issue. He took the basement bedroom. There's a small kitchenette down there and a living room. Not to mention he's got his own entrance. If it weren't a little bit humid down there, I'd have taken the spot, but he likes it, so it worked out that he's got the basement, and Cody and I've got the rest of the place.

Dropping my backpack, I head into the kitchen in search of food. One thing about being an athlete, we're always hungry. For real, 24/7 my stomach growls. I grab yesterday's takeout container and pop open the Styrofoam lid. "Asshole." I look down at a limp piece of lettuce and three hard fries. Cody ate my leftovers. "Fucker," I mutter again. He always eats my shit.

Tossing the white box into the trash, I reach into the freezer for a pizza. While the oven's heating, I make my way into my bedroom. I need a shower, then I need to eat. After that, homework. Stripping out of my clothes, I drop everything into the hamper and walk naked into the kitchen so I can slide the frozen pizza into the oven. Back in the bathroom, I get the water temp the way I like it—hot—and step beneath the spray. That's when my mind turns to Emma and our little interlude in the library. The memory of it makes my dick hard again. My God, the woman can kiss. Sure, she's shy and my guess is she's a little inexperienced, but she's so naturally sweet and sexy at the same time.

Reaching down, I take my hard cock in hand and imagine what it'd be like to be inside Emma Perkins. "Snug." I growl as I pump my dick. God, the thought her small hand doing the work for me makes me throw my head back and come in record time.

## 17

EMMA

"You what?"

My roommate is so nosey. Well, okay, I guess I'm the one that opened our apartment door, dropped my bag, and jogged back to her bedroom and blabbed about my incident in the library. The one with Eli.

"I dry-humped with Eli." I pause for emphasis. "In. The. Library."

"You dry-humped Eli Baxter in the library?"

"In the archives."

"Oh, no." Carley gasps. "That's the place everyone goes to hook up. Was that your idea or his?"

My smile slips over to a frown. "I wondered about that." I did remember. "He knew where the light switch was."

"Of course, he did. Everyone knows where the light switch is."

"Do you?" I mean, this is the first I'm hearing of this. How does Carley know?

She blushes at my question, which gives me the answer.

"Geesh." I cover my face with my hands. "So, do you think he was…."

"I think he wanted to get you alone. I don't think you should read too much into the fact it all happened in one of the most notorious hook-up spots on campus. I mean, you were already *in* the library." She smiles and it looks a little sinister if I'm being honest. "So tell me… and be honest. Did you like it?"

Oh, I see. She's going to talk about my virginity. Again. I'm going to play dumb because I hate this conversation. "Like what?"

Carley is a master eye-roller. This time was no exception. "The dry-humping. Did you enjoy it?"

Fine. "Yes."

"Did you come?" Her question comes out rather soft, like she's a little afraid to ask it.

"Yes."

"What about him?" Her eyebrows wiggle up and down. "Did he––?"

"I assume so."

"You assume so?" She chuckles.

I guess I don't know so I shrug. "Yes. I assume so." You know what they say about assuming? It makes an *ass* out of *U* and *me*. Get it? My high school biology teacher used to say that all the time. It stuck.

"Let me ask you this way. At any point in your little rendezvous, did he throw his head back and roar like a lion?"

What is she talking about? Roar like *a lion*? Now I'm the one who chuckles. "He did throw his head back. But he didn't roar. It was more of a…" What was it? I close my eyes in an attempt to recall. "It was more of a raspy growl."

"Ooh, he's a growler?" She smirks. "That's hot."

I crack up at her words. God, this girl is hilarious. "Whatever." I'm still laughing. "You're insane."

Carley jumps up off her bed and wraps me up in her arms. "You're growing up so fast. Next thing you know, you'll be fucking that guy."

Slapping her arm, I'm still laughing. "Shut up."

Pulling away from me, Carley's knees are bent so she is looking at me at eye level. *My* eye level. "Seriously." And she does look serious. "I'm proud of you."

"I didn't do anything."

"You dry-humped. In. The. Library." She mimics my words from early. "That's huge."

I shrug. "I guess."

"So, when are you gonna see him again?"

"I'm not sure. He said he'd call."

Carley flops back onto her bed. "He'd better do it this time."

"I know. I told him."

Sitting up abruptly, Carley looks surprised. "You did? Did you give him the manners talk?"

"Shut up." I laugh.

"You did. You gave him the manners talk. Did you also talk about kindness? Did you repeat your mom's mantra?"

She's talking about the one my mom has repeated a million times to me. "If you can't be kind, be quiet." I guess working retail for so many years has made her believe that. I guess I do too. "No. I didn't tell him that one. I just told him it was poor manners not to call when you say you're going to call." I shrug. Why wouldn't I tell him that?

"Good for you, hon." She looks as though she really thinks it was good for me. "How did he take it?"

"Fine. Good. I--" Just as I'm about to continue, my phone starts to vibrate in my pocket. Pulling it out, I see Eli's name. Turning it to show Carley, I add, "See? He said he'd call me later." I look down at the phone again. "It's later." Pressing the button, I put the phone to my ear as I leave Carley's bedroom. She follows me. The snoop. "Hello?"

"Hi, Emma," he says in his deep voice. He makes my name sound so nice.

"Hi, Eli."

"I'm calling like I said I would."

"I see that." I walk into my bedroom, turn, and shut the door right in Carley's face and giggle.

"What's so funny?"

"Nothing." No, I'd better say something, so he doesn't think I'm laughing at him. "I was laughing at Carley."

"Oh. I see."

There's a pause. A long one. Should I say something? "What are you wearing?" Okay. What the ever-loving heck? Why would I ask him such a crazy question?

I guess he thinks it's funny because he laughs. I have to wait for him to finish before I can get a word in. You know, to apologize. "No. I mean…"

"I'm wearing a pair of old workout shorts."

Oh. "That's it?" It's getting cold outside. He should have a T-shirt on at the very least.

"That's it." I hear him make a guffawing kind of sound. "Now, beautiful Emma. What are *you* wearing?"

"The same thing as before. I just got home."

"Oh." He's quiet for a moment. "Maybe you should change into something more comfortable."

"I will." Duh. Usually, it's the first thing I do when I get home. "The bra has to come off first." Oh. My. Goodness. *What am I saying?*

"Oh, yeah?" His voice got that husky tone again. "Maybe you should do that now. While we're on the phone?"

"I'm good."

"You sure are. But you kiss like you're naughty." He sighs. "Actually, that whole thing in the library, Em, that was hot. The way you wrapped your legs—"

"Eli," I squeak. I'm not used to talking like this or being talked to like this, I guess.

"Too much?" He chuckles.

"Maybe." I mean. I don't hate this sexy side of Eli. No. I *definitely* don't hate it. "I'm just not ready for phone stuff." I may as well be honest with him. Or talking about what we did in the library. Not in any detail, anyway.

"Fair enough." I hear him moving around on the other end of the line. "Which brings me to the reason for my call."

"Uh-huh." I'm leery. It can't be helped. It's just me.

"I want to take you to a party this weekend."

"A party?" Oh dear. "What kind of party?"

"A hockey party."

I swallow hard. "A hockey party? With hockey people?"

"The team. Yeah."

"Where is this party?"

"At one of the guy's houses."

"Can Carley come too?"

"Sure. That'd be a good way for me to introduce her to Cody."

Oh, right. He thinks they'd hit it off. "Okay."

"Saturday night, then?" he asks. "I'll pick you up early and we can get dinner beforehand."

"Okay."

"Invite Carley and we can double."

"Double?"

"Double date."

"Oh." I'm an idiot. "Right."

"Great," Eli says, sounding chipper. "Well, I'm going to hit the books. Call me later?"

"Me?" He wants *me* to call *him?*

"Yeah. You. You call me."

"Later? Tonight?"

"Sure. If you want. Or tomorrow. Or both."

Both? No. "Okay." Oh, crap. I can't believe I just said I'd call him later. The notion makes my stomach flutter. Truth? I've never called a guy in my life.

Correction, I've called boys about school things. You know,

like lab partners--pretty much it's guys that I never wanted to kiss or do other things with. No. Eli's my first, well, everything, I guess. "Bye." I need to hang up. I need to tell Carley about the party and her date.

## 18

ELI

"Ladies," I say as the apartment door opens to reveal both Emma and her roommate, Carley. They're both dressed in nice jeans and sweaters. Appropriate for the chilly fall weather. Winter is fast approaching for sure. I take special notice of Emma's outfit. Her jeans are tight all the way down her legs. Her deep green sweater, isn't—sadly. It's oversized and it hangs down to midthigh. But the color looks gorgeous with her hair and skin. She's got on some of those short boots women wear now. Her hair is down in waves, which I love. It looks soft and silky. I can't wait to touch it later.

"Hi, Eli," Emma says shyly.

"This is Cody." I reach back and grab Cody's sleeve and bring him forward. "Cody, meet Carley."

"Well, you're as beautiful as Eli described."

I quickly look at Emma at his words. Sure enough, the smile she had on her face when she opened the door is gone.

"Thanks." Carley reaches her hand out to shake Cody's. "Nice to meet you. I've heard about you."

"Oh?" Cody smirks. "My reputation precedes me."

"Sure." She chuckles. "If you want to go there."

"Do not go there, dude," I mutter, still looking at Emma. "May we come in?" We're still standing out in the hallway.

"Sure," Emma says as both she and Carley take several steps back so we can enter. Once we're inside, Carley asks, "Would you two like anything?"

Yes. Absolutely yes. I'd like the little brunette.

"Well…" She laughs a little. "I guess all we've got is water or coffee."

"I'm good." I look over at Cody, who hasn't taken his eyes off Carley. I knew he'd like her. "Cody?" I slug his arm.

"Huh?" He blinks at me like he just realized I was here. "What?"

"Water? Coffee?"

"Oh." He chuckles and looks back at his date. "Nah. Thanks."

"Shall we go then?"

The girls put on jackets and as we approach the door, I hold my hand out for Emma to take. When she slides her palm into mine, I release an inner sigh. Even though her hand is tiny, it feels perfect in mine.

"We thought we'd go to the steak place on Beckett Ave," Cody says looking at Carley like she's the actual Stanley Cup. "Unless you don't care for steak, then we can go somewhere else. Wherever you ladies want to go is fine with me." He glances at me. "Us."

My God. Cody is nervous. I want to laugh and make fun of the guy, but I can't. Not when he's so obviously in uncharted waters. What happened to my smooth best friend?

"No. That sounds fine to me." Carley looks at Em. "What do you think, Emma?"

She shrugs, then nods. She's quiet. Too quiet. So I lean down and whisper in her ear, "What's wrong?"

"Nothing." She gives me a smile, but I can tell it's not a sincere one. How do I know? Because it doesn't reach her eyes.

I watch Cody head down the stairs first, then Carley. I take the opportunity to straighten this out. When they're out of sight, I tug Emma close to me. "If this is about calling Carley beautiful…."

"No." She shakes her head.

"Emma, don't lie to me."

"I didn't…." Emma's lashes flutter. "Okay. It did. It bothered me."

"Well…" Pulling her closer, I bend down and kiss her mouth. "I had to say that to get Cody on board with a blind date."

"She is pretty, though."

"Not as pretty as you."

Her eyes roll hard.

"Don't roll your eyes at me." I slide my palm down to her round little ass and tap it. "I mean it."

A blush spreads across her cheeks in record time. "I--"

Kissing her lips again, fast, I take her hand in mine again. "We'd better get down there."

19

———

EMMA

I can't believe I'm at a party. Not only that, but a party thrown by an athletic team, in this case hockey.

"Would you look at all the smokin' hot guys." That comment courtesy of my roommate. I lost her the minute we stepped into the party as it's packed to the gills in here. We finally found each other again.

"The sheer quantity of testosterone in this room could maim someone." Again. Carley.

She's right, though. "There's a lot."

"Why are you just standing here by the door?"

"Eli went to get us a drink. He told me to stay here."

"How long ago was that?"

I have to give that some thought. "Five songs ago."

"Five songs ago?" Carley screeches. "What the hell, Em? You've just been waiting for him for five songs?"

I shrug. What was I supposed to do? Carley ran off and… "He told me to wait here."

"You're not a fucking dog, hon."

I give her my best scowl. "I know." Ugh. She always knows what to say to make me feel like an idiot. "You ran off and I didn't

111

know what I was doing. Look at all these people." I'm not pointing at the throng on the makeshift dance floor. "I didn't want to get lost."

"Oh, hon," Carley coos as she pats my back. "I'm sorry."

I look up at her and give her the stink eye. "Whatever." She looks beautiful tonight. Well, she's always beautiful but especially tonight with her hair down, straight and shiny. She's also wearing her tightest jeans (her words) with a cute, cropped sweater. Something I'd never get away with because my stomach, well, let's just say it's not cropped-sweater worthy. "Where'd Cody go?"

Carley shrugs. "Who knows. He mumbled something to me then took off. He's been gone about three songs."

"Hm. Maybe we should look for them."

"Better than standing here getting beer spilled on us."

I look at the side of my jean-clad leg and nod. Someone splattered me with beer a few minutes ago. "Good point." I let Carley lead the way since she's taller and can see above some of the crowd. I hang on to her belt loop, so I don't lose her. I should have done that with Eli. When he said, "Gonna get us a drink. Be right back... You stay there," I should have known it wasn't going to end well.

"I see them," she shouts back to me.

I don't bother responding. Instead, I hold a little tighter to the waistband of her jeans as she works her way through the throng of dancers. Ugh. It stinks like sweat.

"Ladies." I think that's Cody's voice. "There you are."

I peek around Carley to see that, yep, it's Cody. He's standing with several girls––and Eli. Both of the guys are holding red cups and look as though they've been having a great time.

Without us.

I don't know why but it bothers me, but it does. A lot. I've been standing near the door for the past twenty minutes or so. Meanwhile, Eli's got a nice red cup full of whatever as he talks to three of the prettiest women I've ever seen. I mean, if he'd been holding another glass, you know, the one for me, I may have been able to overlook it since it probably took him a while to get to the drinks, but he's only got the one.

I'm not going to cry. Okay. Let me rephrase that. I'm not going to cry in front of all these people. Not at my first real college party. There's only one way to ensure that doesn't happen.

Without another thought, I turn on my heel and go back the way I came. To the door. I'm out on the front porch in record time. I guess it pays to be short because I was able to maneuver my way through the crowd easier than Carley. By the time I get to the sidewalk, I hear my name. I'd love to tell you it was Eli's voice.

"What?" I turn quickly.

"Wait for me."

"You don't have to leave."

"Yeah. I do. I'm not staying if you're not."

Nodding, I turn and start walking again. I have no idea what Carley's thinking, but my concern is she's thinking I may have overreacted. "Um...."

"What?"

"I think I may have overreacted by storming out of the party like a house on fire." Just putting it out there. No need for me to hide my thoughts from her.

"Mm, yeah. I was sort of thinking the same thing."

Why do I hate that she said that? She was merely agreeing with me.

"Here's the thing, though," she adds. "It's going to be interesting to see what he does."

"Eli?"

"Yep." She pops the *p* sound at the end. "My theory is that he'll jump into his fancy SUV and be hot on your trail any minute."

I turn my head to look back the way we came. No sign of Eli's vehicle. "You think?"

"I do. And here's what we need to do. We head for Gilly's Fro-Yo. If he doesn't find us before then, we stop for some delicious frozen yogurt."

"And if he does?" I love this girl.

"Then give him a chance to explain himself. If he makes up some bullshit excuse about why he just left you standing at the door, then you know he's not for you. But if he seems sincerely sorry, then maybe you kiss and make up with him while *I* get some delicious frozen yogurt."

I slap her arm and laugh. "Not fair. I want fro-yo too." Even though it's pretty dang cold outside. It's too bad I left my coat in his car.

"I'm sure your boy will buy you some."

As we turn the corner onto one of Madison's main thorough-fares, we hear a horn honk. Looking to our right, we see Eli's sleek black SUV pull into the convenience store parking lot in front of us and stop.

"There he is," Carley hisses. "Listen to me." She bends closer and whispers in my ear, "Do *not* apologize."

I look up at her. "I won't." I didn't do anything terribly wrong. Not really.

"Good." She gives me one good nod. "Because, my virginal little friend, he needs to learn to grovel every now and then."

"That doesn't seem right."

"Right, schmight. If he doesn't see how his actions have consequences... how will he ever learn?

I release a snort that's louder than it should have been. "He's not a dog for crying out loud, Carley."

"Just trust me. He'll kiss your pretty little ass."

"My ass is not little."

"It's perfectly round and perky. I'd kill for your ass."

I grumble at her because she loves to embarrass me like that sometimes. That's when I see Eli has parked his car, opened his door, and stepped out. Carley and I slow slightly as we approach him. "Remember what I told you."

"I will." I'll try anyway.

"Em."

I don't say anything because I'm not sure what to say yet.

"Emma," Eli says again. "Get in the car."

The pair of us continue walking past his shiny vehicle.

"Emma?"

Turning, I finally speak. "What?"

"Why'd you leave the party?"

Seriously? He's asking that question? Maybe this pretending to be mad isn't going to be that difficult. "I--"

"You left her standing by the door. You said you were going to get her a drink. Thirty minutes later, we find you hobnobbing with three co-eds holding one fucking glass."

Wow, she noticed the glass thing too? I'm glad. It means I'm not crazy. Well, yes, okay, I'm crazy but in a good way.

"I--" Eli stops there. "You're right."

"I know." Carley's doing all the talking, but I need to step in.

Ignoring her, Eli takes a step closer to me. "I'm sorry, Em. I ran into some old friends."

"Uh-huh." I look over at his SUV, then back up at him. "Can I get my coat out of your car?" If I can get it, then Gilly's here we come.

"That's it? You're just going to walk away?"

I think I'm doing a good job here, you know, pretending to be mad. Heck, I even shrug as Carley jogs over to his fancy car.

"Why?" Eli's voice sounds downright whiney.

*Why is that endearing?*

"Because I left you for like ten minutes, you're ditching me?"

Moving a little closer, I lower my voice so Carley can't hear. I've only got a minute or so. "That was my first *real* college party." I swallow hard. "You left me at the door." What else do I need to say? I guess I'm still a little miffed by the whole thing.

"Em."

Carley's back. "Got the coats. Let's go."

"Goodbye, Eli."

I take several steps toward Gilly's when he asks in a very soft, sort of sad voice, "That's it? You're just ending things? Because of a stupid party?"

Halting, I turn. "Ending things?" This guy is killing me. Drawing this out is killing me. "Had we started something?" That wasn't meant to be witchy. It's a real question because this thing with Eli is still confusing to me.

"Jesus." He runs his fingers through his hair. "I'm sorry. Okay? I'm *really* sorry." He looks over at a scowling Carley, then back at me. "Will you get in the car so we can talk?" He blinks. "Please?"

I don't even need to look at Carley because she answers for me. "Just get in and talk. I'll meet you at Gilly's when you're done."

"Sure. Yeah." I nod at her. "Good idea." I know the minute I slide into the passenger seat in Eli's truck, I'm going to give in. Heck, just the smell of him makes me weak.

"I turned the seat warmer on for you."

"Thanks." I mean that too. It feels amazing. I've never experienced heated seats before. I'm not surprised his car has them. This thing is f-a-n-c-y. I take a moment to gather myself and to really look around inside his vehicle. I see the logo on the steering wheel and recognize it. BMW. I know, for a fact, those are pricey. No matter… why would I be surprised about the kind of car he drives?

I finally look to my left at Eli. And wow, he looks distraught. I don't like his expression. Since this whole talk in the car was his idea, I remain quiet. He must get that because he finally speaks. "Look." He pauses. "I'm sorry, Emma."

"It's fine." It's not but—

"I screwed up."

I watch as Eli rotates in his seat. A second later, his warm hand touches mine. When our fingers intertwine, my heart starts to beat wildly in my chest. Like a drum beat on some hard rock album. That's what it feels like anyway. "I'm going to confess something to you, Em."

Uh-oh.

I look up and our eyes meet––still, I remain silent.

"I've never had a girlfriend before."

Okay. That shocks me. So much so, I release a tiny gasp. "That can't be true." But if it is, it means we have something in common. I've never had a boyfriend. The question is, do I have one now?

"Yes," he says quickly. "It's true. I've gone on a couple of dates for prom and other events, but I've never technically had a girlfriend."

"That just can't be. You're…" He's gorgeous. There had to have been a million girls and now, women, who have at least tried. Instead of finishing that sentence, I ask, "Why not?"

"Never had time." He shrugs. "Hockey and school have dominated my life."

"Are you saying you think *I'm* your girlfriend?"

"Oh." He pulls his hand away from me so fast I don't have time to grab on. "I guess I thought…."

I reach my hand out to his hand this time. Taking it in mine, I slide my fingers between his until it's back to the way it was moments ago. Only, this time, our hands are resting on his thigh. "I like the idea. I just never thought…. I mean, we've only known each other for a little while." And I know for a fact that it takes people a long time to get to the point where they call each other boyfriend and girlfriend. At least Carley says it takes a long time. According to her, "kids today," take the time to get to know the other person before jumping into anything.

"You're the first girl, woman, I've ever met that made me feel--"

"Feel?" I lean closer to him. "How do I make you feel?" I really want to know.

He looks down into my eyes and a sweet smile appears on his face at the exact moment his hand squeezes mine. The sweetest thing I've ever heard—ever—follows.

"Happy."

*O.M.G.* I swear to you, the burn of tears hits me in zero point one second. But I hold it back. I can't let him see that his one word is making me tear up. No way. He'll think I'm crazy. "I make you happy?"

"You do. You make me smile and laugh and whenever I'm with you, I feel like I could conquer the world."

"*I* do that? For you?" *Seriously?*

"You do."

I shake my head quickly so I can clear my head from this euphoric state. Clarity. I need clarity. "So, you left me at the door and forgot about me because you've never had a girlfriend?"

"Basically. Plus, I assumed you were hanging with Carley."

"Oh, *never* assume."

He holds up his free hand. "I know. I know." He chuckles. "I promise you, Emma. If you ever go to a party with me again, I'll *never* leave your side."

His face, God, he looks so pained. So worried. "Okay."

"Okay?" He looks surprised. "You forgive me?"

"I do. Plus, I could have handled everything better than I did. Next time, I'll make sure I talk to you. I'll tell you if something's bothering me."

"Good." He squeezes my hand again. "That's good. Tell me how you feel." He pauses before asking, "That was your first college party?"

"Yep."

"So I ruined your first college party?"

"Nah." I need to do something to make him stop feeling like crud about this. "You didn't. Let's just forget about it. I'll go to another party with you sometime and we can get a do-over."

"Really?"

"Really."

Eli's smile is sweet and sincere. I love it.

I reach for the door handle. "I need to go meet Carley at Gilly's. She's waiting for me."

"Sit tight. I'll drive you over."

I point to the building two doors down from where we're parked. "I can walk—"

"My girl isn't going to walk in the cold."

I snort at that. "Eli, that's a ridiculous thing to say."

His expression shifts from something smiley to the most serious thing I've ever seen. "You're my girlfriend, Emma Perkins. I won't have you walking in the cold. When you're with me, I'll take care of you."

"Oh."

"Yeah." He nods a little testily. "'Oh' is right." I feel his lips on mine and then they're gone. "Girlfriend."

"Okay, *boyfriend*."

"Damn right," he grumbles.

And I smile.

2 0

---

E L I

*THAT WAS CLOSE.* AND SURPRISING. I CAN'T BELIEVE HOW I FELT AS I watched Emma storm out of the hockey party. Like I'd fucked up big time. So I did what any pathetic fool would do, I handed Cody my full glass of beer and I jumped into my car to go after her.

I had to.

When I saw the pair of them walking, arms wrapped around themselves looking cold, my heart flip-flopped in my chest. A protective instinct I didn't realize I had took over. Emma was cold and I had to do something about it.

"Em." That's what I say as soon as I get close enough to speak to her. It's also the only thing I'm able to get out.

After I convince her to get in the car, I know I've got to confess a thing or two. It was time she understood a few things. Not everything. Not yet.

Luckily, she listened to me, to my reasons for behaving like a complete jackass at the party.

*God, I feel so lucky she's giving me another shot.*

So, now, we're at Gilly's, the three of us, Carley, Emma, and myself. I'd love to tell you that her friend has warmed up to me,

121

but I can't. Not yet. She seems to be holding back. No doubt because Emma is smiling and happy. Me too. I mean, I just bought my girlfriend some ice cream and if that isn't the most cliché date thing in the entire world, I don't know what is. When she stepped up to the counter and placed her order, I half expected her to order a tiny cup of something because that's how my dates have behaved in the past. They barely ate when we went out to eat. But I'm happy to report, Emma didn't. She ordered a hot fudge sundae with nuts. It looked so good, I got one for myself.

"Mm," I say as I take my first bite and nod at my cup of vanilla ice cream covered in warm chocolate fudge. "Delicious."

"You act like you've never had ice cream before," Carley snaps.

"I've never had this before." Using my spoon, I point at the cup in my hand.

"You've never had a hot fudge sundae?" Emma sounds incredulous. "They're the best."

"They are." I nod, then smile.

When she starts to laugh, I know it's at me. "What?"

"You've got hot fudge on your front tooth."

I make a big point to lick it off dramatically, and I make that *mmm* sound again. Because, damn, it's good.

"Ugh. You guys are making me sick." Carley groans. "Take me home, will ya?" She's looking at me. "Then you two can go off and do that romantic stuff alone."

"Romantic stuff?" I wink at Emma. "I like the sound of that."

"She hates winking, by the way," Carley deadpans.

"Right. I forgot." I look over at Emma, who just shrugs.

"You're cute when you do it. As long as you're just winking at me, that is."

"I'd never wink at anyone but you."

Carley makes a disgusted, snorting sound as Emma smiles and that's where my focus lies. On Emma.

"Let's go." Carley is now standing.

I guess we're going.

<hr>

"THANKS FOR COMING OVER." AS SOON AS I PULLED INTO THEIR apartment complex, and Carley exited my vehicle, I asked Emma if she'd like to hang out at my place for a while. Of course, I offered to bring her home at any point. I need her to know I'm not just trying to get laid here. I want her to feel comfortable with me.

So, now we're at my place. Cody's still gone and hopefully that means he'll be gone all night. "Can I get you something to drink?" I look over at Emma, who's looking around my living room. I've got a sectional sofa that sits in front of a huge television mounted above a gas fireplace.

"Water?" Emma asks tentatively.

"Sure." I reach for two glasses out of my cupboard. "If you flip that little switch there on the right, the fireplace will turn on."

I watch her reach for it and flip the switch. "Oh," she says, sounding surprised. "That's cool." She bends closer and I get a glimpse of the shape of her sweet ass through that big sweater.

"Is that blue glass?"

I'm distracted by the growing hard-on in my jeans and that ass of hers. "Uh, what?" I know I sound like an idiot.

"In the fireplace. Is that blue glass?"

"Yeah."

"It's really pretty."

No, *she's* really pretty. "I like it. It's modern."

"Your whole house is cool. How in the world did a bunch of college guys get a place like this?"

"My parents bought it for me to live in while I'm in school. Cody and Mark basically pay the utilities on the place. And groceries. They have to buy their own food."

"Wow. So you live here for free, essentially?"

"Yep. They'll sell it when I'm done with school." I chuckle. "No doubt they'll make a profit."

"Your folks will sell the place after you graduate?"

"That's the plan."

"Smart," she says as she turns away from me. "Very smart."

"My dad's in real estate. He knows how to make a buck." That's an understatement.

"I thought your dad retired from the NBL."

I laugh. "It's the *NHL*, babe."

"Oh. Right," Emma says, blushing. "I don't know anything about hockey."

"Do you want to know?" While I'd like for her to be interested in my sport, for some reason, it doesn't bother me a bit if she only likes me for me rather than for that.

"Sure." She shrugs. "Just expect a lot of questions."

"I'll answer any and all questions you have."

"Good." Emma takes a seat in the middle of my couch.

Once I've got us water, I hand her a glass and settle in next to her, close enough for our thighs to touch. "What do you want to watch?"

"You pick." I stare as she takes a small sip of her water. When she glances at me, she gives me a closed-mouth smile.

Flipping through the channels, I come across a hockey game. "Hockey? We can begin your tutelage right now." It's a game with my dad's old team and their biggest rival from New York.

"Sure. We might as well start my education now since I've never really watched a hockey match. Are you playing matches yet or just practicing?"

*Start her education?* Why does my mind always go into the gutter with this girl? I do my best to think of other things so my dick doesn't take over. *Focus, Eli....* Clearing my throat, I answer, "Our season starts next week. On the fifteenth." I wait for another question. You know, like her asking if she can come to one or all of my games. I go ahead. "You wanna come to watch me play?"

"Sure." She shrugs like it's no big deal. "Can Carley come?"

"Absolutely." As long as she doesn't spend the entire game scowling at me. "If you promise to wait for me after the game."

A shy nod is what I get from her. "If you want me to."

"I do." Reaching out, I take her hand in mine. "I really do."

We both turn to the television to watch Chicago take the puck down the ice to New York's goal.

"Can you start with some rules, the object of the game, you know, things of that nature?"

"Things of that nature?" I chuckle again and add, just in case, "You're fucking adorable." Emma blushes a pretty shade of pink, and smiles.

As we watch, she asks questions now and then and I answer them. Her questions are a little out of the ordinary but so is she. For example, she points the television. "So, the goal minder doesn't leave his spot at his end of the ice?"

*Goal minder?* "Nope. Unless he's called back to the bench..." but that's getting into a whole thing about being behind at the end of the game. "He stays put."

"And your dad was a goal minder?"

"Goaltender. Yes." God, she makes me smile.

"And you play which position?"

"Defender."

She points to the TV again. "Which of those guys is a defender?"

"There are usually two defenders on the ice at all times. One on the left and one on the right side."

"Oh." She blinks as she watches the game. "What are the other guys called?"

"Forwards."

"And they do all the scoring?"

"Hell no," I snap. It catches her off guard, so I squeeze the hand that's wrapped in mine. "No," I say, softer this time. "We can all score if we get the chance. But defensemen are typically responsible for giving our own goalie more protection. We do our best to keep the other team from scoring."

"Okay." She nods. "Sounds pretty straightforward."

"Straightforward." I throw my head back and laugh.

"What? Why are you laughing? Isn't it straightforward?"

I shake my head.

Emma scoots up to the front edge of the couch, pulling our hands apart as she goes. "It is very straightforward." She points at the TV. "There are six players on the ice. Five of whom score and three who try to keep the puck away from the netty-thing."

The netty-thing. I laugh some more. Reaching out for her, I wrap her up in my arms and pull her close. I think I catch her by surprise because her body falls easily against mine. I slide my left hand beneath her knees and lift her until she's on my lap. She's not giving in on her argument even though she's now on top of me.

I love it.

"You need to quit laughing at everything I say. You're making me feel self-conscious."

I stop laughing. For one because I don't want her to feel like that and two, feeling her ass on my lap is making me hard again. I think she notices because she's got a very serious look on her face.

"Eli?"

"Give me a kiss, sweetheart."

And what do you know…? She does it. She leans in slowly, until our lips touch. I slide my fingers into her hair and let them run through the silky strands. My tongue enters her mouth as she opens for me.

God. I could live inside this girl. She's so warm and soft and, and… well, she's *everything*. Moving my arms until they're wrapped around her middle, I pull her closer so her chest is against mine. I run my palm up and down her back, then further until both hands are resting on her butt. Her ass. It's a perfectly round and not too firm ass. It's just right. When I give it a little squeeze, she squirms on top of me.

I'm able to lift her enough so I can get her on her back. I move from beneath her to over her. With her legs open, she cradles my body between her thighs and, using my elbows, I leverage myself all while our lips remain together, tongues intertwined. I lift one hand from the couch and find the edge of her sweater. When my fingers touch skin, I look pull my mouth from hers. Our eyes meet. "Is this okay?" I ask, making sure I'm not moving too fast.

She nods but says nothing.

I touch her skin. "Soft," I say, smiling up at her.

"Lotion" is all she says.

"It works." My palm moves up until I feel the edge of her bra. Arching my brow, I wait for her to give me the go ahead. She nods slowly. "You sure?"

"Yes."

Cupping her breast, I tug on the lacey cup until I feel her erect nipple. God, I want my mouth on her. On every part of her. "Emma...."

She looks at me expectantly.

"Can I see you?"

"See me?" She blinks.

"Will you lift up your sweater for me?"

Emma glances left, then right. "Is there anyone else here?"

"Cody won't be home until late." Or maybe not at all. I think about her question. "Shall we go into my bedroom?"

# 21

## EMMA

"*Shall we go into my bedroom?*"

That's his question? Should we go into his bedroom? I do my best not to overthink this, but overthinking is what I do. On one hand, I'd be humiliated if Cody walked in while I was shirtless. On the other, going into his bedroom spells a whole lot of trouble. If I go in there, is he expecting sex? Because. No. I'm not having sex with Eli Baxter. At least not yet. I'm not ready.

"Emma?"

"Um…," I say, still thinking of the pros and cons.

"Em. We won't do anything you don't want to do. Okay?"

I finally look at Eli. "Okay."

He shakes his head several times. "Just tell me if you want to stop. And I'll stop."

Well, kissing *is* nice but so is having his hands on me. "Okay. Let's go into your bedroom."

Eli jumps up so fast it startles me. When he holds his hand out to me, I take it. He helps me sit up, then stand. Before I can stop him, he bends and picks me up and throws me over his shoulder in what they refer to as a fireman's hold. "Eli!" I screech. "Stop." God, he's going to hurt himself.

I watch the ground as he carries me out of the main room, down the hallway, into his bedroom. I hear the door slam shut before I fall backwards. When I hit his mattress, I bounce up and back down. All the while I'm giggling hysterically. "You're crazy," I finally say. That is until I see he's taking off his shirt.

Wow. Wow-wow-wow, Eli Baxter is so freaking perfect. His body is at least.

"Your turn." He points to the sweater I'm wearing. Before I think too hard, I reach for the bottom and slowly lift it up and off. Luckily, I've still got my bra on, mostly. The one side is still pulled down below my nipple. I blush, thinking about being exposed. I'm about to cover it when Eli says, "No. Please. Let me see."

Carley's right. Guys are so weird.

I move my hand away and I do it. I let him look.

"Fucking perfect."

No. I'm definitely not perfect.

Eli steps up to the bed, and places one knee next to my leg. The room is suddenly silent because I think we're both holding our breath. I know I am. "I've fantasized about you, Emma Perkins."

"You have?" Why does that seem so hard to believe?

"I have. Repeatedly."

"What'd you fantasize about?" *Emma Perkins! What are you doing? You're asking for trouble, girl.*

"Well, you and I were…"

"Were what?" I can't believe I'm asking him about this.

"We were completely naked."

Oh. Wow. I'm not ready for that. I don't think. "Uh-huh." I want to hear where he's going with this.

"I was standing right where I am now. Your legs were spread wide."

Oh. My. *Goodness.*

"You let me touch, kiss, and lick every inch of that beautiful body of yours."

Okay, now I know he's full of crap. *Beautiful body? Ha.*

"What'd I tell you about rolling your eyes at me, Em? I mean every word."

Why is it hard to believe this man would like me, for me?

Answer? Years of self-deprecating thoughts. No matter how many times my mom, dad, or even Carley told me otherwise, there's still a part of me that will always feel insecure about my body But, I'm not going to lie. Eli's words help. I believe him. Heck, I can *feel* how much he likes my curves.

Eli slides over me again. I move my legs, so I've got one on either side of his big body. When he lowers himself, I can feel how hard he is between my legs. His warm palm is on my breast, and I close my eyes to focus on how it feels rather than worry about what he's looking at exactly.

"Can you take the bra off, Em? Do you feel okay doing that?"

I don't answer. Instead, I reach behind me and unhook the bra. My eyes are shut tight. Pulling it away and off, I hold my breath, expecting the worse. But he says nothing and then I feel something new. Something—"Oh my God." I practically arch off the bed. I've got to look now. I peek down as Eli's tongue swipes across first my right nipple, then my left.

"You like that?" He's looking up at me, waiting for my answer.

"I do." *Like* isn't strong enough a word. Love. I love it. When he covers most of my small boob with his mouth and begins to suck, I lose my damn mind. "Wow. Uh, Eli...."

He stops suddenly and I make a sound like a fussy baby who had its bottle taken away. But when he asks, "Is this okay?" I release a breath.

Using my palm, I press his head back down. That's my answer since I'm sort of speechless.

"I guess that's a yes."

"Yes. It's a yes. Now do it again." And never, ever stop.

He works his magic on my chest, back and forth until I'm squirming on the bed. I reach for him and touch whatever is close enough. I want… I want more. I guess he reads my mind because I feel him fiddling at the button on my jeans. I look down at that hand.

When he's got the button undone, he tugs the zipper down. "I'm just going to slide my hand in, okay, Emma?"

"Okay."

"You sure, sweet girl? I don't have to if you don't want to."

I do. That's the thing. I really, really do. "I do."

With the jeans loosened, I watch his hand move in. He hasn't flinched at the feel of my round belly yet so that's good. When his hand slides down into my panties to between my legs, I open up for him like some dang hussy. "Fuck. You're wet, Em."

Not a surprise. All his ministrations with my nipples were very effective.

His fingers move through me, then they return to the front of me. He swirls and twirls his fingers around my clitoris. He's good. *Really* good. In no time, my legs are open wider and I'm running my fingers through his thick hair muttering things— raunchy things that I shouldn't repeat, but I probably will the next time he's got his hands in my pants. "Eli. Wow."

When his finger slides inside me, I freeze for a second. Nothing has ever been in there. Well, except a tampon and that's only if I'm swimming and since I'm not so great at that, it's rare that anything ends up in that particular orifice.

But I need to give it a chance. He's gentle with his finger, which is good. And when he flips his hand around and begins to rub inside toward the front, I grab hold of his hair on the top of his head and move with him. "Ouch." He chuckles. "Don't rip out the hair, honey."

"Sorry." Not sorry.

I need to hold something. Since his hair is out of the question,

I reach down until I feel the front of his pants. He's so hard and I'm very close. So very, very close.

"I feel you getting tight around my finger, Em. You gonna come for me?"

"Uh-huh." I'm trying to focus on what I'm doing to him, but my mind keeps wondering what's going to happen next. My fingers wrap around him from the outside of his pants. He places his free hand on top of mine to show me what to do. What he likes. I do it and it's then that his finger really starts to work magic at a frantic pace.

"Right there, Em. Yeah." He's panting almost has hard as me. "Right there, sweetheart. Right th--" And then the raspy growl like the one I heard in the library slowly rolls out of his mouth. All the while he's still working on me. When his thumb presses on my clitoris, that's what does it. And I let go. And fly.

ELI

"Dad?" I blink a few times, doing my best to wake up. I need to focus on the person now standing in my kitchen. Well, I guess, technically, it's *his* kitchen. "Wh-What are you doing here?"

"I told you I was going to visit."

I look left, then right. "Where's Mom?"

"She had a thing." My dad flips his hand up like whatever my mom's doing isn't important.

"You should've called." I mean, it's eight in the morning. On a Sunday.

"Why would I?" He glares at me. "Unless you've got something to hide."

"Eli?" I hear a sweet voice coming up from behind me. "Have you seen my sw--?"

It's right then she sees my father. Only she doesn't know it's my dad. Emma turns and smiles at the stranger in my kitchen. "Hi."

"Who is *that*?" My father points a finger straight at Emma. It's rude as hell.

"Nobody." I shrug. I look down at her and pretend what I'm

doing isn't going to ruin everything we repaired last night. It can't be helped. "Get your stuff, babe. Time to go."

"Some puck bunny, then?"

"Sure." I shrug, trying to act as nonchalant as I can.

"I'm not a––" Emma looks at me like she hopes I'll defend her, but I can't because if my father thinks Emma means something to me, that she's a distraction, he'll do everything he can to get her away from me. Or me away from her. "Your clothes are sitting on the chair in my room." I point back toward my bedroom.

I see her eyes turn shiny. She's going to cry. I'm making her cry. *Jesus, I'm glad Mom isn't here to see this.*

"She's wearing your fucking sweater." My dad's pissed. So pissed, in fact, his fists are clenched at his side and he's gritting his teeth. Not a good sign.

What he means is Emma's wearing my jersey. The real one for home games. Back in the old days, players wore actual sweaters to play on the ice. The name stuck. "So." I shrug.

"You never let a fucking puck bunny put on your sweater. It's bad luck."

But *I* put it on *her* after I made her come. I wanted to see her in it. It was better than I'd ever imagined. I've never let a girl wear my hockey jersey before, because of what my dad just said. It's always been seen as bad luck to let someone you don't care about wear it. But that's not the case here. I care about Emma. Enough to want to see her in it. The second she donned it I was hard again. She slept in my jersey, wrapped up in my arms. And it was perfect.

And now it's over. My father's seen her. I'd hoped to keep her a secret for a hell of a lot longer than this, but that dream is over.

Emma practically runs away, heading back toward my bedroom. I want to reach out to her, but I can't.

"As soon as she's gone, we're going to sit down and have a little chat."

"Sure thing, Dad."

I move into the kitchen like none of this bothers me. I need coffee, so I take one of my single serve pods and start the machine going. Moments later, I hear footsteps coming from the hallway. It's Emma in my jersey and her jeans. She's carrying her sweater along with her coat. As she speed-walks through the living room past the kitchen, all the while looking down at the ground. Like she did that first time in the library before we went for coffee. I watch her head toward the laundry room, then she stops. She looks to her left and makes her way to the front door. I watch her flip the lock, then turn the knob.

The entire time she's moving, I'm talking to myself in my head. Saying things like. *You let her walk out of here, and it's over.* I know it. And. *Choose: Your girl and your dignity or accept your father's unwavering need to control you?*

"It's not that simple," I say, only loud enough for me to hear.

"You gonna let that girl leave here in your fucking sweater, Eli?"

"I--" I don't know what to do. All I know is she needs to go so my father can't say anything else to her.

Just then, I see Cody stomp up the front steps. I'm about to greet him when he stops in front of Emma. She's saying something to him. Cody looks inside the house, sees my dad and then wraps his arm around my sweet girl and walks her down the front steps. At least she'll have a ride home.

God damn. I'm fucking pathetic. I don't deserve Emma Perkins. I never did.

## 23

EMMA

"Th-Thanks for driving me." I'm sobbing in poor Cody's car. I bet he's sorry he offered to drive me home. I was planning on calling Carley as soon as I got far enough away from Eli's house. "That was so embarrassing."

"I told you. He's got a fucked-up relationship with his father."

"So that gives him the right to treat me like I'm a p-puck bunny?" I stare down at my lap.

"If his father thought Eli had a girlfriend, he'd probably try to ship him off to hockey camp up in Canada."

Wiping my nose with the sleeve of Eli's jersey, I ask, "Why?"

"Because all Jack Baxter wants is for Eli to make the pros."

"I thought Eli wanted that to. I thought he loved hockey."

"He does love hockey, but he's not sure he wants to go pro. His dad, well, let's just say Jack Baxter has one goal and that's to see his son in the NHL, but here's a little secret." Cody looks over at me and winks. I don't bother commenting about the wink. I'm getting used to them. "Our boy is the opposite of that. If he had his druthers--"

Druthers?

"--he'd be at home, on his sofa, watching TV with his wife and kids. That's all he's ever wanted."

"His wife and kids?" I practically scream the words. "He's married?"

"Sorry." Cody waves his hand in the air. "His *future* wife and kids."

"But his dad wants him to play professionally." I'm not asking a question. It still makes no sense. "Isn't Eli an adult? Can't he just tell his dad what he really wants to do?"

"His dad has him by the balls. Eli's plan is to work for the FBI someday, whether that's after hockey or after he graduates. It's been his dream since we were in high school and two agents came and talked to us about working for them. Eli was sold the minute they started talking about cybercrime."

"Wow." I mean, that makes sense why he's a computer programming major.

"But his dad wants him to follow in *his* footsteps. And since Jack Baxter is paying for our house and his tuition, Eli lets him dictate how he lives."

"That's ridiculous." And sad. Plus, it makes me mad. Here I thought Eli Baxter was this strong, stand-up guy, but this makes me wonder if I was wrong.

"It is." Cody nods.

"If you think it's wrong, why don't *you* do something?"

Cody chuckles. "Because my dear, sweet, naïve Emma, I live in the house for practically nothing so I'm not about to rock the boat. I come from a lower-middle class family. I'm living the high life thanks to Jack Baxter."

Ignoring his rationale, I feel like I need to defend myself. "I'm not naïve."

"You are. A little." Cody pats my shoulder and it's not just a little condescending. "Jack Baxter is an asshole. It's easier to go along with it than deal with the fallout." Cody's quiet for a minute or two. "It's too bad Eli's mom wasn't there."

"Why?"

"Because she would have put a stop to all that back there. She's what we call a mild-mannered ballbuster. It's how she and Jack have stayed together all these years. She doesn't put up with his bullshit and she thinks her son farts flowers."

His last two words get a startled laugh out of me. *Farts flowers?*

"It's true. As far as Helene Baxter is concerned, Eli is the Second Coming."

"Reminds me of my sister," I grumble. Only she's the one who thinks she's the holy one.

<hr>

THE MINUTE I GET HOME, CARLEY KNOWS SOMETHING'S WRONG. No doubt thanks to my red, puffy eyes. After I tell her what happened, I half expect her to jump into her car and drive over to Eli's place and kick him in the-- Well, kick him. But that's not what she does. Instead of getting angry and violent, she shrugs and says, "Parents are weird."

That's the understatement of the year, at least as it relates to her parents. Her dad specifically.

"So you're okay with him referring to me as a puck bunny?"

"No. I'm not. But maybe he was trying to protect you or something. I mean, it sounds like his dad's a real asshole."

"It's not right."

"Really?" She arches her perfectly plucked brow at me. "Was it really that bad? Why don't you let him explain everything before you break up with him again?"

*Break up with him again?* I've never broken up with him because before last night, I didn't think there was anything to break up with.

"You like him. He likes you. A lot. You just made up. Sure, he was a jerk for not giving you a heads-up about his dad, but Cody said it was a surprise visit. Eli wouldn't have been prepared."

"It's… it's just…"

"What? It's just shitty? Sad?" Carley reaches out and squeezes my hand. "Relationships are hard. You have to work on them and cut the guy some slack. If you don't, you'll never be able to stick with a guy because I've got a little secret for you."

Ooh, a secret. I nod like a fool.

"Guys are idiots. They fuck up *all* the time. Like *all* the time. So, if you like this guy, wait and see what he does. If he's really sorry, he'll show up here on his hands and knees, begging you for forgiveness." Her face softens. "You gave him back his hockey jersey?"

Carley saw me come in with Cody. The two of them mumbled something to each other and she returned to her bedroom. I have no idea what any of that meant. Anyway, I quickly ran into my room and changed out of Eli's hockey shirt and handed it back to Cody. According to Cody, that was Eli's actual playing jersey and he needed it back for their game this week.

ELI

"I GOT YOUR JERSEY BACK."

I've been sitting on my sofa staring at the wall. I've got no desire to do anything else. All I can think of is Emma and the expression on her face when my dad called her a "bunny." Then there was the fact I did nothing to defend her. "God." I groan as I run my fingers through my dirty hair. I still haven't showered.

"Dude. Did you hear me?"

I turn and see Cody standing a few feet away, eating a giant sandwich. "Huh?"

"Here." Cody steps away but returns, tossing my jersey onto my lap. "She wanted me to make sure you got this back."

Of course she did. She's considerate like that. I pick it up and smell it, hoping some of her scent is left, but all I smell is hockey. That's a thing. Well. To me it is.

"You fucked up." Cody won't go away.

"I know."

"I tried to explain. You know about…." He looks left and right. "Where is he, anyway?"

He's referring to my father. "He's in the office, making calls or something."

I feel the couch move and look over at my best friend who's still eating his sandwich. With his mouth full of meat and cheese, he asks, "How long's he staying?" Only it sounds more like "Ow mong's he faying." I got what he meant.

"He brought an overnight bag."

"Fuck," Cody mutters. This time his pronunciation was spot-on.

"Yep." I nod. "He's coming to practice." Which is gonna happen in less than an hour.

"Aw, fuck. I hate when he does that."

We all do because when the great Jack Baxter shows up to practice, even the coaches bow to him. For some inexplicable reason, my father feels the need to critique everyone, not just me. It's fucking humiliating. When he's done it in the past, the guys were mad at me for days afterward. Take last year, for example, he sat our goalie down after practice and talked *at* him for over twenty minutes. The kid was so pissed at me, he hasn't spoken to me since. Maybe Coach Montross will nip it in the bud. Maybe, for once, he'll tell Jack Baxter to fuck off.

---

Coach Montross is worse than usual. He seems to have crawled so far up my dad's ass, it's fucking embarrassing. Since Coach is from Illinois and he used to be a goalie and because my father is who he is, shit at practice is going downhill pretty fast. One by one, my dad has started picking apart everybody's game. And my dad doesn't mince words.

But neither do my teammates, telling me stuff like "You fucking suck, Baxter." And that's one of the nicer things said by my fellow players. "You're dead, fucker" is also popular. But my personal favorite? "I know where you live. You'd better sleep with one eye open, Bax." That one was said by our captain, a senior goalie from Finland. (If you say that with an angry Finnish accent, you'll appreciate it more.)

The thing is, my father is hardest on me. Appropriate, I suppose. For one, I'm his kid, and two, I've got no energy and also no desire to be at practice. All I want to do is go home and crawl into my bed and sleep for a year. But if I do that, I know my mind will fixate on Emma and what happened this morning. I should ask Cody more about their conversation. If only she'd kept my jersey, I could have used it as an excuse to go over to her place. Hell, why did I do what I did? I like that girl. A lot. I need to do something. I don't want things to end with her. Not that way. But what can I do? Who can I ask for help?

Suddenly, it's like a lightbulb has gone off in my head because I know who'll help... my *mom*. Relief hits me in the chest. But that's not the only place I'm hit because it's at that precise moment, I feel sudden pain in the left side of my head, and everything fades to black.

EMMA

"ELI?" I'M LOOKING DOWN AT HIM. SEEING HIM HERE, IN A hospital bed, hooked up to monitors and an IV is more than distressing. Cody said he was hit by a puck on the side of his head. He was wearing a helmet, but it hit him so hard the helmet cracked. Cody also said the minute he regained consciousness, the first word out of his mouth was "Emma."

Cody did what he thought was right. He grabbed Eli's phone and called me. When I saw his name appear, my first reaction was to let it go to voicemail, but then I thought about what Carley said. So I took the call. I'm glad I did.

Carley dropped me off at the emergency entrance, then went to park the car. I ran to the information desk and asked about Eli. Luckily, Cody appeared and led me back into the emergency department. He stopped in front of a wall made of a blue curtain. Pointing, he said, "He's in there."

I nodded and grasped the edge of the curtain that acted as a partition from the other bays in the ER. Peeking in first, I noticed the room was dim. I saw him on a gurney-like bed with an IV in his arm and a beeping machine behind him. His head was wrapped up in a colorful strip of something and the side where, I assume, he was hit, looked lumpy. I hoped that was an ice pack instead of lump.

"Eli?" I ask as I approach the bed. He doesn't respond which worries me. "Eli?" I repeat as I lean down closer to his face. My voice is soft, barely a whisper. I can't decide if I should wake him up or not.

*He did ask for me.*

"Eli?"

"Emma?" he asks as his eyes flutter open. "Is that you?"

"I'm here." I reach out and touch his arm. It feels cold so I pull up the thin blanket they've got over his legs until it's covering his upper half. "Are you okay?"

"Yeah. Just got the wind knocked out of me."

"You were hit by a puck. In the head. It broke your helmet."

"Oh. Right." His chuckle turns into a wince. "I'm glad you're here."

"Me too."

He lifts his arm off the bed and reaches for my hand. "I'm sorry about earlier." He pauses. "My dad."

"I know. Cody told me that your dad is…."

Eli laughs, then winces again. "…An asshole." With a sigh, he adds, "But he's my dad."

"I get that." I do. My parents look out for me, us, too, but they do it differently.

"I really like you, Emma."

When our eyes meet, I feel something I've never felt before. Not about a boy, anyway. I feel a connection. I think he actually sees *me*. Ordinary and nerdy Emma Perkins. "I like you too."

"Good." Eli squeezes my hand as he closes his eyes. "Need to sleep."

"Do you have a concussion?" If that's the case, I don't think he's supposed to sleep.

"He sure does" says a woman as she pushes through the

curtain. I watch as she washes her hands, then she holds one out to me. "I'm Doctor Striker. I've got an update."

"Um, I'd better get his dad." Or Cody. I start to stand just as the curtain whips open the rest of the way and Jack Baxter appears.

He looks first at Eli, then me, then the doctor. "She can leave." He points to me. Since Eli's asleep, I don't expect him to need me around, so I stand. Keeping my head up, I walk around Mr. Baxter. The minute I'm on the other side of the curtain, Eli says my name again. "Emma?"

"She's gone," his dad says gruffly. "The doctor is here. Let's hear her out."

I don't wait around to eavesdrop on their conversation. If Eli wants me to know what she says, he'll tell me. Instead, I make my way out of the emergency department into the waiting area. I spot Carley right away and move toward her. Cody approaches carrying two cups of coffee. Handing one to Carley, he looks over at me and smiles. "You get a chance to talk to him?"

"For a minute. The doc stepped in, then his father..." I don't know how to tell them that he kicked me out of the room. But he did. "I, uh, left so they could talk."

"That's a nice way of saying that Jack Baxter kicked you out of the room." Cody's chuckle is humorless. "Don't take it personally, Emma. He doesn't even want Eli to hang out with *me*. And we both play hockey. Plus we've known each other for years. We played in the juniors together in Chicago."

I don't know what to say to that. All I know is Eli likes me and I like him. And maybe that's enough for now.

"If you're ready to go, I'll go get the car."

"Yeah. In a sec. I'd like to say goodbye to Eli."

"I'll go get the car. It'll take me fifteen minutes. I'm parked a mile away."

"It's getting dark. I'll walk with you."

Carley stares at Cody for a minute or two, then gives him one nod. "Sure. Thanks." I know why she sounds so tentative. She's not used to anyone, guys in particular, making that kind of gesture. I mean, her father definitely doesn't. Cody's being rather chivalrous.

I watch the pair walk out together, then I turn just as a deep voice snaps, "You." I know who that voice belongs to. Eli's dad.

When I look up, the man is pointing right at me. Without meaning to, I point to myself. "Me?"

"Yeah, *you*." Jack's voice hasn't softened. "What the fuck are you doing here?"

"I'm…" God, what do I say to this man? "He…."

Mocking me, Jack repeats my words in a way that instantly makes me angry. "I'm…. He…." He pauses. "You're what? He what?"

Clearing my throat, I push my shoulders back in a feeble attempt to grow a pair. "He asked for me."

"The fuck he did."

My God, the man likes to cuss. "Cody said—"

"Cody said…," he mocks again. Then the man scoffs as he runs his fingers through his hair. Hair that reminds me a lot of Eli's, except his dad's has a lot of gray running through it. Still, he looks distinguished. It hints at what Eli will look like when he's older. Handsome. It's too bad Mr. Baxter has that look on his face. You know, an angry one.

"He was delirious."

*Was he?*

Mr. Baxter takes a step closer to me and I take one back. I don't like where this conversation is going. "I don't know who you are, but you need to leave. Eli doesn't have time to deal with hangers-on."

"Hangers-on?" What does that even mean?

Jack Baxter scoffs. "I know your type. You're just hoping to get knocked up because Eli's destined for the NHL. He's your gravy train." He looks down at my worn-out T-shirt, jeans, and sneakers. "Yeah, I know your type. You're after the money."

I'm now staring at the man, blinking. Because… "What are you talking about?"

Jack Baxter laughs or scoffs, I'm not sure which. A little bit of both really. "You're not only homely, you're dumb too?"

I believe that's the most offensive thing anyone has ever said to me. "I'm not dumb."

"Then don't look shocked that I figured out your game."

I've had enough of this conversation––enough of Jack Baxter. I'm just going to do it. I'm going to tell this big jerk the truth. "There's no *game*. I'm Eli's girlfriend."

Uh-oh. Maybe I shouldn't have said the *G* word because I swear his face has turned magenta since hearing my confession. His nostrils flare, and his teeth are visibly gritting. He's angry. No. I shake my head. He's more than that. He's pissed.

"That's bullshit. Eli knows better. He doesn't have time for fucking distractions like *you*."

I shrug because I don't know what else to say. Well, I could tell him that he's out of touch. That he can't expect his college-age son to go without relationships in his life for a stupid sport. If I say that, I'm not sure what he'd do. He's *that* angry.

"Don't you fucking shrug me off, you little—"

"Jack." We both turn our heads toward a woman's voice like we're synchronized.

Eli's dad speaks, "Helene."

Helene? Oh, that's Eli's mom. And wow, is she ever beautiful. Petite with shoulder-length hair the color of night. She's very elegant.

As she approaches us, she smiles at me, then she scowls at Jack. I feel him back away from me right after that look's directed at him. I'm adding another word to my description of her: intimidating. To Jack. Not to me. Because if I had to guess, I'd say the man was a little frightened of his wife. A snicker escapes my lips before I can stop it.

"Hello." Helene reaches her hand out for me to shake. So, I do. "Hi."

"You must be Emma."

Okay, how does she know my name?

"I ran into Cody on the way in. He told me all about you. You're Eli's girlfriend?"

Jack makes an angry scoffing sound again. When he does, Helene's head rotates toward him so slowly, I have to hold my breath in anticipation of what she's about to say to him.

I think I love this woman.

"How is he?" she asks Jack.

"He'll be fine."

"You always say that." Mrs. Baxter is now frowning at her husband.

"And I'm always right," Mr. Baxter replies angrily.

She's still glaring, which causes Mr. Baxter. to sigh, adding, "Doc said it's a concussion. He'll need a little time off, but he'll be back in no time."

"Did the doctor say that or is that just Jack Baxter's opinion?"

"Helene."

"Jack."

"He'll be fine after some time at home." Jack gives me side-eye, then quickly returns his gaze to his wife.

"I'm going to go see him." She turns to me. "It was nice to meet you, Emma. We'll have to go to lunch so we can get to know each other a little better."

I've no words so I merely nod.

---

APPARENTLY "HOME" MEANT HIS PARENTS' HOUSE, BECAUSE ONCE Eli was released from the hospital, his parents packed him a bag and drove him back to Chicago. I learned all this from Cody who, for some reason, still had Eli's phone. When I asked when he'd be back, Cody didn't have an answer. "They didn't say. They just grabbed Eli's school stuff, some clothes, and they were gone."

I researched concussions. According to the internet, it may take a week or two to get back to daily activities. He could have headaches afterwards, and sports are not a good idea for a while. I'm sure that's a fact his dad is worried about.

"Will you call me if you hear from him?"

"I sure will, Emma."

ELI

THERE'S SUCH A THING AS TOO MUCH TOGETHERNESS. AT LEAST that's what I've decided after being home for two weeks. I'm ready to get back to Madison, to school, to my roommates, *to Emma*. I haven't heard from her since I've been home, but that's because I left my phone back at my place.

Come to think of it, I haven't talked to Cody either.

All of my information is funneled through Mom and Dad. But enough is enough. I'm ready to head back. I've got a shit ton of work to make up since I haven't been able to do much. My headaches have been so bad, all I want to do is lay around in a dark room and sleep. But those are improving every day. According to my last doctor visit, everything is healing as it should. They haven't cleared me to play hockey just yet and I'm okay with that. I'll need extra time to get caught up with school-work when I get back.

"Honey?" My mom has been tiptoeing around me since I got home. I swear her voice hasn't been above a whisper in two weeks.

"Yeah?"

"Can I turn on the light? I've got your laundry."

"Oh, sure." I sit up from my bed and close my eyes, waiting for the light to shine. It doesn't hurt like it did.

"How are you feeling today?"

"Great," I say with a smile. "I'm ready to get back to school."

"Oh." She stops. Frozen.

"About that…" Here we go. "Your dad and I…"

"Mom." I toss off my blankets and stand. "I'm going back to school."

"Your father thinks—"

"I know what he thinks." And since he left yesterday to go to LA to speak at some conference on selling commercial real estate, he's not here to repeat this bullshit. He's decided that I need to forget about the Badgers hockey season and put all of my focus into the hockey combine. The combine is where all the hockey prospects go so professional scouts can assess them. There are workouts, drills, interviews, the works. If you do a good job at the combine, then your chances of getting drafted are much better. "That's in June. It's now October."

"Yes. But you know your dad." Mom rolls her eyes.

"And you know I want to get my degree, Mom."

"Is that all you want?" She's smirking.

"No." I'm not about to talk to her about Emma because she'll repeat what I say to my father. Wait, that may be a good idea. "I miss Emma."

Mom's smirking again and I don't like it. It's weird.

I shrug. "We just started seeing each other. I'd like to see where it goes." Hell, I'd just like to talk to her. "I need my phone." God, being without has been driving me crazy. It's like I lost a limb at practice.

"So you want to go back." It's not a question. "I suppose you want to go today?" She sighs.

"That'd be great." I give her my best smile.

"Fine. I'll take you back."

Standing up from my bed, I wrap her up in my arms and kiss her cheek. "Thanks, Mom."

"I'll do it if I can spend a little time with your Emma."

My Emma. I like the sound of that.

"I met her at the hospital, remember? I told you that."

She also mentioned that my father was talking to her when she got there. Part of me is terrified to find out what he said to her. What if she doesn't want to see me anymore?

I watch as Mom reaches into my closet for my duffle bag. She quickly places my clean laundry in the bag, then sets it on my desk. "Oh well." She sighs. "We'll figure it out. You can call her when we get there. It's Saturday. Maybe we can take her to lunch."

I look at the clock. It's just after eight in the morning. "We can try. She may have to work."

---

I'M SO NERVOUS TO SEE HER, I'M PRACTICALLY SHAKING IN MY boots. Literally. The minute we get back to my place, I search for my phone and find it charging on the kitchen counter. Pressing her name in my contacts makes the nerves triple. What if she doesn't answer? It rings twice, then I hear her voice. "Hey, Cody." She doesn't sound that excited to hear from him.

"It's not Cody. It's me. Eli."

"Eli?" she squeaks. "Is that really you?"

I smile so hard it almost hurts. "It's me. I'm back. Finally got my phone. The first thing I did was run into the house to find it and call you."

Hell, my mom's not even in the house yet.

"I've missed you." Her voice goes quiet when she speaks.

"I've missed you too. So fucking much. How are things? School? What have you been doing?"

When she laughs, I smile again. "That's a lot of questions at once."

"Did you ask her?" my mom says as she steps into the kitchen.

Holding my hand over the phone, I nod. "I will." With my phone uncovered, I ask Emma, "My mom wants to know if you'd like to have lunch."

"Oh." She sounds hesitant. "Is… um your dad with you?"

"No."

"Oh." There's relief in her voice, which tells me my father wasn't nice to her. And that pisses me off. "Okay. Sure. What time?"

"We'll pick you up in half an hour."

"I'll be ready."

2 7

---

EMMA

"Carley!" I shout as loud as I can.

"What?" She races into the living room.

"You need to help me. I'm going to lunch with Eli and his mom." I mean, this is freaking serious.

"Okay." She holds her palms up at me like she's trying to talk me off the ledge. She sort of is. "Remain calm." Then, she laughs.

"Funny."

"Let's find an outfit. Then we'll do your hair."

"Nothing over the top. I just want to look normal."

"Absolutely. Normal but adorable."

Rolling my eyes, I grumble, "Whatever. Just do your magic."

---

"It's so nice to see you again, Emma," Eli's mom, Helene, says as she disregards the hand I'm holding out for a shake in favor of a full-body hug. A long one.

"Same," I say into her jacket collar. Ugh. *Same?* I couldn't think of something better to say? I'm so bad at this, especially since I'm so preoccupied with the man standing in my tiny living room.

I'm doing my level best not to jump up and wrap myself around Eli like a monkey. He's a sight for sore eyes. He looks good. Tired. But good.

"Where should we have lunch?" Eli asks, which is great because things were just going to get more awkward between his mom and me.

"I don't know. What sounds good to you, Emma?" his mom asks, giving me a sincere smile.

"Well, there's Casetta Kitchen Counter." That place is affordable. Hopefully they don't want to go somewhere fancy. I can't swing that. "There's Monty's if you want comfort food. Or what about DLUX?" I shrug. "I guess it depends what you're hungry for."

Helene responds with "I'd just like a good salad and a cup of soup on this chilly day."

I look at Eli, hoping he's got some suggestions. He doesn't. I guess it's up to me. I suggest, "Zoup?" It's a place known for its healthy soups, salads, and sandwiches. They're big on natural ingredients as well as posting the nutrition information for everything on the menu. How do I know all that? Carley. That's her jam.

"Oh, we've been there before." Helene reaches out and touches Eli's arm. "That place was yummy and very healthy. Let's go there."

Phew. I'm glad that's settled.

At the restaurant, we each order at the counter with me going first. I make my way over to the cashier, ready to pay for my meal, when I feel a hand on my shoulder. "I'm buying you lunch, babe."

Babe. Wow. It seems like so long ago––the last time he used a term of endearment. "You don't have to."

He's now leaning down, his mouth so close to my ear I can feel his warm breath. And by that, I mean I feel it down to my toes. "We've been through this. *We* invited *you*. We pay."

"Fine." I only ordered a side salad and water anyway, so it won't cost much.

"And you're going to have to order something else. Like some soup?" He looks at the cashier. "She'd like to add something to her order. Is that okay?"

The girl behind the register is just staring at Eli like he's the best-looking guy she's ever seen. I suppose he could be.

"Tomato soup, please. A cup."

"Make it a bowl and add a grilled cheese as well."

"Eli."

"I'll eat whatever you can't finish." His lips touch that spot right below my ear and I nearly melt on the spot. Right there in Zoup.

"Now...," Helene says as she settles into her seat with her cup of vegetable soup and her tiny salad.

See... I should've ordered that.

"...tell me about yourself, Emma."

Crap on a cracker. This is it. Oh well, it's got to be done. I tell her I'm a junior in the engineering program, that I'm from Pontiac, a tiny town in Illinois about two hours southwest of Chicago (Go Indians!), that I've got one sister (I leave out the part about her being Satan's mistress), and then I describe my parents.

"Isn't that where the prison is?" Helene's face morphs into a frown.

"Yep." It's our biggest employer. That and the discount store my parents have worked in forever.

"Well..." She sighs like she's resigned to the fact I'm from a prison community. Someone's got to be. Am I right? "...you're not that far from the city. Do you get to Chicago much when you're home?"

"Not really." I shrug. "I don't have a car."

"That reminds me." She looks at Eli. "No driving for you, mister. Doctor's orders."

"I know, Mom."

I want to giggle because he said that in a very whiny voice.

"Maybe Emma could drive you around. You know, if you need to go places." She looks at me. "Have Eli give you his keys. Just drive the car home. If he needs a ride, you can pick him up." Her face brightens up. "Or better yet, you could stay with him." Her expression turns serious, almost grave. "You know, since he's still recovering. It'd be a *big* help to me since I'm going to worry if he's all alone."

"Mom." Eli chuckles. "Stop."

"What?"

"Knock it off."

"I'm not kidding, honey. I'm going to be worried sick about you."

Eli looks over at me. He's had his hand on my upper thigh for most of the meal. When she started in about me taking his car, he squeezed my leg, then rubbed up and down. It was so distracting I barely heard a word his mom said. "The car thing isn't a bad idea. You could take it until I'm able to drive."

"No." I shake my head. "I really haven't driven a car in a long time. I mostly rode my motorcycle."

"Your motorcycle?" Helene squeaks. "You have a motorcycle?"

Holding up my hand to stop her. "I misspoke. I *had* a scooter." I did until my sister took it without my permission one night and wrecked it. I'd saved for two years for that thing and in one night, she totaled it, and my insurance didn't pay out enough to replace it. The money did help me buy my books here at school though. There's that.

"Well, aren't you a surprise!" Helene's smiling from ear to ear.

I suppose I am. I just hope it's a good one.

2 8

EMMA

As soon as his mom's pulls out of the driveway, Eli reaches for me and presses my back against the door we just walked through and kisses the heck out of me before saying, "God, I've missed you so much."

I slide my arms around his neck and kiss him back. It feels right. Perfect actually. I pull away. "I've missed you too."

Now, he's kissing my neck, my chin, my cheek. It feels so damn good. His hands make their way to my back, then down. When his palms slide over my butt, he lifts me. "Eli. I'm too heavy."

"Shush." He nibbles on the side of my neck. I love that. The next thing I know, we're moving. He's practically running down the hallway, no doubt heading to his bedroom.

"You're going to break your back."

Ignoring me, he says, "I thought my mom would *never* leave." Eli's got me on his bed, and his hands have already made their way beneath my top. "I've been rock-hard since the second we stepped foot in your apartment."

I look down at his jeans and see what he means.

When he cups both of my breasts, I moan. I quickly reach

163

down and pull up my shirt before he even asks. Once that's gone, I fumble around until my bra's unhooked. Once I'm free of that proverbial shackle, I see Eli's expression. He looks blissed out at the sight of my naked breasts.

"I've missed you."

Is he talking to me, or them? "They've missed you too." I giggle.

I stop though, the second his mouth is on one of them. My head falls back on the bed as he licks and suckles. "Uh-huh," I mutter. Or maybe I mumble it. Either way, it feels good. *Really* good.

Eli quickly unbuttons my jeans, after asking me if it's okay. I don't bother answering. Instead, I help him. We did all this before. I know what to expect. However, if we go further than we did before, I'll have to think about it.

"Get out of your head, Em." I blink a few times and look into his eyes. "I can practically see the wheels turning. We won't do anything you aren't comfortable with. Yeah?"

"Yeah."

"Good. Now. Take off your pants."

That makes me crack up. But I do as he asks. I wiggle out of the too tight jeans Carley chose for me. All that's left is my underwear. I can't help noticing that Eli's still fully dressed though. "Aren't *you* going to take anything off?"

Without another word, Eli's off the bed. His shirt is off in one second, his jeans in another until he's left standing in boxer briefs and white athletic socks. I'd laugh at the sight if it weren't for his… uh, his penis. That's where my eyes keep going back to. I've been holding my breath, maybe a bit too long because I'm starting to get lightheaded.

"Do you want me to keep going?"

*Do I?* Do I want him to take off the rest of his clothes? The socks, definitely. What is it about a nearly naked man in a pair of socks that makes you laugh?

"Em?"

Instead of answering, I move my head up once, then down.

Eli places his thumbs in the elastic band of his dark gray boxers. Now, I'm holding my breath because, this is it. This will be the first time I see a naked man. In person. And this naked man is unbelievable. You read about bodies like his, you know, with the muscly arms, firm chest, and that stomach with the six bumps. Yes, Eli has all of that. But what those books don't tell you is what it's like realizing that magnificent body is about to be next to my, uh, very soft one. Those bumps on his stomach are going to be pressed against mine.

And that-- Holy shit.

His penis is big.

"Eli?" My voice sounds a bit like Mini Mouse.

"Emma." Yeah, my voice is squeaky and his just went down an octave. It's deep, husky, and rich.

"Um--"

"We don't do anything you don't want to do."

"I know. It's just…." I'm staring at it, and I may or may not be pointing at it. Oh, crud. I can't tell him that it's never going to fit, do I? I don't even like tampons. Sorry. That was probably TMI.

"Why are you opening and closing your mouth like a fish, babe?"

Great. *Like a fish?* I still can't say it. I flop back down onto the bed and cover my face with my hands and laugh.

"You laughin' at my cock, Em?"

"Definitely not." I shake my head back and forth. "You're just…" I push up on my elbows. It's weird. I'm almost completely naked and that's the least of my worries right now.

"I'm just what?"

"Unbelievably gorgeous."

"Aw, thanks." He places a knee on the bed between my legs. Next, I feel his palm on my stomach right over my bellybutton.

It's warm. It begins a slow trek up until it has skimmed over my right boob. "I feel the same about you."

I'm about to argue that point when he uses two fingers to pinch my nipple. After that, my brain turns to mush as he touches me.

Everywhere.

2 9

———————

ELI

THE LOOK ON EMMA'S FACE WHEN I TOOK OFF MY UNDERWEAR IS one I hope I never forget. It was a mix of horror and anticipation. I wanted to tell her it was going to be fine, that'd we fit together like two puzzle pieces, but I figured it was best to show her when the time comes, because she's not ready for that just yet. But she does know how to touch me now. And let me tell you, my girl is a quick study. Even though her hands are tiny, they worked magic. It could be because the thought of Emma Perkins doing *anything* to me makes me hard as stone, but it could also be she's a natural. I'd go so far as to say she's a sensual person. If you asked her, and I did, she'd probably tell you she enjoyed me touching her—my hands and my body touching hers. I call that sensual and I could really get into that.

"Yo. Dude. When will you be cleared to play again?" Cody asks as he brings me a sandwich and milk.

Cody's been hovering like a fucking mother hen. I'm pretty sure my mom put him up to it. She probably told him he needed to make sure I ate, that sort of thing. If she had Emma's number, she'd probably say the same shit to her. Hell, maybe she did when

I left them alone when I went to pee at the restaurant. I should ask Emma about that.

Thinking of my girl, I frown, remembering I haven't seen her for four days. We've texted a lot and even spoke on the phone late at night, but it's not the same. After we messed around in my bedroom on Sunday, she had Carley pick her up. I told her to take my car, but she wouldn't do it. She's stubborn. Maybe I can talk her into taking it today since she's going to take me to my doctor appointment later.

"Eat up, young man," Cody says, standing over me. He's become quite domestic since my concussion. He cleaned the bathroom, something he's never done and now, he's got his hands on his hips staring down at me. Hell, he's even wearing an apron. It's got flowers on it.

*Where did he get an apron?*

"Don't hover," I say, and wait for him to, well, stop hovering, but it doesn't work. So, with a sigh, I take a huge bite of the sandwich he made me. "Peanut butter and jelly?" I ask, still chewing. Yeah, it's impolite but… it's Cody. "On a hot dog bun?"

"We ran out of deli meat." He pauses. "And cheese and bread and chips and mayo." He looks back toward the kitchen. "And—"

"I get it. We need groceries." The fact that my sandwich was made on a stale hot dog bun is proof enough. Setting down the plate that holds the remainder of my sandwich, I add, "Emma's taking me to the doc in a bit. We'll get groceries on the way back."

"Oh, thank fuck." He chuckles, reaching into his apron pocket. "Here's a list."

Reaching for the wadded-up piece of paper, I uncrumple it and read. He's got everything on here but the kitchen sink. "I'm not getting all this." Not today. "I'll get the basics. We can get the rest this weekend."

"Fine. At least get the steaks, baked potatoes, and salad. I want to make that for dinner."

Wow, he is really getting domestic. "Yeah. Okay."

"Oh, and the cereal. We need cereal and milk."

"Uh-huh."

"And—"

Just then, the doorbell rings and I literally think, *Saved by the bell.*

"I'll get it," Cody says, taking off in a jog.

Standing, I take the plate that holds the rest of my PB&J and watch as Emma Perkins steps into my foyer. My smile is instantaneous. She looks adorable with her hair up in a ball on top of her head and her dark-rimmed glasses a little steamed over, which tells me it must be cold outside. Her winter coat is another sign that our beautiful fall weather will be gone soon.

The next moment, the door opens wider and a tall redhead steps in behind Emma. My first thought is, damn, Emma brought a friend. I was hoping for some alone time today. Placing the plate on the kitchen counter, I make my way over to Em. "Hey," I say, trying to sound cool.

"Oh, um, hi." Emma looks at me, then back at the redhead. I can't help noticing Emma looks both nervous and, well, annoyed.

"Eli." She sighs. "This is my little sister, Amber."

I look at the woman behind Emma again. Actually, I'm staring, which is a bit rude, I know. As quickly as possible, I attempt to see if her sister and Emma have any similar characteristics. So far, all I notice are differences. Emma has dark hair, her sister is a redhead. Emma is short, Amber isn't. I can see similarities in the face now that I've taken a moment to look. Same nose, same shaped eyes, although Amber's are brown while Emma's are grayish blue. They've both got freckles. Emma's mouth is fuller and poutier than her sister's, whose mouth, well, her mouth is smiling. A big, wide smile.

"Well, *hello*," she says, holding her hand out to me. Am I supposed to kiss it or shake it? I opt for the latter. "It's *so* nice to meet you, Eli." The way she's emphasizing some words is a little weird.

"Same." I guess.

I attempt to pull my hand away, but Amber's still gripping mine. Looking down at her hand, I watch as Amber steps closer. "I had no idea Emma had such…" She looks me up and down. "…gorgeous friends."

*Friends?* I use my strength to pull my hand away as I look over at Emma. She's frowning so I turn and give her all my attention. "How are you, Emma?"

"Fine," she mutters, but I've heard that "fine" before and know she's full of it.

"Wow, this place is *ah*-mazing." That comes from Amber again. "I had no idea Emma's friends were so…" I can't wait to hear the next words. "…*rich*." Then, she titters. "Heck. I'm surprised she *has* any friends other than Carley." Like we're close, she, Amber, reaches out and touches my arm. "Between you and me, let's just say that our Emma here"—she nods back at her sister—"was *not* popular. On the contrary, she was what one might refer to as a social leper."

*Who the fuck is this girl?*

We don't technically have to leave for twenty minutes, but I'm not sure what's going on here, so I turn to Emma. "Can I speak with you for a moment?" I peek over at Amber, then back at Em. "Alone."

I glance at Amber again. who's now looking around the open-plan space in my house. "Wow, this place is *niiiiiice*. I could get used to living in a place like this."

I turn my head and make eye contact with Emma. "Emma?"

"Sure." She nods, but her expression is flat.

I hold my hand out to her and she takes it. A charge races up my arm at the feel of her touch. It reminds me of Sunday, but I shake off those thoughts. "Be right back." I'm not sure who I'm talking to. Cody's still there watching us, so I use that to my advantage. "Can you entertain Amber?"

"Sure." Cody smirks. "Glad to."

In my bedroom, I shut the door just as Emma flops back on my bed. "Oh, my God. She just showed up at my place last night. I came home from work and she was sitting on the floor by my door with a suitcase." She sits up and glares at me. "A big one."

I'm not sure what to say. "I didn't know you had a sister."

"We're… not close."

"Did she say why she's here?"

Shaking her head, Emma says, "She just said she needed a change of scenery."

"Oh."

"I just don't have time for any of her—" Emma pauses. "I don't have time to entertain my sister."

"She's an adult. Right?"

"Sure. Right."

"She can entertain herself." I feel like I need to say something encouraging. "She seems nice."

The glare she gives me quickly shifts into a smile. "Yep. She's *so* nice. Very, very nice."

Wow, sarcasm isn't a good look for Emma. "Okay then." I slap my palms down on my legs. "We'd better hit the road so I'm not late for my appointment." Standing, I turn and hold my hand out to her. "I also need to stop and get a few groceries afterward. Do you have time for that?"

"Sure." She gives me a smile, sort of. One of those with no teeth showing. "We can do that."

"Good. Thanks." Before we leave my room, I bend down so we're eye to eye. "I mean it. Thanks for doing this." I kiss her pretty lips. A real smile finally emerges, albeit a small one. It's okay. I'll take it.

"No problem."

## 30

EMMA

IT WAS A PROBLEM.

Not the grocery shopping thing. No, I don't mind helping Eli out. The problem has everything to do with my little sister, Amber.

She's less than a year younger than me, but she acts *much* younger. She has always behaved like a petulant child. There's also the fact we've never gotten along. I'm pretty sure she came out of the womb hating my guts. You wouldn't know it by the way she performed at Eli's earlier (and it was a performance), because she's really good at pretending. She pretends to be something she's definitely not. Like nice, for one. Honest for another. Law-abiding is a third one. Maybe the biggest one is the law-abiding one, but I didn't want to tell Eli about any of that. I mean, what would he think of me if he heard about my shoplifting, police-assaulting sister who can't hold a job? He'd think less of me, for sure.

It's why I couldn't leave her at my apartment alone. Or with Carley. Carley is this close to strangling her so having the two in the same room without me as the mediator is a bad idea. But alone, I think Amber is worse. You see, she steals things.

Anything that has any value. Not that I have anything like that. Well, my laptop is a big one. She mostly likes to take small things she can slide into a pocket. It's gotten her fired numerous times.

And then, there's my parents. My poor parents. Amber has been manipulating and milking them dry for as long as I can remember. Heck, lawyers' fees alone have forced them to nearly double their hours at the store, sell one car, and I'm pretty sure they took another mortgage out on the house. Crud, thinking about all of that makes me feel like such a shit-heel. *I* should be helping them.

I *will* help them. When I graduate and get a job, I'll be able to send them money.

---

AMBER WAS BORED AT THE DOCTOR'S OFFICE, SO SHE PACED AROUND the waiting area and complained the entire time. When Eli finally came out, because she was right, the appointment took a long time, she acted like it was no big deal and that her first concern was his health.

*Yeah, right.*

She raced to his side when he stepped through the door that led to the exam rooms. She held his arm like he was some sort of invalid that needed help walking. Eli let her do it too. He's too nice to do otherwise.

In the grocery store, she grabs her own cart and proceeds to fill it with food and other things she deems necessary, like a new coffeemaker, saying, "Yours is old and it sucks."

It was my parents' coffeemaker, and it works great. Okay. Not great because it takes about thirty minutes to brew a pot of coffee, but it's fine for us. No need to spend that kind of money when all you have to do was wait for it.

Because I know my sister, the minute I see the cart, I ask, "Are *you* buying all of that?"

"No." She rolls her eyes. "I'm broke."

*You're broke because you can't hold a job longer than two weeks—*

I don't say that, though. What I do say is "Well, I can't afford to buy it."

"Your *friend* will do it." She keeps doing that. Emphasizing the word "friend" because I haven't told her that Eli and I are… more than that. That we're dating. No matter. I don't want her to know, because if my sister thought Eli and I were, well, together, she'd do whatever she could to change that: Amber has always wanted what I have. I don't know how many times she took my toys, then broke them. Out of spite, probably.

My parents weren't much help with our issues because they were either working or tired from working. So I just got used to it, I guess.

Carley thinks I need to put my foot down especially now. She can't stand my sister because of all the stuff she's pulled on me over the years, but mostly because she thinks Amber is a pain in the ass.

She's right. She is.

Actually, Carley did put her foot down when she came home and saw Amber on our couch, eating our food, with the television remote in her hand. She pulled me into our tiny bathroom and said, "Your bitch of a sister can stay one week. One. Then it's either her or me."

Obviously, my choice is Carley. The thing is, knowing my sister, once she digs in, it's hard to get her out. She's like a leach that way.

"No." Glaring at Amber, I shake my head for emphasis. "Eli's not buying you groceries."

She leans in like she has a secret and whispers loudly, "He's loaded, isn't he?"

"I have no idea." Yes, I did know, but I'm not about to tell her.

"Cody told me their place belonged to Eli."

"It belongs to his parents."

"His parents are rich, which means he's rolling in it too."

I shake my head and point the cart. "Put that away."

"I'm getting most of this. You're out of everything."

"I don't have the money." I growl at her. "Seriously. I'm a broke college student."

"With a scholarship," she snaps. "Plus you've got a job, right?"

"Amber—"

"You ladies ready to go?" Eli asks as he approaches us.

"We would be but Emma forgot her wallet so she can't pay for all of this stuff she wanted."

"Amber." I look at Eli and slowly shake my head.

"I'll get it for you, Emma," he says sweetly.

"See?" Amber smirks. "I told you." She turns to Eli. "Thank you so much. That's the sweetest thing anyone has ever done for... *her*." Amber snickers. "Trust me. Nobody is bending over backward for big, old Emma back there." She points her thumb back at me.

I take the opportunity to grasp the cart handle. "We are *not* getting this stuff, Amber."

She reaches for the handle, which means we've both got hold of the cart. "Yes. We are. Eli said he'd pay for it."

I grit my teeth and do my best to keep my voice down when inside, I'm screaming. "No. He's not going to pay for your stuff."

"But, Emma," Amber whines. "I'm so hungry."

"Ladies." Eli's voice sounds so deep it startles me. "You ready to go?"

"We are. We'll meet you up front." I watch him turn his cart and proceed to roll it up to the cash registers, except he looks back at us several times until he rounds the corner and he's out of sight. That's when I lean into my sister. With my teeth gritted so hard I'm afraid they're going to break, I speak only loud enough for her to hear. "*We* are not asking Eli to buy our groceries." Glaring daggers at my sister, I add, "*You* do not need all of that." I pointed at the cart full of junk food.

"But Emma…," she whines again.

"No." I hold up my finger and point it right at her. Rude, I know. "You're not staying long enough to eat all this anyway."

Her pathetic face suddenly morphs into one I recognize growing up. Her eyes turned squinty and I swear, she snarls. Literally snarls. "I'll stay as long as *I* want." Her voice is as low as mine.

Shaking my head, I say, "No. You won't. There's only two bedrooms." And those are tiny.

"So. We can share."

"The landlord only allows two people in a two-bedroom apartment." I'm actually not sure if that's true. Amber certainly doesn't know if it's true or not.

"Fine." She releases the grocery cart and starts to stomp off, but she stops suddenly. I watch as she reaches back and grabs the box of Fruity-Os cereal. "I *need* this." And off she marches, no doubt to ask Eli to buy it for her.

By the time I get up to the front, she's all smiles with Eli. Heck, she even smiles at me.

Which means one thing… Amber Nicole Perkins is up to something, and I have to do my level best to find out what it is and nip it in the bud.

## 31

ELI

I don't know what's going on with Emma and her sister, but it was tense in the car. From the point we checked out at the store when I offered to buy Em's groceries, all the way back to my place in the truck. No, tense isn't the right word. Strained. Yeah, that's a better word. Amber was the only one who said anything and that was directed at me.

She had lots of questions about my family, which classes I was taking and why, and of course, about hockey asking things like "Just how good *are* you?" and "Are you going pro?"

I gave her clipped, standard answers, because every time one would come out of her mouth from the back seat, I'd look over at Emma to gauge her reaction. To say she was white knuckled is an understatement. The woman never took her eyes off the road for a second, but that doesn't mean I couldn't see her expressions. The ones that really got her going were the hockey questions. I could feel her eye roll from my spot in the car.

Emma pulls my SUV into the garage, turns off the engine, looks back at her sister from the rear-view mirror and snaps, "Wait out front. I'll only be a minute."

"Emma," Amber whines. "I want to hang out with Eli for a while."

Now, I'm pretty easygoing and as we all know, my manners aren't on par with my girl's, but even *I* know that's rude. There was no invite to "hang out" with me. Amber just assumes she can ingratiate herself at my place. Not cool.

"Wait. Out. Front." Emma is having none of it. And I have to say, seeing her take control like this is kinda hot. Also, a tad scary. I don't think *I'd* even mess with her when she's this angry.

"Fine." Amber pushes her door open, jumps out, slams the door hard, and stomps out the open garage bay door to the front of my place.

"I'm sorry about her," Emma says from the open car door. "She's—"

"Spoiled?"

Emma snorts. "The understatement of the year."

When Amber appears again, Emma growls. I want to laugh but think better of it.

"What did I just tell you?" she snaps at her sister.

"I forgot my cereal. And since you have absolutely no food at your place—"

Those words get my attention. Our eyes meet and as I'm about to ask Emma about her food situation, she holds one hand up. "We have food. It's just not up to Amber's high standards."

"Fuck you, Emma," Amber snarls. "Just because I don't want to live off old oatmeal and cheap ramen—"

"There's peanut butter and jelly. And bread too."

"Oh, wow. Gee. That makes it all okay."

"I didn't invite you here, Amber. If you don't like it, go home." Emma goes from standing in her open car door to standing about five inches from her sister. Glaring up at her, Emma has a hand on each hip and her stance, in a word, looks like she's about to knock out her bratty little sister. Like I say, it's hot. Until I hear a sniffle. I know for sure it's not coming from Emma.

"Oh no." Emma shakes her head. "Don't you dare start with the fake tears. I'm not falling for it. You may have Mom and Dad fooled, but not me."

"I'm really crying, you bitch."

"Oh, there's water coming out of your eyes, sure. But there's nothing behind those tears, faker."

"Faker?" Amber sobs. "I'm n-n-not faking it. You're so mean."

I watch Emma's shoulders visibly slump. A heavy, heavy sigh follows, like she's given up. I don't like it. "Just wait out front, Amber. I'll get your stupid cereal."

"Fine," Amber snaps before stomping out of the garage again.

I gently place my hands on Emma's upper arms. My God, she's tense. "You okay?"

"Yes."

"Hey." I bend down until we're eye to eye. "I mean it. You okay?"

"I'm fine." She pauses, looking to her left at the wall where the few manly tools I own hang. "She's up to something," Emma says softly, barely loud enough for me to hear.

"She's up to something?"

Looking up at me, she blinks. "Yeah."

"What? What's she up to?"

"I don't know. But I'm going to find out." Emma's still looking at the wall of my garage like she's really thinking about it.

"When can I see you again?"

"Oh." She looks back up at me. "Not sure." Pulling away, she holds up my car keys. I really wish she'd just take my car. But I know she won't.

"Let me help you get the groceries inside. Then I need to go before Amber decides to do something rash."

"No." I bend and kiss her lips. "Cody can get the groceries. He'll eat most of them so it's only fair."

"You sure?"

"Positive." I kiss her again. This time for a little longer and with tongue. Emma kisses me right back. During the kiss, I keep thinking about us doing more than just kissing and those thoughts make my dick hard, which is a tad inconvenient. Pulling back, I reach my hand around and gently pat her bottom. "I'll call you."

"Okay." She gives me the smallest of smiles, but I take it. I'll just make it my mission to get her to smile bigger next time.

3 2

---

EMMA

WE DON'T SPEAK THE ENTIRE WAY BACK TO MY APARTMENT, WHICH is fine with me. She stomped to the bus stop, then sat three rows behind me on the city bus. Probably so she could make sure she got off at the right stop. Smart, really. Now, as I step off the bus, I peek back and see her stand. I only live a half block from this particular stop, so as soon as she's off, she starts to jog past me. I don't know why she's bothering to beat me home because she doesn't have a key to my place and Carley isn't home. Unless she plans to pick the lock—

I stop suddenly. She could probably do that. Or kick in the door. I wouldn't put it past her to do that. So I pick up my own pace. When I get to my door, I sigh with relief. Amber's sitting on the floor with her back against the door. Reaching into my pocket, I grab my key.

"You should just make me a copy of that key."

*Yeah, right. That's never going to happen.*

Ignoring her, I unlock the door and push it open. Since she's blocking my path, I wait for her to go in first. As soon as she's over the threshold, she drops her purse on the floor and makes her way to the couch where she's set up a temporary bed.

*God, I hope it's temporary.*

No. I know it is. Carley gave me an ultimatum and she's not one to pussyfoot around about ultimatums.

"Make me a bowl of cereal, would you?" Amber's on the couch with an old magazine in her hand.

Setting my purse on our tiny counter, I rotate my head slowly, for emphasis. I don't know why I bothered because she's not looking my way. "Get your own cereal." I move toward my bedroom, but then it hits me. And it makes me smile as I say, "We're out of milk."

The scream's loud. Louder than necessary, for sure. Then, in an equally loud voice, she adds, "You *fucking* suck."

"Yep," I reply, just as I open my bedroom door and slip inside.

---

"I CAN'T TAKE MUCH MORE OF HER."

Carley's finally home. I think she spent extra time away after class, so she didn't have to deal with my little sister. I don't blame her. I switched shifts at the library so I could take Eli to the doctor and to keep an eye on Amber. I don't know what's going to happen when both Carley and I are gone.

"She'll probably steal the silverware while we're gone."

"It's from the thrift store." I blink at her. "Nothing matches." Literally. No two utensils are the same. We kind of like it that way. It's the same with our dishes and glasses. A hodgepodge.

Carley stares at me like I'm crazy. "I wouldn't put anything past her. When you go to class tomorrow, you'd better take all of your electronics."

Ugh. My backpack is already ridiculously heavy, but she's right. Anything of value needs to travel with us.

"Did you call your parents?"

I was supposed to call them to ask them why Amber's here,

but I'm afraid to. The last thing they need is more Amber drama. "What if she's on the lam or something?"

"Well, then she's fucked because she crossed state lines." Carley gets a gleam in her eye. Her voice suddenly wistful as she adds, "Federal prison."

It cracks me up. Not the idea that my sister would end up in federal prison, but the way Carley said it. Like it'd be a dream come true for her. "She's not *that* bad."

The look on Carley's pretty face suddenly morphs into one of shock. "Yes. She is. She's one bust away from going away for a good, long time."

"Most of her things have been misdemeanors."

"Thanks to your poor parents and good lawyers."

True.

"Call them. See if you can find out why she's here. What if we get in trouble for aiding and abetting?"

"You've been watching too many true crime dramas."

"Have not."

"Have too."

"Call. Them."

"Fine." I search around my bed for my phone. It must still be in my purse. When she sees I don't have my phone handy, she passes me hers and steps out of the room. "I've got your mom's number on there."

Not surprising. Growing up, Carley was at my house as much as I was at hers. We were always together. Pressing my mom's name, it rings several times. "What's wrong with Emma?" Are the first words out of my mom's mouth.

"It's me. Emma. I'm fine."

"Oh, thank God." I can hear the relief in her voice, and it makes me smile. I mean, she loves me, that I know.

"How are you?"

"Good." But she sounds tired even over the phone. "We worked a double today."

A double means a double shift. Two eight-hour shifts in one day. That's a lot. "I'm sorry, Mom."

"No worries, my sweet. How's school?"

"Good. I'm doing well. I'm going to graduate on time."

"Wonderful." Her voice sounds much cheerier now. "I hope you find a job close by."

"I'm planning on it." Most of the places in Illinois that would hire someone like me are in Chicago, which is an easy drive home. I'm quiet for a bit too long.

Mom must sense the change because she speaks first. "Is she with you?"

Wait a second. Mom didn't even know where she went? "She is."

"And you don't want her there." This time, it's not a question.

I shake my head, knowing my mom can't see it. I'm forced to say, "She's too much."

Mom chuckles. "Oh, I know."

"What is she doing here? What happened?"

"She was fired again."

Shocker.

"They accused her of…" Mom hesitates.

Oh, shit.

"Of what? What'd they accuse her of?" Her most recent job was at a truck stop slash convenience store just outside of town on the interstate, so I can imagine her doing all sorts of things there. Like…

"Selling…."

"Selling?" Oh no. Has my sister really gone there? "Drugs? Was she selling drugs?" She's always been a petty thief. Never anything that serious. I mean, Amber Perkins is no criminal mastermind.

"I'm not sure." Mom's not being honest with me. I can tell by her voice. I've heard it many times before when she's doing her best not to think about the illegal stuff my sister has done.

"Mom."

"I don't know, honey. The police wouldn't say much." Mom sighs and it makes me so sad. "I honestly don't know, sweetheart. Our lawyer was supposed to talk to the police today. I'm hoping we can just pay a fine and—"

"Mom." I interrupt her. "If she was doing something like that, selling drugs…" Then, a lightbulb flickers on above my head like one of those in cartoons. If she's selling drugs, then I know why she's here. Why she came to a college campus. To a place that has hundreds, maybe thousands of potential customers. "I've gotta go, Mom. I'll call you back soon."

"Emma—"

"Love you. Bye." I hit the button to disconnect our call. Setting the phone on the bed next to me, I rub my face with both hands. If my sister is selling drugs, then she'd have them with her, I assume. Which means, she's got them in her suitcase or her purse.

Which also means she's got them in my apartment. And if that's the case, Carley will go ballistic, which means I can't tell Carley about my suspicions. No, what I need to do is get them both out of here for a while so I can search her stuff. The question is, if there are drugs, what kind of drugs? I mean, I just assumed that's what she was selling. Maybe I should have talked to Dad. He would have been straight with me. Mom just can't see the bad in Amber, in anyone, really.

Deciding I need more information, I step out into the living room in search of my purse. Spotting it on the counter, I reach for it as Amber asks, "So, what's for dinner?"

She cannot be serious.

"Cereal." I grab hold of the handle on my bag.

I turn and make a beeline for my bedroom just as Amber whines, "But you're out of milk."

"Go get some. There's a convenience store about a block from here."

"Fine." She gripes. "I need money."

For crying out loud.

"What?" She stares at me. "I spent all my cash to get up here."

"And that's my problem, because?"

"Just give me a couple bucks. Jesus. You're such a bitch."

I can't take this. I really can't. Reaching into my purse, I take out my wallet. Opening, I see only a ten-dollar bill, which means I won't see any change. "Here." I hold it out to her. "I need my change back."

"Sure thing, sis." She smirks. "Back in a jiffy."

*How do I know she's lying?*

Because that's what Amber does. She lies.

As soon as she's out the door, I pause. I could call my father first, or I can go through her luggage while she's gone. Opting for the luggage, I set my purse back down and make my way over to her stuff.

"Damn it." Nothing. There's nothing in her bags.

"What are you doing?" Carley asks from somewhere behind me.

"Searching her luggage."

"For what?"

"Just trying to figure out what she's *really* doing here." But, honestly, I'm not sure.

"What aren't you telling me, Em?" Carley has her hands on her hips. She knows something's up.

"I don't know for sure." I push myself up onto my feet. "Mom said she got in trouble for selling something back home. I just assumed it was drugs, but I need to call my dad to find out because there's nothing in her suitcase other than clothes and makeup."

"Jesus," Carley mutters.

Picking up my purse, I head into my bedroom. Reaching inside, I fish around for my phone. When I don't find it, I dump out the contents. "Crap." Out in the living area, I ask Carley if she's seen it.

"Nope. Maybe you left it at Eli's?"

"Or in his car."

"I'd tell you to call him but—"

"Ha. Right." Looking up at her, I ask, "Can you call my phone. Maybe it fell underneath something."

After several failed attempts to find my phone, I sigh and ask Carley, "Is my dad's number on your phone?"

"Of course."

Back in my room, I pick up Carley's cell and search for his number. Pressing on his name, I wait. It rings only once when he answers, sounding groggy. "Is Emma okay?"

I'd love to laugh because that's pretty much what Mom said. "Hey Daddy. It's me, Emma."

"Oh, phew, peanut." He chuckles. "What's up?"

I may as well just get right to it. "What was Amber selling?"

There's a long pause. I hear rustling like he's moving around. "Hang on," he whispers into the phone.

I don't like this. Not one bit. In the background, I hear the click of a shutting door. "You there?" he asks.

"Yeah."

He releases a gust of air. "Emma…"

My goodness, what the heck is the deal? "Dad?"

"Herself."

"Huh?" Herself? What is he talking about? "What do you mean?"

"She was selling herself."

Herself? Selling hers… "Pros-titution?" My voice cracks in the middle of that word. I can barely get the rest out. "She was pros-tituting her… herself?"

"That's what they're saying."

This, that's— "No."

"Yes."

## 33

---

### ELI

I'VE TRIED TO CALL EMMA TWICE NOW. SHE HASN'T ANSWERED either time. I've left a voicemail too.

Okay, before you think I'm completely pussy-whipped, I'll just say, hell yes, I am. I was away from school, my house, and her for two weeks. Now, I'm just stuck at home. Sure, I got to see her for a few hours today, but it's not the same has having her nearby. Hell, just sitting on the sofa, watching TV would be enough for me. I'll opt for the next best thing––hearing her sweet voice.

Since it's late, very late, I don't feel like calling is the right thing to do. A text message will have to do.

**Me**: Hey, babe. I've been trying to call. Miss you.

See? Pussy-whipped.

I stare at the screen of my phone watching for those three little vibrating dots to appear. You know the ones that tell me she's writing back. I glance at the clock on the screen. 1:37 a.m. That's not late for a student. Not for me but maybe it is for her. I stare for several more minutes but give up.

I'll take a shower and grab something to eat before I crawl into bed. Maybe by then, she'll have sent me a response.

By the time I get back to my room, I see my phone is glowing. Grabbing it up, I flop back on my bed, ready to talk to my girl. But the second I read the screen, a feeling of hurt so deep strikes me to the core.

> **Emma:** Thank you so much for tonight. I've never felt
> such passion. Your touch burned my skin. I can't wait to
> see you again. Just name the time and the place.

I stare at the screen, doing my best to process what I'm reading. "Thank you so much for tonight?" I guess I enjoy torturing myself because reading it silently isn't enough for me. I need to hear the words too. *Your touch burned my skin.*

"Fuck." I read on: "I can't wait to see you again."

This can't be right.

This has to be a mistake.

Emma wouldn't cheat on me.

Would she?

I stare at the screen again. Reread it a third time.

And then it hits me.

I don't really know Emma. Not well.

I only thought I knew her.

But this message says everything I need to know.

She's not the girl I thought she was.

I thought she was *my* girl.

Apparently… she's someone else's.

***

"Fuck, Bax." Cody sounds angry. "You've got to get over that girl. Get back on the fucking horse." He chuckles. "I mean that. The *fucking* horse. The best way to get over a girl is to get under another one."

He thinks he's so funny.

"It's been two fucking weeks and all you've done is mope. You've been back on the ice for a week and your game is pathetic. Coach is going to bench you, which means your dad is going to lose his shit."

He's right. About everything. It was two weeks ago today that Emma sent me that text. Well, she sent it to me on accident. I know because a few minutes after that one came, another one appeared.

**Emma:** Golly, Eli. I didn't mean to send that to you.

Well, fucking *duh*.

I was pissed but that passed. It's the melancholy I haven't been able to shake that's the problem. I've never cried over a girl. Not until the night Emma Perkins broke my heart.

"Party tonight at Bridge's place. Lots of lovely puck bunnies for you to choose from." Cody won't let up. "That one chick, Shannon, has been asking about you."

*Shannon. Which one is she?* Oh, I remember. "She's been with a half dozen of the guys."

"So. She's a modern woman. She's in charge of her own sexuality."

"Whatever." I'd just be a notch for her. I'm not ready to be someone's notch. Wait. *Was I one for Emma?*

"If you don't go, I'm going to call your mom."

"The fuck?" I spit.

"I will. Don't you dare underestimate me."

"My mom—"

"Loves me," Cody smirks. "MILFs love me."

"Do not refer to my mother as a MILF." Argh. I can't unhear that.

"Why not? She is one. She's one of the hottest older ladies I've ever seen."

Clenching my fist, I'm about to punch him in his stupid mouth when he laughs. "Glad to see there's still some life in you."

"Fucker."

"Come to the party. It'll make you feel better." He punches my arm but not hard. "Besides, I heard Calvert say he wanted to do more nude hockey videos."

"God. When will you guys grow up?"

"Hopefully never." Cody laughs. "So, is that a yes?"

"Fine. Yes."

"Sweet. Change your clothes. I'm sick of seeing you in the same pair of dirty sweats and an even more disgusting shirt." He claps his hands in front of my face while shouting, "Let's go, let's go, let's go."

So, I do. I go. Why the hell not?

3 4

EMMA



"Tell me why we're doing this again?"

It's been two weeks since the last time I saw Eli. It was the day I took him to the doctor. That's also the day I lost my phone. I hope I find it soon because I can't afford to replace it. I should cancel my plan, but that's such a hassle, and I know the minute I do it, I'll find my stupid phone. And don't worry, the lack of phone didn't stop me from trying to get in touch with him. I did. Carley had Cody's number so when she sent him a text asking for Eli's number, he sent a very rude reply. Something like "Fuck off, bitches." That didn't prevent me from stopping by his house. Again, Cody answered the door and told me, in no uncertain terms, that "Eli wasn't home and if he was, he didn't want to see me. Ever." When I asked when he would be home, he just glared at me, saying, "Don't fucking toy with my boy's head, Emma."

*Toy with his head?* I wouldn't. I hadn't.

To say it was unexpected well, it was an understatement. What had I done? Everything seemed fine when I dropped him at his house after the doctor's visit and the store.

I still have no idea what happened. Carley told me to write

him a real letter asking him. Her theory is that Eli's dad somehow convinced him to stop seeing me. I could see that happening, I guess. Honestly, I have no clue what happened, and I'm not going to lie. It hurts. A lot. Not knowing is almost worse than the feeling of my heart breaking into a gazillion pieces. Almost.

"I told you. We're getting you closure. You've done nothing but mope for the last two weeks, and I don't foresee that changing until you know what happened. That's the closure I'm talking about."

She's right, I suppose. The thing is, I don't know if I want to see him. What's going to happen if we end up in the same room? Is he going to turn and walk away? Will he get angry and make a scene? I just don't have a clue.

My focus returns to Carley as she adds, "Anyhoo, I heard about this hockey party and figured it'd be a chance for you to bump into him."

"Bump into him?" I hope she doesn't mean literally. Like I said, just being in the same room with him is going to be too much.

"Sure." She shrugs. "Let's see what he does when he sees you looking all hot like that." She points to my bare legs. She's got me in that short dress again. At least I talked her out of the big hair and the over-the-top makeup.

*I have no idea why I agreed to any of this.*

The minute she pulls onto the street where the party is being held, my stomach flips over, my mouth gets suddenly dry, and sweat beads at my hairline. "This is a bad idea."

Carley points to my right. "Ooh, look. There's Eli's car."

I stare at the Illinois license plate and feel nauseous. "Terrible idea," I mumble to myself.

"Nope. This is the perfect idea."

It's not. "I don't think I can do this."

"You always say that. Do I need to double-dog da—"

"No." I hold up my hand to stop her from finishing that

sentence. "I'm here, aren't I?" *Stupid double-dog dares.* That's what got us into this situation in the first place. "Let's just get this over with." *So I can go home and eat my weight in cookies.*

---

"OKAY. I SPOTTED HIM. HE JUST WALKED INTO THE KITCHEN."

I've been standing by the front door while Carley does reconnaissance. You have no idea how many times I reached for the doorknob, plotting my escape. Twenty times? Thirty?

"I'll lead the way, but before we get there, then I'm going to disappear."

"You're not going to leave, right?" I swear, if she takes off without me, I'm going to kick her perfect little butt.

"No. I'll be around. I'll keep my eye on you, so *you* don't take off on me."

"I wouldn't…."

She rolls her eyes. "You so would."

She's right. I feel like running now. "Fine."

We get about five feet from the swinging door that leads to the kitchen and I halt. That's when Carley reaches back, grabs my arm, and pulls me in front of her. Then, with her hands on my lower back, she gently pushes me closer to the door. "Go on. Just get it over with. Let's see what he does."

I watch her walk off into the crowd of people. With courage I didn't know I had, I place my hand on the door, ready to push through when the door suddenly flies in my direction, hard. Hard enough that I'm launched backwards. I swear I'm airborne at one point. When I land with a thud on the ground, I feel pain on the back of my head, but that's not the part that's terrifying. It's the fact that my dress is now up around my waist.

Thank God I wore my best black spanx-like underwear. I can't afford the real kind so generic will do.

As fast as I can, I try to work my dress back down over my thighs, but his voice gives me pause. "Emma?"

I don't bother responding because, well, my dress. Working it down until I'm sort of covered, I then reach back and touch my head. It's wet. "Am I bleeding?" Pulling my hand forward, I hold my breath, expecting the worst but all I see is clear wetness.

"Probably beer," Cody mutters. "It's all over the place."

When I feel wetness seep through my dress into the back of my underwear, I realize he's right. "Gross," I mutter.

"Emma?" Eli asks again. "What are you doing here?"

He doesn't sound pleased to see me.

"Isn't it obvious, bro?" Cody slaps Eli's back.

"She came back for the Bax special." Even though Cody's words sound humorous, the glare he's giving me says otherwise. He's warned me away enough times.

Eli extends his hand to me and I take it. The feeling when our hands touch doesn't surprise me. The guy makes me feel charged, alive.

When I'm on my feet, Eli reaches back to touch my head. "You hit your head?"

"Yeah. I'm okay, though."

Eli merely nods. "Is Cody right? Did you come here to see if I was here?"

I shrug. "Maybe."

"Why would you bother?" Eli's face looks tired. And irritated. His brows are pushed tightly together making one.

"Why would I bother? I've been trying to talk to you for two weeks. I've talked to Cody on the phone and at your front door. He said you didn't want to talk to me. *Ever.*"

I don't know what I expected Eli to do. No. That's false. What I expected, or maybe fantasized is a better word. I fantasized he would wrap me up in his arms and kiss the crud out of me. That he'd tell me he was sorry he blew me off without an explanation. But that's not what I get. Instead of that, I get the opposite.

"Why the fuck would I want to see *you*?"

I blink a few times. Which turns into more of a flutter of my lashes as I do my damn best to keep the tears from falling. It's not working, though. "B-because I'm your g-girlfriend."

Eli stares at me. Hard. I watch as his lips draw into a thin line on his handsome face. His nostrils flare. When his eyes get all squinty, I know he's going to say something that's gonna hurt.

"You fucking cheated on me. Why the hell would you think you're my girlfriend?"

"I--" The words aren't coming. I mean. He thinks I cheated on him? "I didn't cheat on you." I didn't.

"Are you fucking serious right now?" He reaches into his back pocket and pulls out his phone. I watch him click around a little bit, then he pushes it in my face. It's so close, I have to work to get the thing into focus. When I do, I see it. The text.

**Emma:** Thank you so much for tonight. I've never felt such passion. Your touch burned my skin. I can't wait to see you again. Just name the time and the place.

I'm speechless. I lean in a little closer to his screen just to make sure I'm reading it correctly. "I don't understand."

"You're a smart girl. What don't you get? You sent me a text intended for whoever you were fucking while we were together." He looks around the party then back at me. "Is he here now?"

"He who?" I'm so confused. "I didn't send that text message."

"Yeah. You did." He clicks around on his phone and shows me:

**Emma:** Golly, Eli. I didn't mean to send that to you.

I reach for his phone because I've got questions. He quickly pulls it out of reach. So, I ask, "Golly?" I would never say "golly." "When was this sent?"

Running his hand through his hair, he sighs. "I'm not doing

this. I'm not going to entertain this little fucking twisted game you seem intent on playing."

"It's not a game." I stare at Eli, and I know he believes I sent that text message. "I lost my phone."

Scoffing, Eli glares down at me. "Yeah. Right."

"I did. The day I took you to the doctor."

Bending down so we're close enough to kiss, he hisses, "You expect me to believe that you lost your phone and somehow, a mystery person decided to send me those text messages?"

And then it hits me.

"Amber."

That little bitch. I'm going to murder her and I'm not even going to wait until she's sleeping. I'm going to do it in broad daylight. I want her to know it was me.

"You expect me to believe your *sister* did this?"

I feel a hand on my shoulder and know it's Carley. "It makes sense. That little bitch is a snake in the grass. She was pissed that day."

Carley's right. She was angry about the milk. Then right before she went to the store, she suddenly changed her tune. When she got back, Amber was all smiles as she packed her bag. She claimed "we were right" and that she was going to head home and face the music first thing in the morning. She was gone before we woke up.

That's not what she did, though.

She didn't head home to face any music. My parents haven't heard from her. They've been worried sick too. But now I know who has my phone. *Why didn't I think of that?* Of course, Amber would do something like this. *Of course* she would steal my phone and mess with my life.

I can't think about her right now, though, because that's not the issue at hand. No, the issue is Eli believing I'd cheat on him.

I guess if I'd gotten a text like that, I'd believe it too.

"Eli." It's Carley speaking. "Amber got into trouble back home.

She came up here to hide out or something. She told us she was going home to deal with it."

It's quiet. At least it is to me. Sure, there are a hundred people drinking and dancing around us, but I can't hear a thing because Eli is staring down at me. Blinking. He no longer looks angry. He still looks really tired--the same as me. I haven't gotten much sleep lately.

"Are you saying you didn't cheat on me?"

"Of course she didn't cheat on you." Carley is still defending me.

"Do you mind?" Eli glares at Carley. "Can I talk to Emma alone, please?"

"Sure thing." Carley looks at me, smiles, pats my shoulder, then winks.

*Stupid winking.* I guess it's okay if Carley does it. I watch her walk away with Cody right behind her as Eli says, "Come on. Let's go somewhere more private."

Turning, Eli looks back at me and points to a stairway that leads down. "Let's head to the basement."

Without a word, I follow him down a rickety old set of stairs. When we get to the bottom, I'm a little surprised to see a fairly nice family room. It's crowded with partiers too, so Eli bypasses them and leads me down a long hallway to a door at the end. He knocks once and waits. When he gets no response, he turns the knob and pushes the door open. Reaching in, he does something to make an overhead light flick on. "This is a spare bedroom. We can talk in here."

"Okay." I step into the small space and notice there's only a double bed and a dresser. Not knowing what to do, I step in far enough for Eli to enter. When he shuts the door, I hold my breath. I don't know why. Anticipation, perhaps.

When he looks at me, his face is unreadable. "You really didn't cheat on me?"

"Of course not. I—"

I don't get a chance to finish my sentence because right then, Eli's lips are on mine. It's a sweet, soft kiss that only lasts a few seconds. "I've missed you so much, Em."

"I've missed you too."

His arms are wrapped around me and I'm pressed against his body. He feels tense. Raising my arms, I place one on each of his broad shoulders, then join my hands behind his neck. "I'm sorry."

"Why would your sister do that to us?"

"She--" I shake my head. "Can we not talk about her? I promise to tell you everything about her, but I want to do that later. Right now, I just want you to keep doing what you're doing right now."

"Holding you?"

"Yeah. And kissing me."

"Kissing you, huh. Like this?" Eli moves in closer.

When our eyes meet, I smile. "Yeah. Like this."

After a long and sensuous kiss, Eli pulls me over to the bed. He sits first, then pulls me with him until I'm standing between his legs. His hands slide around me until one is on my lower back, the other resting on my bottom. I love Eli's hands on me.

I bend down until our lips are almost touching. I feel like I need to say what's on my mind. "I'd never cheat on you, Eli. Nobody has ever or will ever make me feel like you do."

"And how do I make you feel, Em?"

"Alive."

I guess my words have impact because Eli stands quickly. "Let's get out of here."

"Okay. Can you send Cody a text? Ask him to tell Carley we're leaving."

Eli looks confused, so I clarify, "I don't have a phone."

After the message is sent, Eli takes me by the hand and leads me back out the door, down the hallway, up the steps, and out the back door. We round the house and practically run to his parked SUV.

Sliding up into the passenger seat, I wince at the chill from the leather, thanks to the beer that seeped through my dress. And then there's the fact there isn't much to said dress.

"Where are we going?"

"My place."

I visibly shiver.

"You cold, Em?" I watch as Eli reaches down to the bottom of his sweater. As it rises up and off, I see he's wearing a Wisconsin hockey tee beneath. "Here. Put this on. Your seat's gonna warm up quick, but the sweater will get you there faster."

He places the neck opening of his dark blue sweater above me. I lean forward so he can pull it over. I lift my arms until he's tugging the sweater down over my top half. "Thanks." The thing is warm, soft, and it smells like him—amazing.

We're silent on the ride to his house. I stare out the window as Eli pulls into the driveway of his large ranch-style house with a three-car garage. The largest door rolls open and Eli drives slowly into an open parking spot.

My door opens and Eli's hand appears. I take it and scoot out of my seat. I let Eli lead me through the one and only door in the huge garage that opens to that kitchen I could only dream about.

"You hungry?" he asks without even looking at me.

"Um…" I am. Starving actually. I didn't eat before the party—too nervous. "A little."

"Good." He turns his head. When he sees me, the smile on his face is unbelievable. It's the first real Eli smile I've seen all night. It's also the first time I've felt like things are going to be okay with us.

"I've got leftover pad Thai from Taste of Thailand, or I can make us a turkey sandwich." He looks back at me, expectantly.

"Turkey sandwich." I've never had pad whatever, so if I say yes to that and don't like it, I'll look like an idiot.

"Turkey it is."

Moving closer to the kitchen, I pull out a stool and sit. One by one, he's setting down sandwich toppings like they have at the fancy sub shops. It's unbelievable. "Do you need help?"

"Nope. Just tell me what you like." He holds up a loaf of wheat bread and a french loaf. I point to the french bread.

"Mayo?"

I shake my head and make a face. One that makes him laugh.

"Hates mayonnaise. Got it."

"Mustard?" I nod. We go through the list until he's made me the perfect turkey sandwich with mustard, pickles, lettuce, and tomato. I watch him build his own. He uses the same as me, except he adds mayo, black olives, and hot peppers to his.

With those on plates, he pours some chips next to each sandwich and walks around the counter. "Let's eat in here." He nods toward the room with the large sofa. "We can watch something."

"Okay." I hop down from the tall stool.

"What would you like to drink?" He sets our plates down on the stone coffee table.

"Water's fine."

It feels like the first time I was here with Eli. Only way more tense. And not in the sexual kind of way. Well, okay, there's that too, but this feels more like Eli's still unsure about me––that text message––and I'm not sure what to do about that. Is there a way to convince him that I didn't send that message? I guess I could track down my sister and make her confess—

Wait one dang second. I look over at Eli. "Can I use your phone?"

"You need to talk to Carley?"

I shake my head. "I feel like I need to prove to you that I'm not the bad guy here."

"I believe you, Em."

Does he? Really?

"Just let me see your phone."

After reaching into his back pocket, he hands it to me.

Scooting closer to him so he can see what I'm doing, I press his text message icon and search for my name. "You didn't delete me."

He shrugs.

"I'm glad," I say, without looking at him. I'm a little afraid at his expression.

But then he finally says, "Me too."

Thank goodness.

"Okay. Here we go. We'll see if Amber still has my phone."

"Wait. You haven't tried to call it? To find it?"

"Oh, I've tried but nobody ever answers." Because she would have seen Carley's name appear on the screen. No way would she answer if it was Carley.

So, I type:

**Eli**: Emma. I miss you. Can we talk?

I look over and up at Eli. He smiles. "Clever."

"Now, let's see if she takes the bait."

We don't have to wait long. Moment later, those three vibrating dots appear on the screen. "She's typing."

**Emma:** Wow. Why? I've moved on. Found someone better.

Our eyes meet and I feel like I have to say it. "There's nobody better than you, Eli."

A small smile appears on his face. "I don't know about that, Emma."

The phone chimes in my hand as another text appears.

**Emma:** I mean, are you that desperate? I guess I could fuck you again. For old time's sake.

"Jesus," he mutters. "How are you even related? Does she know anything about you?"

"No." I quickly begin to type my message.

**Eli:** I'm horny, yeah. Had a few…

I look up at Eli and mouth, "Sorry."

He laughs. "Go for it." He nods at the phone. "Let's see if we can draw her out."

That's what I was going for.

**Eli:** Where r u? How soon can you get here?
**Emma:** Not far.

I stare at the screen. That little bitch. "She's still in Madison."

**Eli:** You remember where I live?

I don't hit Send. "Oops." I forgot I'm supposed to be texting myself. I quickly delete that text and write.

**Eli:** How long will it take you to get here? I'm pretty wasted.
**Emma:** You got a problem with whiskey dick or something? LOL.

"What's whiskey dick?" The question is out of my mouth before even giving it some thought. Eli laughs. "Oh."

**Eli:** Nah. How soon can you get here?
**Emma:** I'll be there in ten.

"She's ten minutes away?" I'm talking to myself. Where could she be and where has she been staying for two weeks? Things I want to know but am afraid to ask.

"Now what?" Eli's question is valid.

"Well, let's see what she does. Will she show up?" Only time will tell.

He scoffs. "You two have *nothing* in common."

Except our parents.

We quickly clean up our turkey sandwich mess. "I'll hide in the laundry room." I point to the door right off the kitchen. From that vantage point, I'll be able to see the front door as well as the living area.

"Here." Eli grabs a dining chair and places it next to the dryer. "I want you to be comfortable."

I blush a little at his gesture. He's such a good guy. Oh, crud. I feel that stupid burn of tears again.

Eli can tell I'm getting emotional. "What's wrong, babe?"

I repeat what I'd been thinking. "You're such a good guy."

He doesn't respond to my statement. Well, he does, with a little kiss just as the doorbell rings.

"She's here." Fear rushes through me. I don't know why.

"Ready?" he whispers.

"No." Then I giggle. "Yes."

I push the door closed enough for me to see them, but they can't see me. Hopefully. Eli reaches for the doorknob and looks back at me, smiles, then turns the handle. When it's fully open, I see her. Amber. Wearing one of Carley's favorite dresses.

That little witch. Carley's been looking for that dress.

"You're not Emma," Eli says like he's a natural.

"She sent me. Said she didn't want to see you again. She said, and I quote, 'You can have him.'"

Wow, that's a terrible thing to say to a guy.

"Oh." Eli's acting skills just took a dive. I'd laugh if this wasn't so sickening. He follows up with a shrug. "Whatever. Come on in."

Amber steps into the living room and looks around. "I forgot how nice this place was."

*Sure* she did. I'm tempted to step out of the laundry room, but I sort of want to wait. Hear what else she'll say.

"Can I get you something to drink?"

"Beer?" she asks as she walks around his living room, touching things like the silver frame on the shelf next to the fireplace. There's an old box next to that that seems to make Amber pause. When she picks it up and looks inside, I see the glint in her eyes from here. There must be something good inside.

Eli walks into the living room with Amber's beer, so she quickly places the box back on the shelf. "Thanks." She taps her bottle against his. "To being single."

Eli releases an awkward chuckle. "Single. Yeah."

"You doing okay after my sister dumped you?"

Like she cares.

"I'm doing just fine." Eli nods, then winks at my sister. Now I *really* hate winking.

"I've gotta say, Eli. You dodged a bullet with that one."

Is she for real? Dodged a bullet?

"How so?"

This ought to be good. Or bad, I suppose.

"She was a problem child. Had to see therapists growing up. My parents are pretty convinced she's got some sort of psychopathy."

No, that was her. Not me.

"Psychopathy?" Eli's doing a good job playing along. At least I hope it's an act.

"You know, like someone who only thinks of themselves." Amber rolls her eyes. "That's her in a nutshell. She doesn't care about anyone but herself."

"That isn't the Emma I know. Or knew."

"Well," she scoffs, "she was great at hiding it." Stepping closer to Eli, she smiles at him. "See? You dodged a bullet." Setting her beer next to the little wooden box, she reaches for his shirt and that's it. I'm not about to let that sister of mine touch my boyfriend.

"You're horny, huh?" I watch as she runs her hands up his chest. "Fifty for a blowy. A hundred for a fuck. Three hundred for anal."

My mouth drops open. Why would it not? Shock does that. She literally just asked him to pay her for sex. I can't imagine what Eli must be thinking.

"Well…" He chuckles. "Those prices sound—"

Amber interrupts him. "Fair. They're very fair. Market value and all that."

I've heard enough. Pulling the door open, I step into the doorway. "What the hell are you doing, Amber?"

Amber drops her hands from Eli's chest. "Of course you're here." She laughs, but there's no humor in her voice. Turning to me, the expression on her face is one I've seen a time or two. One word describes it. Hatred. For me. "God, Emma, why can't you just *die*?"

It's best to ignore her when she says things like that. Even though I know, in my heart, she doesn't want me to die, I'm not so sure she'd mourn me if I did. "You need help."

"Fuck you."

"Where have you been for two weeks?"

"Staying with some friends."

"Friends? Who?" She's never been to Madison in her life, and she has no friends at home that I recall. How would she have friends here?

Amber takes a few steps closer to me. "You wouldn't know them. They're cool."

"Who are they, Amber?"

"None of your fucking business, Emma." She's a foot from me now and I don't like it. There's something off about her tonight.

I scoff at my own thoughts.

Amber has always been *off*, but it's different. "Are you prostituting yourself?"

She crosses her arms and juts her hip out in a casual stance. "You think I'd need to get paid to fuck? Look at me? Now you—" –She arches her brow and snickers. "—you'd probably have to pay them."

I choose to ignore her little jab. Because them? "Who is them?"

Amber leans forward and growls. "I. Told. You. They're friends."

"Mom and Dad are worried about you." I take another approach.

"That's too bad." She's back to looking casual again. Actually, she's looking at her fingernails like she's not got a care in the world. "I'm a grown up. I can do whatever the fuck I want."

That's not true. Any of it. "Amber—"

"No." She holds up her palm. "I'm sick of perfect Emma telling me how to live my life. I'm happy, okay. I met some people. *They* like me."

I just bet they do.

"I'm not going home to that po-dunk town, so deal with it."

I stare at my sister as she glares back at me. I don't know how long we do that, but Eli's voice breaks it up. "Time for you to go," he says to Amber as he makes his way over to the front door.

"Fine." She turns to leave.

"I want my phone."

"I don't have your fucking phone."

Is she for real?

From the corner of my eye, I watch as Eli's picks up Amber's purse. Peering inside, he reaches in and retrieves a cell phone. "This it?"

I nod as Amber turns to see what he's got in his hand. She must not appreciate the fact that he has her purse because she races over to him and grabs it out of his hand. The motion causes them both to lose grip on it. When it falls to the ground, the contents end up all over the tile floored entrance.

I stare down at the mess. She's got the typical things we carry in our bags, lip gloss, nail file, receipts, and money. A lot of money. Twenties and tens. If I had to guess, I'd say she had several hundred dollars floating around in her purse.

"Amber, where…?" I start to ask. But she's on her hands and knees grabbing at every item on the floor, stuffing them back into her purse.

"None of your fucking business, *Emma*," she snarls.

Standing, she reaches for the door and steps out onto his front stoop. We follow her. I keep my mouth shut because, she's right, she's an adult now. There's nothing I can do to stop her. The three of us stare at one another for a beat. I figured if I said nothing more, Amber would take the three steps down to the sidewalk and be on her way. Instead, she looks at Eli and asks, "Can I use your bathroom?"

We both stare at her.

"Hello?" Amber waves her hand in front of both our faces. "I'm going to pee my pants." Neither of us speaks. "Jesus." She crosses her legs over one another and bounces up and down like she's holding it in. "You're not going to let me leave like this? You can't be that big of an asshole."

"Fine." Eli sighs as he points back into the house. Take a right. First door on your left."

"Great," she chirps. "Be right back."

After she reenters the house, Eli wraps his arm around me. "It's gonna be okay, babe."

"I don't think so. I have a feeling I'm going to get a call in the middle of the night."

"All set." Amber steps back out onto the stoop. She's got a huge smile on her face. I'm immediately suspicious because there's no way she used the bathroom that fast.

"Hang on a second, Amber." I attempt to smile sweetly at her.

I need her to stay put for a minute or two. "I want to give you something."

ELI

It's still hard to believe they're related. There have never been two more opposite siblings. As I watch and listen to Emma and Amber go back and forth, I can't help thinking about their differences.

Amber's about to leave when Emma says she had something for her. Once she's inside, she calls her sister to step back into the house. Of course, I follow her in. That's when I see Emma holding my phone. We set it up to record everything that happened with Amber. In Emma's words, "to protect ourselves."

Emma lifts her head from the screen and glares at her sister. "Give it back."

"Excuse me?" Amber sounds sincerely confused.

"Whatever was in that little box." She points at the small wooden box that was on the shelf near the fireplace. "Give it back. Now, Amber."

"I have no idea what you're talking about, Emma."

Emma turns the phone in our direction. We're too far away to make out the details but I watch as Amber reenters the house and walks directly to the shelf, picks up the box, and empties the contents into her hand. She drops them into her purse. I had to think about what was in the box. Coins that belonged to my grandfather. They probably aren't worth anything. But I'm not sure about that. I've had them since I was little. He used to hand me one every birthday. None of them were common coins like we use today, and they were all unique, so I'd place them in that little box for safekeeping.

I'm quickly pulled from my ponderings, though, when Amber launches herself at Emma. Luckily, Emma's far enough away from Amber she's able to run into the kitchen before Amber makes contact. That's when Amber picks up a ceramic dish Mom added to "liven up the space" and chucks it at Emma. Luckily, my girl is quick. She ducked just in time, but the dish didn't make it. Once it hit the granite counter tops, it broke into a million pieces.

"Emma," I say, rushing over to her. "You okay?"

"Yeah." Looking behind her, she says, "Your counter got the brunt of it."

"No, bitch." Amber spits. She's on us before I even realize she was on the move. "You're going to get the fucking brunt of it." It's then Amber raises her hand, rolling it into a fist. It all happens so fast; I barely have enough time to stop it from making contact with Emma. I quickly step in front of the swinging hand just as it makes contact with my chest. And fuck. It hurts. Amber's got a pretty potent right hook.

"Amber!" Emma shouts. "You just hit Eli." Turning to me, she touches my chest and looks up at me. "Are you okay?"

"I'm fine." I take her hand in mine. "No worries."

"I didn't mean to hit *him*. He got in the way. That was meant for *you*." Amber's still trying to get past me to get at Emma again. Her arm is reaching around, her hand in a clawlike formation in an attempt to scratch at Emma. I move my body around until I'm completely blocking her from harm's way. Strange. It feels like I'm in a hockey game--caught in the middle of a fight between our enforcer and the other team's. It's not ideal.

"Amber. Stop." God, I want to laugh, but I know none of this is funny to Emma. How do I know? Because the woman is so red with anger, I'm fearful she's going to pass out from it.

"She started it," Amber whines.

"No." I shake my head and glare down at Amber. "You started all of this."

"Of course you'd side with her." Amber rolls her eyes. "She cheated on you."

"No. I didn't." Emma steps out from behind me but far enough away from Amber's talons. "I think this entire episode proves I didn't cheat on him. Why would I? Look at the man."

Both women turn to look at me then back at each other.

Holding out my hand, I say as gently as possible, "Give me the coins."

"*Coins*," Emma emphasizes.

"Fine." Amber reaches into her purse and digs around a minute or two, pulling out three small silver discs.

"The rest." I know how many are there. Thirteen. He died when I was fifteen and he started giving me those when I was two. "There are thirteen."

"Jesus," she grumbles. Stepping over to the counter, she dumps her purse out, counts out the remaining coins, and hands them back to him. "Happy?" she snaps.

Looking over at Emma, I smile. "Yeah."

Shoving her stuff back into her back, Amber mutters. "God, you make me sick."

---

"I'M REALLY SORRY ABOUT EVERYTHING, ELI."

"Why are you sorry? That's all on your sister." And thankfully, the woman is now gone. Hopefully on her way back to Illinois. She promised to leave Madison if we didn't call the police and show them the video of her antics tonight. Yes, we recorded the entire episode. Emma's idea. "If she doesn't leave town, we'll call the police."

"Speaking of calls, I got in touch with my parents." Emma looks exhausted and defeated. I don't blame her. It's obvious Amber needs help. Professional help. "I told them everything. They were horrified when I told them she tried to walk out of here with your old coins. I knew she was up to something when, after she was out of the house, she said she had to use the bath-room before she left. That's why I went back into the house." We had her out the door--on the front porch--doing our damn best to get her to leave.

"That's because you're smart, Em."

I watch as Emma flips through her phone messages. "You should read the stuff she told my parents the night before she took off."

Apparently, Amber used Emma's phone to message her about how great Amber was doing. That Emma was convinced Amber was going to turn a new leaf up here in Madison. Complete bullshit.

Reaching out, I hold my palm up. "Come on. Stop with the phone. Let's get into bed. We're both wiped out."

She places it in my palm, and I set it on top of my dresser. Before crawling in, I take a minute to look at Emma. I've got her in one of my Wisconsin Badger Hockey T-shirts and I'm not going to lie, she looks hot as fuck. When she stepped out of my en-suite bathroom in it, I nearly choked she looked so damn good. I even told her I could get used to seeing her in my clothes.

When I had, she fiddled nervously with the bottom of the shirt, saying, "Kinda long."

Immediately, I answered, "That's because you're tiny."

I guess those weren't words Emma was expecting because she rolled her eyes and scoffed, "Right."

I wasn't going to argue with her about that negative bullshit that came out of her mouth. Not after everything that happened tonight. But, tomorrow, hell yes. No, now I just want to focus on the beautiful girl who's only wearing underwear beneath the light gray fabric of my favorite shirt. It's too bad I'm so tired.

Lifting up my quilt and sheet, I slide onto the cool cotton sheets. I move closer to the middle of the bed and reach out for her. "Come 'ere." She gives me that shy smile I love and moves in, turning her back to me so we're spooning.

"God, I've missed you."

"Me too."

With my arms around her, I nestle in until there's no light or air between us.

"Don't you think it's weird that this is so comfortable?" Emma asks softly. "It seems too easy."

I nearly choke. "Too easy?" I feel a laugh start, and it's one that I won't be able to stop anytime soon.

Rolling over to face me, Emma looks confused. "What?" She's frowning now. "What's so funny about that?"

I stop laughing, but only for a second. "Nothing about you and me has been fucking easy, sweetheart."

"Oh." She looks to her right like she's got to think about it, then back at me. "I guess you're right."

Leaning into her, I press her shoulders down onto the mattress. Not hard or anything. It's just so I can look down into her eyes. "You're worth it, Emma. All the misunderstandings, the crazy sisters, overbearing best friends—"

Emma has one to add, "The jerky fathers. Yours. Not mine."

I nod. "You're worth all of it."

Her lashes flutter and her cheeks turn pink. "Thank you."

"You're welcome. Now give me a goodnight kiss and let's get some shut-eye."

3 6

---

EMMA

HIS HANDS ARE EVERYWHERE, AND IT FEELS SO GOOD. "ELI," I SAY, breathless.

"I love waking up with you in my bed, Em."

"Me too." I really do. His warm hands dip beneath the hockey T-shirt he loaned me. I hold my breath as they skim up over my stomach until they're cupping my breasts. "Oh, God." I moan as he tickles the peaks of each with his fingertips.

"Love your tits, Emma," he says before kissing my neck. "The perfect size."

"Thanks." I reach back in an attempt to touch him too, but I have to stop when his right hand moves down and slides into the front of my panties.

When his finger dips through me, he moans into my ear. "So wet."

I wiggle a little at the sensation. In the process of my wiggle, I press my butt up against him. He's hard. Very hard. I feel him press in closer and move against me. "You make me so goddamn hard, Emma."

"Yeah?" One word is all I can muster.

"Yeah. Take off your panties, honey."

The thing is, I don't think I can do it. No. Not because I don't want to, but because I'm afraid if I move, he'll stop what he's doing with his fingers and I really, really need him to keep doing what he's doing with his fingers.

"Don't stop, Eli."

"You gonna come on my hand, babe?"

"Uh-huh." It comes out as more of a whine and… ugh, I sound like one of those women in the porn movies Carley made me watch that one time.

Okay, it's been more than once, but she felt it was important for my sex-tutelage.

"You needy, honey? You need to come?"

"Yeah." I do it again. It can't be helped.

"That's right, angel." Eli sounds so frigging sexy. His voice is husky and he sounds a little desperate too. "Come for me. Do it. Come."

I do it. I come right then. Sure, he told me too, but his hands did the work. "Eli…." I'm still really breathless.

"Jesus." Eli's on the move. He's got me flat on my back now. In seconds, the tee is off and my panties are on the floor. I stare as he strips himself down to nothing but socks. My focus is now on his dick. The one that's long and hard and jutting out toward me. "Emma?" Eli asks, stroking himself. "We don't do anything you don't—"

I don't even let him finish. I place my feet on the bed and slowly open my legs. "Eli?"

"Jesus, baby girl." He's staring down at my… well, my center. "You sure?"

"Yes. I want you." And I do. I want him so much.

Eli reaches into the table next to the bed and pulls out a foil square. I stare as he places it in his mouth and tears it open. Next, he slides the condom down his shaft, and I can't help thinking it's about the sexiest thing I've ever seen. Eli naked with his muscles flexing in anticipation and his hand on his… his… manhood.

"I'll go slow, but it's gonna hurt, Em."

"I know." Carley told me.

"You sure?" he asks again.

"Positive." Holding my arms out to him, I hope he sees I want him to come closer. "Come on."

Moving onto the bed, I open my legs wider so he's got room. He's looking at me. All of me reverently. "You're so fucking beautiful, Emma."

I smile at his words. I know he means them. There's no doubt in my mind this is the man I was always supposed to do this with. To make love with.

This isn't just sex to me. It's more important than just sex. This is a very big deal. I need to be sure he knows I'm all in and that I trust him to make this good and right and special.

"So are you." I slide my hands over his shoulders, down his arms and to his waist. "I trust you to make this…" What's a good word for all of those things I just thought about? "…first-rate, Eli."

He chuckles. "First-rate?"

"Yep. Of the best class or quality; excellent." I give him a broad smile. "Now, let's do this thing." I'm so ready to be his.

He chuckles again and kisses me softly. "I'll do my best to make it *first-rate*, but it's gonna hurt. The next time will be much better."

I love that he's talking about next time. Smiling at him, I lift my head and touch my lips to his. "I trust you."

With a sigh, Eli leans down and kisses me softly again, but it quickly turns into more. Our tongues find each other, and his hands move over my breasts, tweaking them several times. I squirm beneath him and know I'm close to ready for him. When his hand slides between my legs, he does magic things with his fingers. I watch as he looks down between us and that's when I know it's about to start. "I'll go slow."

And he does. He enters me slowly as I hold my breath.

"Relax, Em. Breathe."

I release the air I was holding in my lungs, and Eli kisses me, which helps distract me a little. As he moves further inside, I adjust my hips, because it feels like the right thing to do. When he stops moving, I whimper which, for some reason, make Eli chuckle. "Needy little thing." I look up into his eyes.

He kisses me and then it happens. I feel a sharp pain that quickly turns into more of an ache. "You okay?"

"Yeah." I blow air in and out like I'm in labor or something. But it doesn't take long for the pain to subside. "Yes," I say with some relief. "It's better."

Without another word, Eli moves again and while there's a little pain, it soon turns into something else. He leans in closer, kissing my face and neck. I feel his breath on me and smell his scent, but the best part is what he's saying to me. "You're mine now, Emma. You're fucking mine."

Without any prompting, I say what I feel too. "And you're mine."

"Yessss. I'm yours." He hisses in my ear, right before I hear his growly moan. And I've gotta say. I like that sound. I like it a lot.

## 37

ELI

"WELL, MAN—" CODY SLAPS MY BACK. "GLAD TO SEE THE OLD ELI back."

"Great to be back." It's been a week since Emma and I got back together. In that time, she's slept over at my place three times. Three amazing times. I can't get enough of the girl.

"Jesus," our bitter goalie grunts. "You disgust me."

They all know about me and my girl. Hell, I can't help but talk about her, and we've got hours on the team bus together, so they've also listened in while I was on the phone with her. I've heard everything from "you sicken me" to "lucky bastard" from my teammates.

It doesn't matter what anyone says. The fact of the matter is, I'm the happiest I've ever been. I smile constantly and not just when she's with me. Hell, I'm grinning from ear to ear as I speak.

"So you're going out with your parents this weekend? The four of you?"

"Yes." My smile fades. "Mom loves her."

"Probably a good thing we didn't mention that whole cheating thing."

"She didn't cheat on me and you know it. It was her sister." A sister who hasn't reappeared since that night. A fact that worries Emma because she didn't go home.

"I know. It's just a good thing Helene Baxter doesn't know about it."

True. Or Jack Baxter for that matter. "Well, neither of them knows about any of it, so there's no need to worry about it."

"Guess not." Cody slaps my back again. "I'd love to be a fly on the wall at the restaurant just to watch your dad."

"He'll come around." He has to.

---

"You look lovely tonight, Emma," my mom says as we sit down at our table at Chez Paul. The spot of our first date--the one that didn't happen. Well, it did, but I wouldn't call it an official first date. Which makes me think, we haven't really had a real first date. I'll need to remedy that.

"Thank you, Mrs. Baxter. So do you." My girl is so nervous. I can practically feel her shaking from my seat next to her. Reaching out, I place my palm on her upper thigh and give it a little squeeze. I hear her release a breath and know that it's helping, so I keep my hand there. It's the least I can do.

"Helene, honey. Call me Helene."

"Helene," Emma repeats.

I look over at my dad who's sipping from a short glass of amber liquid. Bourbon. The man loves the stuff, but he can only handle one glass. If he has two or more, he becomes a bigger asshole than usual. One is just enough to soothe the savage beast.

"And you can call him Jack." Mom says with a smirk.

Dad remains silent.

I hate it.

Why does he have to be such an asshole?

I give Emma's thigh another squeeze and look over at her and smile. I hope it's a reassuring smile for her.

"What does your father do, Emily?"

And there he is. The fucker I've known my whole life. "It's Emma, Dad."

He shrugs.

"Both of my parents work at Wal-Shop."

Jack Baxter scoffs. "So landing Eli's really going to help your family out. Especially when he gets to the pros."

"Jack," my mom growls. "Enough."

The man knows better than to anger Helene Baxter. She's a force to be reckoned with, let me tell you.

"I––I have my own career—"

Dad scoffs again as he empties his glass, then raises his hand for our waitress.

"No." Mom shakes her head. "No more."

My dad is being an extra-large asshole tonight because he turns to Mom and says, "I'll drink as much as I fucking want."

"Fine." She turns to face Emma and me, forcing a smile on her face. "So, you're an engineering major?"

Dad scoffs again. I'm getting pretty damn sick of that sound.

The conversation gets stilted pretty fast especially since Dad did, in fact, get a second drink. We place our food orders and watch him order a third.

This is going to get ugly.

Uglier.

Holding Emma's hand, I hear the buzz of a phone. It's not mine so it must be hers. I watch as she reaches into her purse. When she sees the screen, she excuses herself. "It's my mom. I'll be right back."

As soon as she steps away from the table, Dad says, "I've called in a favor."

Here we go.

"Uh-huh." I take a long pull from my beer.

"I got you a tryout with New York."

"New York?" I can't believe this shit.

"Dad—"

Holding up his giant paw, he stops me from finishing. "Next week. You fly out on Wednesday."

"Jack..." My mom's voice is short. "You said we'd talk about this."

Ignoring her, he glares at me. "Enough of this fucking school bullshit, Eli. "It's time you stopped fucking around."

"I'm not fucking around."

Dad glances in the direction that Emma just walked. "You're distracted."

"Jack...," Mom again.

When he gives her his hand, that's when she's had enough. Tossing her cloth napkin on the table, Mom stands and follows Emma's path.

Great. Now it's just the two of us.

"I had to pull some strings to get this for you so there's no backing out. I'll text you the itinerary. I'll already be in New York, so I'll be able to watch your tryout. Make sure you don't fuck it up."

Jesus. "Dad. No." I shake my head.

"Do it or I'm cutting you off. Your friends will have to find a new place to live."

"Dad." Why the hell does he have to be like this? "Come on."

"No," he grunts, lifting his glass. "I'm not fucking around this time. I've let you and your mother dictate how this is going to go for far too long." He glances to his left. "And look where that left us."

Us? Like my life has anything to do with his. And... he's referring to Emma. "I love her, Dad." I surprise myself with those words. I certainly haven't said them to Emma. Not yet. But I mean them. I love Emma Perkins. More than anything.

He slams the glass down onto the table and some of the golden fluid sloshes out over the side. "And that right there is precisely why it's time to go."

"Dad—"

"Do you think she'll stick around if she knows you've got nothing, Eli?"

Yes.

"Eli?"

I turn to see Emma approach the table with Mom in tow. She's pale as a ghost. I quickly stand. "What's wrong?"

"Um." She looks over at my dad, then at me.

Mom's got her hand on Emma's shoulder as she says to me, "Honey. You need to go."

I grasp Emma's jacket from the back of her chair, then pick up her bag. "Right. Let's go." Reaching for her hand, she places hers in mine.

"I'm sorry, Mrs. and, erm, Mr. Baxter."

"Go on, honey. Don't worry," my mom says with a reassuring smile.

I lead Emma out the door of the restaurant and the second we're on the sidewalk, she bursts into tears. "Oh, Eli. She's been arrested."

I don't even have to ask who she's talking about. "Where?"

"Here. In Madison. Mom called. She wants me to bail her out."

"Okay. Do you know where she is?" There's more than one police station in town.

"Yes." With her phone in hand, she holds up the address. Between snobs, she adds, "Sh-She's transferring the bail money into my account."

"Good. Okay. Let's go."

WE'RE ASKED TO TAKE A SEAT IN THE LOBBY OF THE POLICE station. I stand to get Emma a cup of coffee from one of those machines in the lobby. I'm sure it tastes like shit, but I think she needs something. As soon as I'm far enough away, I check my phone. I felt it vibrate long after we left the restaurant. Pulling it from my pocket, I see Dad's text.

**Dad:** Her sister's a whore? Jesus. Good job, Eli. Way to pick 'em. Now more important than ever to get you to New York away from that trash.

Mom must've told him what's going on. No doubt he insisted he know. But he's right about one thing. Amber was arrested in Madison for prostitution. The rest of his statement is pure bullshit.

## 38

---

EMMA

SHE LOOKS LIKE HELL. MY SISTER LOOKS LIKE SHE'S BEEN UP FOR days and hasn't showered in any of that time. "Amber." It's all I can say at the sight of her. When she emerges from some back room in the Madison police station, she's wearing the shortest skirt I've ever seen. She's paired it with a cropped tank top and no bra that I can see. The heels she's wearing look like they're six inches tall.

Who can walk in those things?

Amber, I guess.

"Don't say a word." Amber grunts at me.

I'm shocked. "Don't say a word?" I can't believe… yes, I can. "What the heck are you thinking?"

As soon as we're out of the station and on the sidewalk, Amber turns, places her hands on her narrow hips and snaps, "I'm thinking this is none of your fucking business, you snooty bitch."

Snooty bitch.

"That's enough." Eli says those two words like he means them. "You." He points at Amber. "Shut the fuck up and don't talk to Emma like that."

"Whatever." Amber rolls the eyes that are thick with eye shadow and extra-long fake eyelashes.

"Where are you staying?"

"Don't worry about it." Amber starts to walk away.

"You can't walk around like that," I shout. "You'll get picked up again."

Amber turns quickly. "You know what. Fuck. Off. Emma."

"Come home with me. Mom told me to buy you a bus ticket."

"No way." She shakes her head. "I found a cash cow here. I'm finally making some money. College boys love a good blowy and the frat guys have the bank to pay for it."

"Geesh, Amber. Listen to yourself…."

"I am. I'm all I've got."

"That's not true. Mom and Dad…"

"Are tired of me. I get it." She turns like she's leaving again. "Tell them thanks for bailing me out."

I half expect her to add "Tell them I'll pay them back" but that's six words she'll never say. "Amber?"

"Leave me alone, Emma."

I feel Eli's arm wrap around me. "Let her go."

*Let her go.*

Three little words that hold so much meaning.

EMMA

"WHEN'S ELI GETTING BACK?"

Good question. He's already been gone a few weeks. Oh, who am I kidding. I act like I don't know exactly how long he's been gone. Eighteen days, six hours, and forty-two minutes. That's how long he's been gone.

And honestly, I don't know when he's coming back. Or worse, *if* he's coming back. After the night dealing with Amber, we spent it at Eli's place. I knew something was wrong and I assumed it had to do with my sister--that maybe Eli couldn't handle the drama. He was quiet all night. Too quiet. Plus, he barely touched me, which is saying something because every time we've slept in the same bed, he's always wanted to.

That wasn't what was wrong, though. He told me about his dad. About New York. The tryout. While the thought of him leaving made my heart feel like it was dying, I knew I had to support him. This has been in the works since long before we met. It wouldn't have been right to try to stop him, so I acted happy for him. I encouraged him to go, saying things like "Besides the computer stuff, this is something you've always wanted, right?"

He nods. "Pretty much."

"If it's your dream, then you've *got* to try, Eli. You have an opportunity that not many people get. And if you make it, which I'm sure you will because you're so good at the hockey, think of the money." I mean, why would I stand in his way? Besides, I'm in no place to argue with the likes of Jack Baxter.

It was weird though. After I said all those things, Eli's expression changed from concern to something resembling irritation or even anger. The conversation ended abruptly with him telling me he was going.

I'd love to tell you I've since found out why that was, why he got angry all of a sudden, but I can't because I haven't spoken to him. Sure, he's sent me texts. Two, to be exact. The first:

**Eli:** Landed safely.

That one came the day he left, obviously and, in retrospect, I believe the only reason he sent it was because I made him promise he'd let me know he got there in one piece. The second came three days later.

**Eli:** Made it through the initial round.

I sent him several responses to each, but none of them garnered a response.

Heck, I've heard from his mom way more than him. She's called me half a dozen times checking on me and letting me know what Eli's been up to. I'm glad she has, because if I didn't know just how busy Eli really was, I'd probably be sobbing in my bed worrying that Eli and I are over. But according to Helene, he's not just playing hockey. Part of the tryouts include weekly physicals, two psychological evaluations, weights and conditioning, plus he spends all day with the team. Helene also told me he spends his evenings doing his best to keep up with his classes. I'm aware his professors gave him permission to continue working remotely. I know he's busy. Too busy for me, apparently.

Eighteen days later, I still can't help wondering why he hasn't called me. Not once. And why only two tiny text messages. At first, I sent him several messages a day, most with a photo of me doing something mundane. After a few days of getting no responses, I trimmed it down to one message per day. Now, I'm at one message every three or four days and it's killing me. I have no idea what I did to deserve to be ghosted by the guy who claimed I was his and he was mine. The man I love.

*God, I miss him so much.*

## 40

ELI

WALKING INTO MY PARENTS' APARTMENT, I TOSS MY WORKOUT BAG down in the foyer and make my way into the kitchen. I'm starving and something smells good. Strange, because Dad doesn't cook. Turning the corner from the hallway into the living room that's open to the kitchen, I halt in my tracks. "Emma?"

I think I'm seeing things because how could she be here? In New York.

"Surprise?" she says with a cautious expression. Hell, she even said it like a question.

"What are you doing here?" I know I don't sound excited to see her. I am. Well, part of me is excited to see her. The other part is wary. Wary because the girl I thought she was--was exactly the girl my dad said she was.

"*...think of the money.*"

That statement right there gave me pause. How well did I really know Emma? I certainly got to know her sister. Maybe Amber and Emma are more alike than she leads on?

Looking at her now, though, all I see is the sweet girl I fell in love with, not the mercenary I've conjured up in my head. Or did I conjure it?

"Your mom thought a visit would cheer you up."

She was wrong about that. All this visit is doing is making everything hurt more. "I was okay."

"Right." I catch something in Emma's eyes that makes me feel guilty. They're glossy like she's about to cry. I should go to her.

I can't.

"Eli?" I turn to see my mom in the kitchen. "Emma and I made your favorite. Lasagna."

Shit. That's why it smells so damn good in here. "Great." I turn and step over to the expansive kitchen. My dad bought this place for a song, and Mom redesigned the interior. It's beautiful. It overlooks Central Park so it's an awesome location. "I'm starving."

"Your father will be here soon so go shower. By the time you're out, dinner will be ready."

"Great."

Why do I keep saying that word? Nothing is great.

41

EMMA

THIS WAS A MISTAKE. A HORRIBLE, HORRENDOUS, MASSIVE MISTAKE. He doesn't want me here. Heck, he doesn't want me at all. I'm doing my best to fight the tears, but it's not working. I quickly wipe away the one that escaped. Then I make a beeline for the hall bathroom. I've already had a tour of the apartment. It's gigantic with three bedrooms and three baths. It's got floor-to-ceiling windows that look out at Central Park. I can only imagine how much this place must be worth. Not that I care. I don't. The only thing I care, or cared about, was seeing Eli because Helene had me convinced that Eli was depressed because he missed me.

One minute after seeing him, I know she was wrong. The question is why? Why, all of a sudden, is he done with me?

Grabbing a tissue from the box on the bathroom counter, I blow my nose but do it quietly. I don't want them to know.

———

"DINNER IS SERVED."

Helene lowers the large pan of lasagna down onto the table. Minutes earlier, I'd placed the salad and garlic bread down and

237

found a seat next to Eli. Ordinarily, he'd reach over and place his hand on my leg but not today. No. Today he can barely look at me.

"So, where did you find the money to fly to New York?"

You'd think that was Jack Baxter asking that question but it wasn't. It was Eli.

"Eli. That's rude," his mom interjects.

"So you bought it?" He looks at her pointedly.

"I did not. I offered but she insisted on paying her own way."

Eli makes a scoffing sound.

I lift my plate and watch as Helene serves me a slice of steaming lasagna. Placing it in front of me, I pick up a fork and begin to play with it. I can't eat. That's for sure. Because I have to think instead. Eli's question makes no sense. Why would he suddenly ask me about money like that? I know his dad probably thinks I'm after his money but surely Eli doesn't think—

"When will you leave?"

When *will* I leave? Eli's question is strange. Specific.

"Eli. What is wrong with you?" His mom is asking all the right questions. It's too bad I have to be here for them.

Wait. I guess I don't need to be here. "Will you excuse me?"

"Of course."

Standing, I walk to the front entrance, grab my purse that's hanging by the door, and I leave. I'd already taken a walk around the block since we had hours to wait for Eli to get home. We flew out on a 6:00 a.m. flight from Madison arriving in New York after 9:00 a.m. By the time we got to the apartment, I had time to kill. Helene encouraged me to walk around the neighborhood to "get to know the place." The thought that this could be a place that Eli and I could visit sometimes was exciting. Heck, if he made the team, it may be a place I visited frequently.

But now that it's dark outside, the city is even more beautiful than it was earlier. The lights from the cars and taxis and buildings make the city feel like it's alive. I recall someone referring to

New York as the city that never sleeps. I can see why that is. Why would you go to bed when there's always something good going on? Knowing I can stay out for as long as I want, as long as I need, fills me with a sense of relief. I don't know how long I can take being in the same room with a man who obviously hates me. Maybe that's too harsh. Hate is a strong word.

"Emma?"

I'm startled by the voice. Looking up, I see Helene approach.

"Honey. What's wrong? Why are you crying?"

I didn't realize I was. Swiping at my face, I'm able to remove some of the evidence of the tears. "No reason."

"Honey…."

"I'm fine." The smile I give her is forced, but it must be somewhat convincing.

"Don't worry about Eli. He's just tired."

Too tired to come down here, himself, evidently. "Right. Sure." I nod. "Of course he is."

"Come up and eat. The guys are done. Eli's finishing up some homework. You and I can watch something and relax."

"Sure." I swallow, hoping the lump in my throat will go away.

It doesn't.

4 2

<hr>

ELI

"WHAT THE HECK IS YOUR PROBLEM?"

Not the words I want waking me up on a Sunday morning, especially when it's my mother delivering them. Shielding my eyes because she turned the light on without warning, I have to force my voice to work. "I don't have a problem."

"You do now. Your girlfriend is gone."

Gone? Girlfriend? "Emma?"

"Do you have other girlfriends?"

I barely have one. "No." I push the covers down and slide my sore legs out and place my feet on the floor. "Did she go on another walk?"

"No. She left a note saying she took a taxi to the airport. Alone."

"Shit." I run my fingers through my hair. I need a cut. "Why?"

"Why?" Mom's voice has gotten progressively louder and with that, the pitch has increased. She's at least two octaves higher than her normal voice. "You're asking me why? Of course she left. You treated her like crap the second you walked in the door. And I want to know why."

"Mom—"

241

"Don't *Mom* me. Spit it out right now, Elijah James Baxter."

*Crap.* She used all three of my names which means she's not messing around. Placing my head in my hands, I squeeze my eyes shut, recalling the night I told her about the tryout. "Dad was right about her."

"Oh, pah-lease… your father is rarely right about anything."

Choosing not to address that comment, I tell her the truth. "The night I told her about the tryout she said she was glad I was going. She told me to think of the money."

Mom is silent. For a long time. Maybe three or four minutes. It feels like an hour. When she finally speaks, she asks, "What else did she say?"

"When?"

"That night. When you told her about the tryout. What else did she say?"

I have to think about it. "Um… I'm not sure I remember." I know she said some other things. "She asked me if this is something I really wanted."

"How did you respond."

"I said yes."

"What else did she say?"

"She, uh, said that if it's my dream, I had to try. That I was getting a chance that a lot of other people didn't have. That I was good at the hockey—"

Mom smirks. "Good at *the* hockey?"

"She knows nothing about the sport." Nothing. Still. Even after us being together for a while, she hasn't yet made it to a game. "It's then she mentioned the money part."

Mom approaches my bed and sits next to me. Placing her hand over the top of mine, she gives it a squeeze. "Do you want to know how I see her words?"

No. "Yes."

"I think she was telling you to follow your dreams. Not to let her stand in your way—"

"Mom…." I groan and rub my face with my hands, trying to wipe the sleep away. Then it hits me. She's right. I can see that. It's exactly what Emma was trying to tell me. She told me to go. To follow my dreams. And without uttering the words, she was telling me to do it even if it meant leaving her behind. "Shit." Emotion hits me like no other time in my life. I feel the burn of tears and don't bother trying to hold them inside. "I'm such a fucking idiot."

"Yes." She pats my hand. "You are." Muttering, she adds, "More like your father than I care to admit."

"When did she leave?" Because maybe I can catch her.

"The note didn't say."

I glance at the clock, almost seven. "I'm going to try and catch her."

"You've got practice in an hour," my dad says the second he appears in my doorway.

"I'll try to make it back in time."

"You'll do no such thing. Practice is more important—"

"Jack." My mom's voice sounds ominous. "Stay out of this."

"Helene."

"Not this time, Jack. Not this time."

"Jesus," my dad snaps. "Fine. I'll call them." Glaring at me, he adds, "Get there as soon as you can."

---

MOM TOLD ME THE AIRLINE THEY FLEW IN ON SO THAT'S WHERE I start. At the terminal, I check the departure board and see there's one flight to Madison leaving in forty minutes. Because of all the TSA guidelines, there's no way I can go to the gate unless I've got a ticket. Therefore, a ticket I shall buy.

With that in hand, I make it through security fast since I've got no luggage. I make it to the gate just as people are starting to board. I could have made it sooner except I did something to my ankle at practice and it's bothering me. I scan the line but don't see her. Next, I hobble through the waiting area, hoping she hasn't already gotten on the plane. I'm about to give up when I spot something red. Wisconsin Badger red. "Emma?" I say as I reach her. She's asleep on the floor near a wall in a little ball. "Emma?" I reach down and touch her arm.

"No, Mom. Let me sleep."

I chuckle at her words. "Babe. Wake up."

"Huh?" She startles awake. Looking around, she seems to realize where she is. When her eyes meet mine, her face drains of color. "What are you doing here?"

"I came to stop you from leaving."

Pushing herself up to sitting, she gathers up her phone and charger, placing it in her bag. "No. I've got to go."

I need to try harder. "I'm sorry." I can't think what else to say.

"Nothing to be sorry about. You've got a new life now."

"No, I don't." I want to say something about my life being shit without her, but how can I after I've spent the last month treating her like she doesn't matter.

"Please stay. Let's talk."

"No, thank you."

*No, thank you?* "Please, Emma?"

Emma stands and reaches down, picking up her bag before she drags the strap over her shoulder. "Please, Emma, what?"

"Stay. Talk to me?"

"You mean like you've been talking to me for the last twenty-six days?" She scowls. "Oh, wait. That's right. You haven't been talking to me for the last twenty-six days." Stepping around me, she makes her way to the line to board the plane.

I follow and stand behind her. "Emma. I'm not going to give up."

Her back is to me, but I can see she's shaking her head. "It doesn't matter, Eli. I gave up yesterday."

Her words hit me like a punch in the gut, hard, like

Muhammad Ali got me with his anchor punch. My breath is gone for a second. "Babe."

Her head swivels quickly so I can see her face. "Don't."

"Emma. Come on."

She remains silent until it's time to hand over our tickets. When I follow her onto the plane, she asks, "You bought a ticket?"

"How do you think I got to the gate?"

"Stupid rich jerk."

Now that's the girl I love.

"I bet you're even in first class," she deadpans.

Sadly, she's right. "Only because there were no other coach seats available on this flight."

"Seriously?" She glares back at me.

I can't think of anything to say, so I merely shrug.

## 43

## EMMA

"Carley picking you up?"

"Yes." He's followed me off the plane and out the main doors of the airport. Now, I'm standing at the curb waiting for my best friend to pick me up.

"Mind if I catch a ride with you two?"

I'd love to roll my eyes at him, but I'm too tired. Not to mention the fact that he hasn't left my side since the layover in Chicago's O'Hare airport. That was two hours of him sitting silently next to me, periodically offering to buy me coffee or food. He's wearing me down. "You should call an Uber or better yet"—I point to the line of taxis—"take a cab."

"I'd rather catch a ride with you, thanks."

I'm too tired to argue. Literally. I'm exhausted from the flights and the shortest trip to New York City in history, but mostly I'm emotionally drained. This thing with Eli has sucked all the energy out of me. All I want to do now is sleep. "Fine. I'll ask her when she drives up."

Carley's tiny blue car comes to a stop in front of me, and I watch as she leans over to peer out of the passenger-door window. Her brow arches and I know what that's about as I've texted her about everything. And I mean *everything*. When I open the door, she asks, "What's *he* doing here?"

"Following me."

"Ah." She nods and sits up in her seat.

"Can I have a lift back to my place?" the jerk asks.

"No." Surely Carley isn't going to let him—

"Sure." She smiles at him. "Jump in."

"Carley?" I whine. "No."

"It's twenty minutes. Thirty tops. It's not going to be a problem."

I growl as I slide the seat belt over myself and snap it into place. She's supposed to be on my side. As Carley pulls away from the curb, I reach to turn up the music. Not that it's a good song or anything since Carley has the worst taste in music, but I figure if it's loud, he won't try to talk. My plan was working. I say *was*, because for some insane reason, the second she's got a chance, Carley pulls the car off the road into a field that probably used to grow corn, but because it's winter it's got nothing but dirt. After slamming the car into Park, she shuts off the radio, and turns in her seat to face Eli.

"Why the fuck did you ghost my best friend, you asshole?"

I peek back and see Eli start to respond, but Carley's not having it. "She flew halfway across America to visit your sorry ass, and you treated her like dirt. I swear, I have half a mind to grab my tire iron and beat you with it, you arrogant prick. She's in love with you, asshat, and this is how you treat your *girlfriend*? Seriously. Who does that? Oh, I know, pricks like you, Eli Baxter."

"I--" Eli attempts to speak but Carley's not having it.

God, I love her.

"You must have some massive balls to think you can just stroll over to my car and ask for a ride."

"I--"

"Guess what, I'm not taking you anywhere. Get out."

Eli's starting to look a little stricken. The spot she's parked is sort of desolate. There's nothing for miles around. I believe there's an old farmhouse off in the distance. "Here?" His voice sounds sort of squeaky.

"Here."

"Really?" He points downward. "Here." When he looks up at me, I can see he's worried.

"Right. Here. Get. Out." Carley isn't letting it go.

I have no words except I hope she's only teasing him. Even though I'm mad at him, I don't want him stranded in the middle of nowhere.

"Fine." Eli pushes his door open and slips out.

I hear the door slam shut and then Carley races out of the lot, leaving a trail of dust in her wake. "That fucker," she mutters as she hits the gas.

"You're not going to leave him there, right?"

"Yes." She glances over at me, but her shoulders slump. "Fine." She hits the brake and makes a U-turn.

I spot Eli sitting on the ground, leaning forward, clutching his foot. I lean forward. "Is he hurt?"

"Hope so."

I snort at her statement, but not because I want him to be hurt, but because my best friend is funny. She doesn't really mean it. She wouldn't wish anyone hurt.

When she pulls up next to him, she rolls down her window. "What's the matter with you?"

"I did something to my foot trying to jump away from your car before you ran me over."

"Eli?" I push my door open and race over to him. "You okay?"

"Your friend drives like a maniac."

"What's wrong?" I lean down to look at it.

"I think it's just a sprain. I've had enough of those over the years to know but… I also did something to it at practice."

"Do we need to go to the ER?"

He looks up at me with a pained expression. "To be safe, I think we should."

"Great," Carley mutters from beside me. "But if you tell them I had anything to do with it, you'd better sleep with one eye open. It's not my fault you're slow."

"Carley."

"What?" she snaps. I can tell she's still really angry with him. I am too, it's just now replaced with worry over his foot.

Helping him off the ground, I reach my hand out until he places his in mine. "Your dad isn't going to be happy about this."

"That's an understatement." He's able to stand keeping his injured foot in the air. "My foot is going to be the least of my worries." I hold his hand and arm as he hops back over to Carley's car. He slips into the back seat. I shut the door as soon as I know he's inside.

"To the closest hospital, James," Eli says with a chuckle.

I know Carley probably has something to say in response to that, but she only makes muttering noises from the driver seat. The rest of the ride is quiet, which is a relief. This entire day, no, the weekend has been exhausting.

<hr>

"Let her sleep." I hear Eli's voice.

"She'll want to go in with you," Carley replies. "Even though I don't know why. If I were her, I'd bail on your sorry ass."

"Me too."

"At least we agree on one thing."

I feel my body being jostled. "Wake up, sleeping beauty. The wicked asshole needs help going into the ER."

"Oh." I quickly sit up. "Right." Opening my door, I'm a little wobbly after my fitful nap. Leaning on the car, I shake off my drowsiness and reach for the door. When Eli places his injured foot onto the ground, I frown. "It's really swollen. Hang on. Let me get a wheelchair."

Jogging into the lobby of the ER, I spot a row of wheelchairs on the left. Grasping the handles of the one closest, I roll it out to the waiting car. "I know there's a way to lock this thing." I'm talking to myself as I search around the chair for a button that activates the brakes when Carley gently nudges me aside.

"Right here." She points to a lever next to the wheel. I watch as she presses it down to lock the right wheel. She does the same with the left. "I'll park and wait for you in the waiting area."

I'm sure the pair of us will be waiting together. "Sure."

Rolling him into the building, I pull up to the admitting desk. Eli hands over his insurance card and explains his situation to the woman as she presents him with a clipboard holding a number of forms. She types some things on her computer and says, "Fill those out. They'll call you when they're ready for you. Give them those"—she points to the clipboard—"when they call you back."

"Okay," we say simultaneously.

I pull him away from the desk and sit quietly as he fills in all the blanks. It doesn't take Carley long to park and find us. "I figured you'd already be in a room."

"Too many forms," Eli mutters as he scribbles down answers.

"Eli Baxter," a voice from behind us says loudly.

"Here," I say as I jump up from my seat so I can wheel him back.

"He can wheel himself back there," Carley grumbles.

Eli looks up from his papers and addresses Carley, "I want Emma with me."

"*Now* you do." She crosses her arms and leans back into her chair. "Now that you need something."

I should say something to defend him, but I'm sort of in agreement with her, so I keep quiet and turn his chair so I can roll him straight toward the person waiting to lead us onward.

"Right in here," the nurse or orderly or whatever he is says.

"Hop up on the bed if you can, Mr. Baxter. A nurse will be in shortly."

As we wait, I address something important. "Do your parents know you flew back home?"

"Yes. I sent them a text before we took off from New York, but I haven't taken my phone off of airplane mode."

"Why not?"

I know why. He's afraid of their response.

"How's your sister?" he asks, changing the subject.

"You should call them. Let them know you hurt your foot."

Reaching into his back pocket, Eli retrieves his phone. "Yeah. Okay."

"Would you like me to leave?" Because I'm not so sure I want to hear this conversation.

"Stay."

"Sure. Okay." I nod as I sit back in the chair. I watch as he fiddles with his phone. It dings multiple times.

"Lots of angry texts," Eli says absently. "Just going to call Mom first."

"Wise plan." That's who I'd rather talk to as well.

Placing the phone over his ear, I hear her voice from where I'm sitting. "Eli Franklin Baxter…"

Uh, oh. She broke out the middle name. He's in trouble for sure.

"How dare you fly off—"

Wisely, he interrupts her. "I'm in the ER."

"What?" I hear her voice and it sounded like more of a screech.

"I twisted my ankle. Well, actually, I exacerbated an injury I got at practice on Saturday."

He listens as his mom talks on the other end. "Yes, Dad knew about it. He was at practice." He pauses. "Yes, the trainers looked at it. Said it wasn't anything to worry about."

Interesting. I don't recall him limping, but I was doing my level-best to avoid looking at him that night.

"No. I don't want to talk to Dad." He blows out a gust of air. "Dad…" He stops. "Listen to me…" He stops again. He looks over at me and mouths, "He's pissed."

I nod and grimace. It's not a surprise.

"Dad. Listen to me. You know I did something to it at practice…" His father must be talking nonstop because all he's doing now is listening and making faces. Angry and irritated faces. That is until a nurse enters the room. "Dad. The doctor's here. I gotta go." He presses on his screen and ends the call.

Standing, I decide to wait out with Carley.

"No." Eli's arm juts out and his hand grasps my arm. "Stay, Em."

I look at the nurse, who's just about to take his vitals then back at Eli. "I'm…" I don't know what to say. "We're…."

"We're what?" Eli looks a bit panicked. "We're okay, Em. We need to talk. That's all."

That's all? Is he nuts? "Eli, you didn't talk—"

I'm interrupted by the nurse, who starts to ask Eli about his ankle. While she does that, I slip out of the room, pausing to take a deep breath before I head out to the waiting area. Everything is confusing. I know I need to take a moment and think about Eli. Not just about the stuff between us but about him. His life. I'm just so muddled. I care about him so much, but I'm not sure I've got what it takes to be Eli's. I'm never going to be one of those women who just goes with the flow.

I make that heinous snorting noise again because I just made a water reference. While I love hydropower, I'm just not built that way. I need to know what's going on in his mind. Not only that, I want him to be happy, and if that means he's no longer with me, well, so be it.

And what about his ankle? How long will that take to heal? Will he be able to go back to New York?

And how romantic was he? I mean, he raced to the airport, bought a plane ticket… all for me. "Gah!" So many questions, and the only way I'm going to get answers is to ask him.

Eli's right. We need to talk.

I'm just not sure I'm quite ready for that because, truthfully, I'm hurt and still a bit angry.

44

ELI

As I'm wheeled out of the ER into the waiting area, I scan the place. For all I know, they left. I sigh with relief when I see the pair of them sitting in the same spot as before. "All set."

"Need help?" Emma asks, reaching for the wheelchair.

"Nope." I don't need help from anybody. Well, I need a ride home but even that, I can call and Uber or something. No way am I going to force myself onto a woman who no longer wants me around. I mean, Emma never came back to the room. Not even after I asked her to talk to me.

"I'll get the car," her best friend and thorn in my side says as she sweeps past me.

I merely nod.

"What'd they say?"

Oh, so now she wants to know how I am? That's rich. "Sprain."

"That's good. I guess." Emma sounds unsure. "High or low?"

I slowly turn my head to look up at her. How would she know the difference? She doesn't care about sports like she doesn't care about me. "High."

"Oh. That's the good kind."

*The good kind?* Is she nuts? "Sure. Right," I snap, and reach down for the wheel on my chair and head toward the door. The sooner her stupid roommate gets here, the sooner I can go home and wallow in self-pity.

"Here. Let me." Emma steps up behind me to push the chair. I'm tempted to tell her I don't need her, but I'm not in the mood to talk. Not to her anyway.

At the glass doors, we stand in silence waiting for Carley to pick us up. Well, it was silent until Emma decided to speak. "Look, Eli."

When I hold up my hand, she stops. I rotate the chair enough so I can look at her without straining my neck along with my ankle. "I get it. You're done with me."

Her mouth opens then closes. That happens several times. "*I'm* done with *you*?" She does the mouth thing two more times. "I'm pretty sure *you're* the one who's done with me." She points at herself. "You ghosted me the entire time you were in New York. I had no idea what was going on. Then--" Her voice is getting angrier, "Your mom practically dragged me to New York to surprise you even though I knew--" She tilts her head up and pauses like she needs to gather herself. When she looks back at me, her eyes are shining. With her voice cracking, she continues, "--even though I knew you wouldn't want to see me."

"I--"

"You what?" I watch a tear slide down her cheek and my hand twitches, wanting to reach up and take that tear away so badly.

"Emma, I thought--"

"You thought what?"

"I thought you wanted the money."

"Money? What money?" Her face... she looks confused. Sincerely confused.

"The money I'd make playing professional hockey."

I hold my breath, waiting for her response. When nothing happens, when she says nothing, I feel as though I need to keep going. "You said, 'Think of all the money you'll make.'" Or something along those lines.

"When? When did I say that?" She's no longer leaking tears and her face is very red. "When did I say that? That I hoped you would go away so you can make a bunch of money. Money that would belong to *you*. Not to *me* because we"—she jabs herself in the chest—"aren't married. Heck, we're not even together anymore."

"Yes, we are--"

She shakes her head. "No. You took care of that. We're not together. So why would I give two figs about your stupid money?"

I open my mouth to respond, but she isn't finished.

"You know what I think?"

I slowly move my head left then right. And I wait.

"I think you let your dad's feelings about me get into that thick skull of yours. He's got so much sway with you, it's ridiculous. But that's fine. That's your problem." She sighs, turns, and mutters, "I've got my own family drama."

"Your sister?"

She doesn't get to answer. Carley's old blue car pulls up in front of the building. I let Emma wheel me out. She locks the thing into place, and I hop up and into the back seat. I watch her take the chair back into the building and return, her face never changing from the angry one I caused inside.

"What's wrong?" Carley asks as soon as Emma's in the passenger seat.

I half expect her to shrug it off, but she doesn't. "This entire thing with him ghosting me is because he thought I wanted him to go to New York so he could make tons of money as a pro."

"What?" Carley hasn't pulled out of her spot at the curb yet. Probably good since she's now turned to glare at me. "You think she's after you for your money?" Her laughter swiftly follows. It's not a happy laugh. It was more along the lines of a scoff.

"Did you tell him you sold your bike just to go visit him in New York?"

I quickly look over at Emma, then back at Carley as she adds, "And that you wouldn't let his mom buy your ticket?"

"Emma—"

Carley holds her hand up to stop me. "Does he also know that you've been resigned to the fact that he's moved on. That he was better off without you and that you hoped he was happy?"

This time Emma doesn't make a move.

Carley looks back over her shoulder and gives me the look of death. "Here's how this is gonna go." I look up at her best friend and nod. "I'm going to drive your sorry ass home. You're going to hobble out of my car and into your fancy-ass house. Then you're going to leave my sweet, loving, caring best friend the fuck alone. You get me?"

I nod.

"Because she doesn't deserve to be treated like that. Why in the fuck would you ever think she was after you for your money? It was always about your body."

"Carley!" Emma shouts. "Stop."

I can't help but chuckle.

I guess Carley was serious. "Laugh it up, asswipe. You fucked up the best thing that ever happened to you, and I don't feel sorry for you."

The chuckle is long gone. "I know."

None of us makes a sound on the ride to my house. Once the car stops and I open the door, I've got to say something. I can't just leave without letting Emma know how I feel. "Emma?"

She doesn't turn. Only Carley does and the glare is back. "I'm going to call you. I hope you'll answer because I'm not giving up."

"You gave up when you didn't bother answering her calls while you were in New York."

"You're right." She's absolutely right. "But Emma's not an asshole like I am."

"No shit," Carley mutters.

I wish Emma would respond. I'm tired of hearing Carley's voice right now. "Will you answer the phone?"

"I don't know." Em's voice is husky with emotion. I believe her when she says she's doesn't know if she'll talk to me or not. I guess that's better than a no. I'll take it. Hopping out of the car, literally, I make good use of my right leg and bounce up to my garage where I enter the code for the opener and watch it rise up. Turning, I see the blue car reverse out of my driveway, well, my dad's driveway, and tear down the street. Emma didn't even look at me. And that right there, that moment, hurts more than anything I've ever experienced in my life thus far.

***

"JESUS, DUDE," CODY SAYS, PRACTICALLY CHOKING ON A SANDWICH. "What the fuck are you doing here?"

I grabbed a pair of crutches from the garage. I've got several sets. Using them, I'm able to move pretty quickly into the kitchen.

"Oh no. You got hurt and had to head home?"

Okay. I like that excuse. It's going to play well with the rest of the guys on the team. "Yeah. High ankle sprain. I'm out for four to six weeks." Actually, it could take up to eight to get back onto the ice, but I don't want to believe that.

"Fucking bummer, man." Cody reaches out and slaps my shoulder. "What happens when you're back on your feet?" He chuckles. "Get it?" He laughs again. "Will you head back to New York?"

"Uh." No. The answer is no. The fact of the matter is, I could go back and play on the taxi squad. That's basically a practice squad that travels with the team and are the backup players if someone on the actual team gets hurt. After that, I'd go down to the AHL or New York's third-tier team that plays in Maine.

My dad was thrilled with the outcome of our trip to New York. Me? Not so much. Sure, I had a great place to stay in the Big Apple, but I hated the routine of getting up at the ass crack of dawn to work out with the team. I ate with them, attended meetings with the other taxis, and then played. After that, we worked with their strength and conditioning team. Then, when I got home, it was all about catching up with school. Couple all of that with the fact I missed Emma. Even though I was angry with her about the money comment, I still missed her. Seeing her when I walked into the apartment last night was the best surprise of my life. But the second I saw her, I remembered.

Sitting on one of the kitchen stools, I pull my phone out and see twenty new text messages from my folks. Glancing at my mom's first, she's asking things like: Are you home? Do you have your foot elevated? Did they prescribe anything for pain or swelling? Remember alternating between ice and heat is best.

That sort of thing.

I click on my father's texts and read shit like: That's it. I'm done. I can't believe the shit you just pulled. Ownership says they don't have time to deal with you. Neither do I. Pack your shit. I'm selling the house.

I knew it was coming. How I'm going to break it to Cody, that's another story.

"Dude. What happened with you and Emma?"

"I fucked up." I'm not sure how else to describe it.

"You blew her off, man. That's not like you." He snorts. "Well, yes, it is, but with puck bunnies, not your girlfriend."

"I know." I nod, staring at my phone. Part of me wants to argue my point with my dad so we can stay in this house. The other part is relieved. How awesome would it be *not* to be under my father's thumb? To be on my own. To live in a place like Emma's. I'd have to get a job, for sure. I've got a scholarship that covers my classes, or I did before I left. I'll have to see if that's still on the table. I'd probably have to give up my car too. That's okay.

The transit system in Madison is above average. I could save for something like Carley drives.

"Are you listening to me?"

I look up at my best friend as he slides a sandwich in front of me. Picking it up, I take a big bite and moan. "Good," I say with a mouth full of bread and turkey.

"Are you going to tell me what the fuck's going on with you or do I have to beat it out of you?"

Setting the food down, I chew, swallow, and tell him everything. The truth. And it goes better than I expected. Turns out, Cody's tired of living under my father's thumb too. "Hopefully he gives us a few weeks to find a place to live."

"I'm sure we have a little time."

Picking up my phone, I send a text to my father––one I should've sent years ago.

**Me:** Let me know when we need to be out of the house.

I half expect him to respond with something like *tomorrow*, but I get nothing. Not one message with an answer to my question. I'm not sure what it means, but I'm guessing we don't have a lot of time. "We'd better be out by the end of the month."

"Right on, man. Right on." Cody raises his fist for me to bump. "We can look for a kick-ass pad closer to campus. Then, my friend, we can walk home from the bars."

Cody's right. "True." Also a good idea since I won't have a car anymore.

## 45

EMMA

"Are you ever going to answer your stupid phone?" Carley sounds exasperated. "He's called a million times. For the love of cookies, answer it. Or mute it. Just end the ringing."

She's right. He's called a lot. Not a million times but a lot. I sort of like that he's not giving up. "I will. The next time he calls, I'll answer it." I'd already decided that. I mean, it's been over a week. Eight days that he's spent doing sweet things like sending me flowers, a box of candy, and several letters, one of which was four pages long.

And yes, I read them.

They were mostly about his time in New York and what happened with the team and how he spent his days. I guess it was his way of explaining that he was very busy. I don't buy that he was so busy he couldn't speak with me. Besides, I now know the reason he ghosted me. He addressed that in the first letter. That he was sorry for thinking the worst of me and that I'd been right when he'd let his father's words play havoc with his own beliefs.

I feel the phone vibrate in my hand and look down.

**Amber:** I need help.

"What now?" I grumble.

"What? Did he finally give up?"

"It's Amber."

"What the hell does she want?"

Carley is over Amber. Correction. Carley's been over Amber since high school but especially now. She still hasn't left Madison. They dropped the charges back home due to lack of evidence. It was only suspected she was approaching truck drivers to, well, you know. That's not the case, here, though. She was definitely caught attempting to solicit. At least that's what the investigative officer said. And because I haven't heard from her since the night Eli and I bailed her out, I assumed she'd stopped. Never assume…

No matter. I still have to find out what she needs.

**Me:** What'd you do now?

Okay, that doesn't seem like the nicest response, but can you blame me?

**Amber:** I need a ride.

Carley is now planted herself beside me and has read the text. "Why am I relieved my car is in the shop?"

I give Carley stink eyes. "And even if there wasn't something wrong with the alternator-thingy, I wouldn't agree to do shit to help her."

"I wouldn't have asked you anyway."

I turn my head and look at her and arch my brow. That's when I say, "Yeah, I would have." Just as Carley mutters, "Yeah, you would have."

It makes me laugh. But then I get serious.

**Me:** I don't have a car. Carley's is in the shop.

**Amber:** Get your boyfriend. I really need help. I'm stranded in the middle of butt-fuck Wisconsin. I wouldn't ask if it wasn't an emergency because I know you've given up on me.

Oh, geesh. Now she's laying on the guilt. She's good at that.

Carley must agree, "Definitely. Call Eli. He'll jump at the chance to see you."

Crud.

I guess that means I'm not done with Eli Baxter.

*Duh.*

**Me:** Where are you? Exactly.

**Amber:** Concord

*Concord? Where the heck is Concord?*

**Me:** Are you in Wisconsin?

**Amber:** Jesus. Yes. I'm at the big truck stop on I-94. Will you hurry?

Great. She's at a truck stop. I hope that doesn't mean what I think it means.

"She's hooking at a truck stop again." Carley's voice is deadpan. "You'd better be careful. The cops could be involved."

**Me:** I'll try.

Without even thinking, I press Eli's number. He picks up on the first ring. "Emma?" His voice sounds like a combination of surprise and glee. Seriously, he sounds happy to hear from me. He'll probably change his tune when he finds out why I called.

"Um. Eli?"

"What's wrong?"

I guess I'm not hiding anything. "I need a ride." Might as well cut to the chase. "Well, I need a ride out to a place called Concord."

"Wisconsin?" His question makes me smile.

"Yeah. My sister—"

"Amber?"

"My sister's in trouble. She needs a ride and Carley's car is in the shop."

There's a long pause. I sense hesitation. It's too much, especially since I haven't actually spoken to the man in over a week. "I'm sorry," I blurt. "I shouldn't have—"

"No. No. I'm glad you called. I was just looking up Concord, Wisconsin on my phone. I'll be there to pick you up in fifteen minutes. You can fill me in on the details then."

My stomach hurts, like someone just punched me, because Eli

shouldn't be helping me. Not after everything. "Okay. Th-Thank you, Eli."

"Of course. No problem. See you in a minute." The phone clicks. I press the red circle to make sure we're disconnected. Turning to Carly, I say, "He's coming."

"Of course he his, silly girl."

I don't respond because I'm too busy thinking about everything he said and the things I said.

"Do you want me to go along?"

Shaking my head, I reach out and take her hand and give it a squeeze. "Nah. I think I need this time to talk to him."

Carly laugh-snorts. "Finally. Your sister is doing something to help you."

"I wouldn't go that far."

---

"Thanks again, Eli."

He glances over at me and smiles. "Happy to help."

We've been on the road for fifteen minutes and neither of us have said much. I wanted this drive to be a chance for us to talk it out, but I'm not sure where to start. Looking at the navigation screen on his car, I see we've got just over thirty minutes before we're set to arrive at the truck stop. "I, um, really appreciate this."

Eli looks over at me and smiles warmly. "I'd do anything for you, Em."

Anything? Funny. Before everything that happened when he went to New York, I'd have believed him, but now? I don't know what to believe. I decide not to overanalyze his statement. Instead, I go with the banal. "How's your ankle?" I could tell it was better earlier because he walked up to my apartment to get me and wasn't limping or using any crutches or anything.

"Getting better. I've got it wrapped up pretty tight. I was sick of the crutches."

"That's good."

We're quiet for another five minutes or more before he asks, "So what kind of trouble is your sister in this time?"

"Honestly, I didn't ask her. Well, I did but she didn't say. All I know is she's stranded at the truck stop."

"So we don't know what we're walking into?"

That's a good question and the way he asked it, all calm and collected, puts me at ease, but it also gives me pause. "Yeah. I'm not sure."

"Maybe you should call her or better yet, text her to get more information for us."

"Good idea."

**Me**: We're on our way. ETA about twenty-five minutes. Do we need to be worried?

I stare at my phone waiting for her to respond. After a few minutes, I look at Eli. "She's not responding."

"Okay." Eli reaches out and places his big, warm hand over mine and squeezes. "I'm sure everything's okay. She's fine."

I turn my hand over beneath his and let my fingers intertwine with his. He presses his palm closer and his fingers wrap around my hand. At the contact, I look up at him and see he's turned his head to me.

"I've missed you."

"I've missed you more, Em. I'm sorry about everything. I'm sorry I was a dick--that I questioned your motives even when I knew deep down that you're one of the kindest, most honest people I'd ever met and that you want the best for me."

"I accept your apology."

"Does that mean you're going to give me another shot?"

"Yes."

The car suddenly lurches to the right. When I look out the windshield, I see Eli's taken an exit ramp. "Is this it?" I know it can't be. We're still a good twenty minutes out. I watch as Eli turns onto a two-lane highway, then into a dirt driveway where he stops the car, throws it into Park, and reaches for my seat belt. Unlatched, Eli leans over the center console, places one hand on either side of my face and kisses me.

It takes me moment to react, but when I feel his tongue seeking entrance, I open for him and kiss him back. I also lean into him until our upper bodies are pressed together right above the gear shifter. Sliding my hands into his hair, I whisper his name, "Eli."

What I don't expect to hear is his reply. "Emma. I love you. I love you so much."

Jerking away from him an inch or two, I can't believe my ears. "What did you say?"

With concern written all over his face, Eli adds, "It's okay of you aren't there yet, but I am. I think I've known for a long time it was just... I've never been in love before, so I didn't recognize it."

"Say it again." I need to hear those words. Over and over again.

Eli's mouth slides from concern into a toothy grin. "I love you, Emma Perkins. I love you so much."

"I love you too, Eli."

"You do?" He sounds sincerely surprised.

"I do."

Moving in slowly, Eli gives me a soft, chaste kiss. "I knew you were mine the minute you said your awesome pickup line."

Grumbling, I feel the heat of a blush on my cheeks. "Don't remind me." I mean it. Don't.

"What? You don't want to hear *'Do you generate electricity with water through the process of hydropower? Because dammmmm.'?*"

"Please stop." I giggle. A giggle that's muffled by Eli's lips meeting mine once again.

"Never."

ELI

To say the mood in the car has shifted is an understatement. It all happens the minute we pull into the truck stop parking lot. Right after Emma sent Amber a text letting her know we were here, we watch as a tall, thin figure steps out from behind a brick retaining wall. At first, I don't think much about it, but the closer it gets, I realize it's Amber.

But not the Amber from before.

No, this Amber has torn clothing and bruises that are already turning black on blue.

"Jesus," Emma squeaks. She throws open her door and shouts, "Amber!"

I quickly jump out of the car because I don't know what we're up against here. She's obviously been assaulted; one look at her tells me that. But that's all I know.

She lets us take her to the ER, which I think sort of surprises Emma. She also lets Emma hold her hand while she tells an officer what happened to her. When Emma steps out of the exam room, I can tell she's been crying. "She wasn't raped but close. She was convinced the guy was going to kill her."

"Did she know him?"

Emma shakes her head. "No, but the guy's truck was bright yellow. Hard to miss."

I wrap my arms around my girl. "Do you think this will scare her straight?"

Emma makes that funny little snorting sound she makes sometimes. "I sure as shit hope so." She looks up at me. "Honestly. I think so. I've never seen Amber so scared. Ever."

---

"YOU SURE YOU TWO WILL BE OKAY? YOU COULD STAY AT MY place." We're finally back in Madison. After spending four hours at the county hospital, they released Amber with some pain medication and strict orders to rest. The trooper assigned to her case, Officer Renate, said he'd be in touch as soon as they were able to track down the truck. He also said there has been other, similar assaults at that truck stop and more troubling, at least one missing person. Another young woman.

Inside her apartment, I watch Emma make her way to the sofa. "No. I'm going to give Amber my bed. I'll sleep in the floor so I can keep an eye on her.

"Emma," Amber mumbles sleepily from the couch. "I'm okay. I can sleep right here."

"No. You're sleeping in my bed." Emma's voice cracks at those words. "You could have been killed."

"But I wasn't."

"We're going to have to call Mom and Dad."

"Tomorrow," Amber mutters. "I'll tell them I fucked up again."

"Hey!" Emma pronounces angrily. "It's not your fault that guy—"

"Yeah. It is. It's 100 percent my doing."

Deciding it's time for everyone to get some sleep, I give Emma a quick kiss and whisper, "I love you."

The smile I get is tired but sincere. "Love you too."

"I'll be back first thing in the morning. I'll bring donuts or something."

"Glazed" comes from the woman on the sofa.

Sure, she's been terrible to Emma in the past, but there's no reason to use that against her right now. "Glazed it is." I mean, who doesn't love a good glazed donut?

"I can't believe this day is finally here."

"I know, right?" Amber says, adding another curl to my hair. She's a natural at hair. She always has been. "You look beautiful."

"Thanks to you. If I had to do my hair all fancy like this, it'd end up looking like a bird's nest.

"Well, lucky for you, I'm here."

"Are you bitches about ready to do this thing?" Carley says, strolling into the room with a champagne bottle in one hand and two glasses in the other. Handing a glass to Amber, she fills the glass, then adds the bubbly to the other one. Lifting it, the two click them together. "To getting this shit over with and on to the party."

"Hear, hear," Amber says, tipping her glass back.

I frown at the sight.

"Sorry, Mama-to-be. No booze for you."

"You could have brought me apple juice," I grumble. "Or better yet, chocolate. Ooh, or a steak."

"Jesus." Carley laughs. "I can't wait for you to pop that kid out. You're gonna be as big as a house by the time she's born."

"Only two more weeks." Eli can't wait. He's more excited

about this baby than I am, which is saying something because I'm so thrilled. Heck, I tried to talk the doctor into an early c-section. They said no.

Speaking of Eli and me. We made it.

Yay!

After I graduated, we moved from Wisconsin to Chicago so he could work on his master's degree in computer programming with the hope of applying to work for the FBI afterwards. In the meantime, I work for a not-for-profit clean energy company that is working to develop renewable energy resources to protect natural areas and wildlife habitat in communities across Illinois. I love the job, but the closer I get to having our baby girl, the more I wish I could spend more time with her.

I know how terrible that sounds. I should relish my opportunity to be a career woman. I guess we'll have to see.

Eli's father really wants Eli to join his commercial real-estate company but Eli's adamant that he steers clear of doing anything that would give his father control over him. He feels like they need to stick to golfing and doing other father-son things. And soon, grandfather-son-and-granddaughter things. As for Helene, well, she's amazing. She and my mom have formed a bond that I love. Couple that with the fact that my sister... well, she's finally got her shit together.

"Drink up. Let's get this party started."

When did Carley get so bossy?

Oh, right. She's always been that bossy.

With the toast done, the three of us step out into the hallway. Carley wraps her arms around us and says, "We look fabulous. Don't we, girls?"

"We do," Amber adds with a smile.

Making our way down a long hallway, we take a right at the end and stop. Music is playing a song I recognize because I chose it. When the doors open, I take in a deep breath for courage. "I don't think I can do this."

"Do I need to double-dog dare you again?" Carley snickers.

"Um. No." I shake my head. "That's not what I mean."

"You know what, sis. This isn't about you. Now, scoot on down there and stand next to your man."

"I can't."

"The hell you can't," Amber says angrily. "If you screw this up now, after all this time."

"Come on. Seriously." Carley's getting testy with me too. Taking my arm, she starts to tug me down the aisle. Because she's right and I don't want to make a scene, I go. At the end of the aisle I see Eli and do my best to smile.

He must see something isn't right because he mouths, "You okay?"

I grit my teeth and nod.

Moving to the right, I stand perfectly still as the music changes.

Everyone in the place stands and turns in time to see my sister, looking absolutely stunning in the same lace wedding dress our mom wore when she married our dad. I can tell he's touched by the whole thing because the poor man is bawling his eyes out. "Dad," I whisper to myself as I watch Amber approach her husband-to-be.

I move into place and wince as pain shoots through my abdomen. I know what it means. I'm in labor. But I'm not about to ruin this day for my sister. She's come so far. *So* far.

In three years she's grown from the problem child to a woman with a bright future as a hairstylist, marrying the man, the police officer who saw through all of the crud Amber had done and saw the woman within. Oh, sure, she's still a pain in the ass, but she's nothing compared to who she was before.

I grit my teeth until the pain ebbs. I missed a bunch of what the minister says, thanks to my contractions but I'm able to hear the good part.

"Amber Nicole Perkins. Do you take this man to be your lawfully wedded husband?"

I can't see my sister's face because I'm behind her, but I know she's smiling. "I do." I know the minister is asking her more questions. I remember them from when Eli and I did this over a year ago. I know the words by heart, but I can't think with the pain that's shooting through my belly. I do my level best to pretend nothing is wrong. With practiced breathing, I'm able to get myself under control in time to hear:

"Ordell Oliver Renate. Do you take this woman to be your lawfully wedded wife?"

"Hell yes."

The audience laughs. I wish I could. I really do. Except I can't, due to the fact that I've just felt warm liquid gush down my legs onto my feet and the floor. "Oh, shit," I say, loud enough for the entire church to hear.

"Shh," Amber says as she turns to look back at me. Heck, she's even got her finger over her lips like I'm a child that needs chastising.

"Screw you. My water just broke."

She quickly glances down at my feet and laughs. "Of course your water broke. You just had to make this about you, didn't you?"

When she laughs, I cry. "I'm sorry." I really am. "I didn't mean to go into labor on your we-wedding day."

"Oh, Emma." Amber's voice sounds sincere. "I was kidding, honey." Her arms wrap around me just as pain so intense shoots through me all I want to do is lay down.

"Emma, babe." Eli's next to me. He's got his arms beneath my knees and one around my back, lifting me. "You all finish up here. We'll meet you at the hospital." As he carries me down the aisle, I watch the group at the front of the church.

"Good plan," Carley says with a nod. Waving at the minister like she's in charge, she says, "Please continue." People around us laugh. "But make it snappy. *Our* niece"—she winks at Amber—"is about to come into this world, and we need to be there."

Turning to face the guests, Carley adds, "After this, the rest of you head to the reception. Have a good time. Lift a glass to the bride and groom, and baby Carley."

And that, right there, is why I love her.

"Baby Carley," I whisper into Eli's ear.

"No way in hell, Angel. We're sticking with the name we agreed on."

"I know." We chose a good one. "Amelia."

"Exactly."

By the time he's walked us out to the car, the pain has eased. "You want to know a secret?" I say as Eli buckles me into my seat.

"Sure." But he doesn't wait to hear it. Instead, he carefully shuts my door and runs to the driver side. He's in with the engine running and in gear in seconds.

"My secret is—"

"Uh-huh," he says absently as he carefully checks for traffic as he pulls out of the parking lot. "We put your bag in the car, right?"

"Right. We did just as they told us. Just in case."

"Good." He glances at me and smiles. Reaching out with his right hand, he takes mine in his. "I love you, babe."

"Me too."

"Now, tell me your secret."

"Well, it's not a secret, secret. It's more of something I know that you don't."

"Sounds like a secret to me."

"I guess." I pause when I feel a flutter in my belly. When there isn't pain, I sigh with relief.

"Are you going to tell me?"

"Tell you what?" Then I giggle. "Right. My secret."

"Your secret."

"Here goes." I place my palm on my belly and say, "The minute

I saw you at The Dirty Rabbit that night, I wanted you to impregnate me."

Eli's car jerks a little to the left, but he quickly gets it under control. He laughs. Hard. "Jesus, Em." Then he laughs some more.

"Well, maybe I said it wrong. I think my ovaries exploded that night." I look over at him. He's still laughing. "Better?"

"Oh, yeah. *So* much better."

Now we're both laughing. Until I feel the telltale sign another contraction has started.

By the time this one eases, we're in the valet parking line at the hospital. "I've got a secret of my own."

"Oh? Please don't tell me that you had a boner the second you saw me."

"No." He snickers. "Well, maybe."

"What's your secret?"

"The day I saw you in the library…?"

"Yeah."

"The day after The Dirty Rabbit, I saw you walk into the library. I followed you. After you went upstairs, I searched the library for over an hour until I spotted you."

"No." My voice sounds breathless. "Seriously?"

"Seriously. You were a surprise. I had to know who you were."

"Obviously, it was all due to my amazing pickup line."

"Obviously."

"I love you, Eli."

"I love you more, Em." When it's our turn at the hospital valet, Eli jumps out and tosses the keys to the woman who'll park our SUV. Opening my door, he unbuckles me, then lifts me out and keeps hold of me. "Now. Let's go have a baby."

"Yes. Let's."


Amelia Rose Baxter

7 pounds, 4 ounces

21 inches long

And beyond beautiful. Just like her mom.

---

Thank you for reading Double-Dog Dare: Pick-up Lines Book 3. I hope you loved meeting Emma and Eli.

If you enjoyed this series, be sure to check some of Kayt's other series like Bedhead: A Romance.

*"Unputdownable! I enjoyed it soooooo much!"* - *Amazon Customer*

**Quinn Maxwell.** Student. Dork. And a woman in love with a guy who doesn't know she exists.

**Cooke Thompson**. British. Hottie. Rugby Star. Chick Magnet. And a guy trying to FaceChat with his old mate Maxwell Quinn.

Sure, it was a wrong number but sometimes, wrong ends up being so-so right.

Don't miss a release, SIGN UP FOR KAYT MILLER'S NEWSLETTER: https://kaytmiller.com/subscribe

I appreciate your help spreading the word, including telling a friend who loves a steamy rom-com. Reviews help readers find books. Please leave a review on your favorite book site.

THANK YOU!

# SNEAK PEEK: DREAM MAN (COMING SOON)

## BASED ON A SHORT STORY ORIGINALLY TITLED: THE NEW NEIGHBOR

**Chapter 1: Level-Ten Hot**

*"Hooooly shit,"* I whisper to myself while squatting down beside my large front window. I'm peeking through the blinds doing my best not to be discovered perving on my new neighbor who's level-ten hot. And right now, he's shirtless and a little wet due to the fact he's hosing down his big truck. "Oh yeah, scrub that truck. Do it harder." I giggle at myself because, lord knows, Henry Miller isn't going to laugh, because cats do *not* find humor in *anything*.

Leaning closer to the window, my hot breath hits the glass and starts to steam up my little corner view of Mr. Sexy—sure, I know his name thanks to the mailman accidentally delivering his mail to my box a couple of weeks ago, but the nickname is perfect for him. With a sigh, I say his name. "Sam Griffin." God, isn't that rugged sounding? I pause, knowing I shouldn't say shit like this, but what the hell? Henry Miller won't tell. "Colette Griffin." Wow. I like the sound of that. It's so much better than the one I was born with—Munsel. Ugh, no matter how you say it, it sounds depressing. Go ahead, say "Munsel" aloud.

A griffin is a mythological beast, and let me tell you, Sam fits that to a T because the man is b-i-g, and I'm not talking about dad-bod big. Peeking out again, I'd guess him to be six three or four, so a foot taller than me. His legs are long and muscular, and his shoulders… God, his shoulders make me swoon. I know some women like a guy's butt, but I'm a shoulder girl, hands down. I could just picture myself hanging on to those as he….

Oops, never mind.

On top of all that yumminess lies a face that could launch a thousand orgasms. Square jaw that's always got a little scruff like he wakes up, shaves, and BAM, it grows back. *Thank you, testosterone.* As for the rest of his face, I can only say, from a distance, he's handsome. I wish I could tell you about his eye color or how soft his lips look, but I can't. I haven't actually met him in person.

Why not just go introduce myself to him? Well, because level-ten hot doesn't mix with level-five meh—and *that's* after I've showered, done my hair, and put on makeup. Since I've done none of those things, it means I'm currently level-three scary.

Anyhoo, he moved in about a month ago. I wasn't home when the truck arrived to set him up in the home attached to mine. I live in what's called a duplex. I only rent, which I know for a thirty-two-year-old woman, it's sort of sad. I should own real estate by now, but I like renting. I mean, if something goes wrong, I just call the management company, and two or three weeks later, it's fixed, pretty much, which is good because I don't have a handy bone in my body.

Outside, I see Sam use some kind of soft cloth to buff his truck to a glossy shine. "I'd like to shine his−−" I mumble to myself. Then I crack up because sometimes my dirty thoughts… well, they'd make a sailor blush.

The way his back muscles are flexing and contracting makes me dizzy. I need to pull away from this and get back to work. "Shit's not going to edit itself." And Mama needs a new vibrator, apparently.

I plop back on my butt, then crawl the short distance into my small living room. Once I make it to the coffee table, I use that to help push me up. I walk the five steps it takes to make it back to my desk.

My little place is perfect for me. It's one bedroom, one bath, with a living room big enough for a sofa, chair, and television stand. There's what I call a dining nook off the kitchen that I've set up as my office. It's an ideal spot for easy coffee refills and access to life-sustaining snacks. But the best part is the sliding doors that lead to my deck––my little slice of heaven. It's small, only about eight by eight feet so I've got room enough for a chaise lounge and a tiny side table.

Three steps down from the deck leads to a small grassy area I share with Sam. It's big enough for Henry Miller to roll around in when the sun is out, like it is today. It's finally nice enough outside for me to leave the slider open so the slight breeze can come through the screen door.

Yeah, I like my little place. And now with the new neighbor, I *love* my place. Granted, it's not as nice as the place next door. I saw it a time or two when the last neighbor lived there. That place is set up in a similar manner as mine, but it's much bigger. Even the deck.

I sigh, imagining what Sam's place is like. I just need to figure out a way to meet him without making it seem intentional, but I suck at meeting guys––and not in a good way.

# THANK YOU!

Thank you so much for reading! When I start a story, it begins with an outline, notes, and lots of crazy thoughts running through my head. When I actually start writing, the characters take over, leading me through the story like they're holding my hand--guiding me. The process is exciting and cathartic. With that said, I hope you enjoy the story.

If you did, please go to my website, www.kaytmiller.com, and join my newsletter so you can be the first to know what's coming up next. And...

*And remember...Please, leave a review!*

Thank you!

Sadie: The Palmer Sisters Book 3

Cortland: The Palmer Sisters Book 4

Keely: The Palmer Sisters Book 5

Violet: The Palmer Sisters Book 6

Molly: The Palmer Sisters Book 7

The Portrait Painter

Hopeful Romantic

Thanks to Margie Dill

ACKNOWLEDGMENTS

Thank you to Olivia and Becky at Hot Tree Editing for editing
this book from start to finish.

And an extra special thank you to Becky at Hot Tree Promotions
for your advice, expertise, and your positivity.

And for my beta readers.
Thank you so much for your time and feedback!

## ABOUT THE AUTHOR

Kayt grew up in the midwest surrounded by a loving family which included three brothers, one sister, and parents who always fostered her creative side.

Kayt wrote her first book when she couldn't find a story about a certain type of a woman and a specific kind of man. She called it *Game Changer* and it couldn't have been a more appropriate title. It changed her life in many ways.

Her goal, as a writer, is to write stories that relate to all of us, to make readers laugh and maybe cry sometimes. Kayt hopes her readers can escape into a fantasy, one that's actually possible. Sure, some of the stories are dubbed "Insta-love" but that's okay. She fell in love with her husband pretty damn fast and with her daughter the second she saw her. So, it's a thing, she swears.

facebook.com/authorkaytmiller
twitter.com/kaytmiller1
instagram.com/kaytmiller1
bookbub.com/profile/kayt-miller